"Hello, Beau," Diedra purred. "I'm back."

Glenna felt as if her mouth were filled with sawdust. This was Beau's ex-wife? She could never compete with a woman who oozed sex from every pore!

"Mom!" Kelly launched herself at Diedra.

"Easy, babe. Don't pull on my dress," Diedra said. "My goodness, Beau, we made a beauty, didn't we?"

"What are you doing here in Sweet Gum?" Beau said at last.

"I told you, I came to see you. Kelly says you've been missing me lately."

Glenna couldn't take any more. "Beau, I'm not feeling well. A headache. I have a headache."

Beau called after her as she walked away, but she didn't look back. Halfway up the steps, she lowered her face into her hands and began to cry.

ABOUT THE AUTHOR

Dan and Lynda Trent need no introduction to fans of romance fiction. Coauthors of more than thirty books, this husband-and-wife team continues to craft award-winning fiction in both the historical and contemporary genres. In *Jordan's Wife*, they have written about a subject that's close to their hearts— the complexities of single parents combining their families and having to cope with teenagers who are resistant to change.

Dan and Lynda enjoy hearing from their readers and will answer all letters personally. Please write them at the following address:

Dan and Lynda Trent
P.O. Box 1782
Henderson, TX 75653

Books by Lynda Trent

HARLEQUIN SUPERROMANCE
348—THE GIFT OF SUMMER
430—WORDS TO TREASURE

Jordan's Wife

LYNDA TRENT

Harlequin Books

TORONTO • NEW YORK • LONDON
AMSTERDAM • PARIS • SYDNEY • HAMBURG
STOCKHOLM • ATHENS • TOKYO • MILAN
MADRID • WARSAW • BUDAPEST • AUCKLAND

Published June 1992

ISBN 0-373-70504-2

JORDAN'S WIFE

PROLOGUE

JORDAN KING had just been named Easton County's Man of the Year. This was his second consecutive year to be given the title, and he was the first recipient to be chosen twice. Glenna was so proud of her husband she felt as if she were floating on air. The attendance at the banquet in Jordan's honor had been enormous, but given Jordan's popularity it was hardly surprising.

"Jordan, I wish Chad could have come to see you accept the plaque," Glenna said. "He's so proud of you."

"He's still a little young to enjoy a banquet. I'm sure he would rather watch television."

"You underestimate his maturity. He got a phone call from a girl today. From the giggle in her voice and the expression on his face when he picked up the receiver, I don't think he'll want to wait until his first year in high school to start dating."

Jordan reached over and covered Glenna's hand with his. "We began seeing each other the summer before we started high school. Remember?"

"I'm not likely to forget. You were the only boy I ever really dated."

"Maybe you should have shopped around more, played the field," her husband teased. "Maybe you would have found someone you like better."

Glenna's laughter ended abruptly when she saw the truck ahead of them. It was an eighteen-wheeler, and it was bearing down on them on their side of the road. "Jordan!" she screamed. "Look out!"

Jordan pressed on his car horn, but the truck driver showed no response. As if it were happening in slow motion, Glenna watched the silver bulldog on the truck's hood tower higher and higher as the truck closed the space between them at full speed. Jordan's grip tightened on the wheel and his jaw muscles clenched. He, too, knew a wreck was unavoidable.

At the last instant, Jordan jerked the steering wheel hard to the right and took the impact on his side of the car.

Glenna had almost no recollection of the next few minutes except for a kaleidoscope of flashing red and blue lights and the wail of a siren. Someone was speaking to her, and she tried to respond but couldn't. Pain shot through her body as she was lifted from the mangled car seat and placed on a stretcher. She tried to focus her eyes and find Jordan, but people were in the way. When she tried to say his name, a man in a white jacket told her to lie still.

Time lost all meaning. Sometimes she was aware of footsteps on an uncarpeted floor, of cool hands and unemotional voices mixed with voices that were pained with too much emotion, of lights that came and went with confusing irregularity. When she was finally able to comprehend her surroundings, she found she was in a hospital room. Her mother was seated beside her bed.

"Lie still," her mother said.

"Jordan?" Glenna uttered almost inaudibly. Her mouth was dry and her tongue felt swollen. "Is Jordan here?"

"Now lie quietly," Betsy Gibson said again. "Try not to get upset."

Glenna was regaining consciousness quickly. "Chad? Is Chad okay?"

"Chad is fine. He'll be in to see you after school."

After school? This made no sense to Glenna. Wasn't this Saturday night? Why was it daylight outside her window? For that matter, why was her mother here? Glenna's stepfather and Betsy lived in Dallas now, not Sweet Gum, Texas. "Why are..." When she tried to move, she found her right arm and leg were immobile. She stared for a moment at the cast on her arm and was suddenly filled with alarm. Not daring to speak, she looked at her mother. The soft, gentle face she expected to see was drawn and swollen as if her mother had been crying. Something was very wrong. "Tell me," she said, her voice tight with mounting apprehension.

"There was a wreck. Don't you remember?"

Glenna nodded. She had a vague memory of a silver bulldog and a truck.

"You broke both bones in your forearm and in your right leg. Your left arm is cut badly, but the doctor was able to stitch it in such a way that there won't be much of a scar."

"Jordan?" Glenna couldn't get her voice above a whisper past the knot in her throat. She already knew the answer.

"Jordan didn't make it," Betsy said miserably. "He never felt any pain, the doctor said. At least he never suffered."

"He turned the wheel," Glenna said as the memories came back in spite of herself. "He turned the wheel so the truck would hit his side and not mine. He did it so I wouldn't be hurt." Her voice caught and the tears burned as they streamed down her face.

Betsy rang for the nurse, but Glenna couldn't get away from the memory of Jordan—her beloved Jordan—deliberately giving up his life so that she might go on. She cried until the medication the nurse gave her put her back to sleep.

CHAPTER ONE

GLENNA GOT OUT of her car and stared with trepidation at the building. Although Monroe College was a familiar sight, as she had lived in Sweet Gum, Texas, all her life and her house was only a few blocks away, she had never attended classes here. As always when she was nervous, Glenna rubbed the pale scar on her left forearm in a gesture that had become so automatic she was never aware she was doing it.

In the three years since Jordan had died, Glenna had gone through the painful process of grieving. At first she had been too devastated to do anything but cry. Later had come denial, as Jordan had been buried in the shadowy days before Glenna became fully aware of the impact of her loss. Then anger. Anger at the senseless tragedy caused by a truck driver who had fallen asleep at the wheel rather than lose a few hours in reaching his destination by pulling off at the side of the road to sleep. Anger at losing the only man she had ever loved. Finally had come acceptance, and relief that her days were no longer filled with the emotional stress of trying to cope. At the insistence of Jordan's mother, who lived nearby, Glenna had resumed her social club activities, but nevertheless she still had too much time on her hands.

It was Glenna's best friend and confidante, Margo Johnson, who had urged her to take a few courses at the local college to fill her days. At first Glenna had laughed at the idea of going back to school. She was thirty-six years old—and it had been too long since she had graduated from high school. And besides, she didn't need more education in order to be able to join the work force. Thanks to the wealth Jordan had accumulated and the wise investments he had made, she would never have to work. But the more she thought about Margo's suggestion, the more it made sense. Chad was now a junior in high school, and all too soon she would be completely alone at home, with nothing to do but think of how she and Jordan used to occupy their leisure time. With school and her club work during the days and homework to be done at night, Glenna would hardly have time to think at all. Before she could change her mind again, she had registered for the fall semester, her first college course.

Glenna had chosen a class in English literature because she had always loved to read and thought that this would be a good class in which to learn to study again. But now that she was on her way to her first college class ever, she was filled with doubts. She hadn't been in a classroom in years, and she wasn't at all sure she could compete with students half her age. The parking lot she was crossing was full of students, mere boys and girls, and they all appeared to know each other. She tightened her grip on her books and walked resolutely toward the English building.

With little difficulty, she found her classroom and was jostled into it by students who were apparently more interested in their conversations than in who they might run over. She chose a desk near the window and slid into it. For a moment, her eyes darted around at the others who were occupying desks nearby, then she opened her book of English poetry and pretended to be reading in hopes that she would appear more self-confident than she felt. Everyone in the class was closer to her son's age than to hers, and she suspected that they, too, had noticed this and were wondering why she was there.

Two weeks earlier, in the registration line, she had learned that the instructor for this class was a new-comer to Sweet Gum, and it was rumored among the students that he was "ancient." Glenna had trans-lated "ancient" to "mature and knowledgeable, if not wise." Or at least she hoped so.

The students in the desks nearest Glenna's had turned their conversation to Old Man Fletcher, and they were speculating among themselves as to why he would come to a small college like Monroe when he had been teaching at the much larger University of North Texas. Glenna tried not to eavesdrop, but her classmates' voices were too loud to ignore.

At last the final bell rang and a hush came over the room as the door to the hallway opened. As a well-dressed, attractive man strode to the front of the room and stepped behind the instructor's desk, Glenna could hear audible sighs from the young women. It was obvious that if this man was their instructor, he must have taken Old Man Fletcher's place, for she doubted he was much older than she was. In deeply resonant tones, he announced the name of the class he had come to teach and introduced himself as Beau Fletcher.

At first Glenna's jaw went slack as she was taken aback by the disparity between her expectations and reality. Feeling self-conscious, Glenna continued to stare, but soon her mind unwittingly drifted from thoughts of herself to a comparison of this man to Jordan. He wasn't as classically handsome as Jordan had been, but his face held rugged character that piqued her interest. His hair, more brown than blond, was wavy, as if it had a life all its own. Although his expressive eyes seemed to be the same shade of moss green as his sweater, she suspected they were actually hazel and likely to appear to be other colors, as well, depending on what he was wearing at any given time. He was tall, perhaps as tall as Jordan had been, and although his shoulders were broad over a lean waist, he didn't look as if he was the athletic type.

Fletcher called the roll, making notes beside some of the names. Glenna was curious about what he had put beside hers, but she was too far from his desk to see. She caught herself feeling self-conscious again, so she tried to concentrate on what her instructor had to say.

"First," he said, "we will study poetry." When most of the class moaned, a broad grin covered his face. "That's why I start with poetry. That way you'll have nothing to dread. And some of you may actually learn to like it."

He picked up a book from his desk and thumbed through its well-worn pages. "'How do I love thee? Let me count the ways.'"

Glenna had heard the poem he was reading many times, but this man's baritone articulation of the familiar words gave them new depths of meaning that touched her as personally as a caress. He read as would a person who enjoyed words and emotions, one who could see beyond the printed page and into the heart of the semi-invalid poet who had penned those words after giving up hope of ever loving and being loved.

"'I love thee to the depth and breadth and height my soul can reach.'" His voice was gentle, melodic, caressing.

Glenna was entranced. She had forgotten her classmates and what they might be thinking about her presence and about her apprehension that college might prove to be more difficult than she could handle. She was lost in Beau Fletcher's voice.

"'I love thee with the breath, smiles, tears, of all my life!'" He quietly closed the book and quoted the last line from memory. "'And, if God choose, I shall but love thee better after death.'"

In the silence that followed, Glenna remembered to breathe. She had never heard poetry read this way before. Evidently no one else in the class had, either, because everyone was perfectly still.

"Elizabeth Barrett Browning wrote those words to Robert Browning, the man who would become her husband, well over a hundred years ago. They were not only two of the world's most accomplished poets, but lived one of the greatest love stories of all times. Whenever possible, we will examine the lives of the poets we study and try to determine what their writings meant to them and speculate as to what may have inspired the author to write a particular poem at that particular time. I believe all of you will come away from this class with a greater knowledge, if not a greater enjoyment, of poets and their work.''

Glenna found herself leaning forward to catch every word. Her pen raced over her notebook as she took copious notes. She was truly glad that she had decided to sign up for this course instead of the American literature course she had at one time considered. Fletcher continued by reading several more selections from the Brownings, and with each one his voice seemed to touch Glenna's very soul. Too soon the hour was over.

Once Glenna was in her car and on her way home, the romantic stirring Fletcher's poetry reading had left her with became an unsettling reminder that she was alone. To ease the familiar twinge of loss, she turned her thoughts toward Jordan, promising herself that she would visit her memories of him for only a short time, then get on with whatever she needed to do.

Although Jordan had never been one to read poetry, he had been an all-star athlete in high school and had led his football team to two consecutive state championships. In college he had been Sweet Gum's only athlete to make it to the Olympics and had been favored to win the pole-vaulting event until he pulled a ligament a week before he was to compete. As an adult Jordan had coached a Little League baseball team even before his own son was old enough to play. Jordan had had great physical ability and business acumen, but he had never been one to read poetry.

Glenna now wished that he had. The thought made her feel guilty, as if she had found fault with Jordan, and that, of course, was unfair and unreasonable.

That night, as Glenna and her son were eating dinner, Glenna noticed herself paying closer attention to him than usual. Chad was so much like his father that she was sometimes caught up in her memories. Like Jordan, Chad had pale gold hair and eyes so blue that strangers often asked if he wore tinted contact lenses. Even his voice was a replica of Jordan's, as were many of his everyday gestures and the way he stood and walked.

"Mom, there's something I want to talk to you about," Chad said as he reached for another roll. "I've asked Diana Murdock to go out with me again."

"Again? Weren't you out with her two nights last week?"

"That's what I wanted to tell you. We've decided to go steady." Chad grinned. "I gave her my letter jacket."

Glenna carefully put down her fork and reached for her iced tea. She knew of Diana as she knew of all Chad's friends, but she wasn't fond of the girl. "Oh?" she said noncommittally.

"We're in love."

Glenna stared at her son in disbelief. "You can't be in love. You're only sixteen years old."

"Mom, get real. We're in the nineties, not the Stone Age. I know a lot of couples at school who are in love."

"Aren't you the one who told me just last month that you intended to date every pretty girl in school and not think about settling down until you're out of college? I could have sworn that was you."

"That was before Diana said she wanted to go steady. I never thought I would have a chance with her. She was going with Randy Stottard all summer."

"That's what I thought. Why did they break up?"

"Who knows? Randy can be a dweeb at times."

"I see." She wondered what "dweeb" meant. "All the same, you seem pretty young to think you may be in love."

Chad was silent. Glenna glanced at him and concern crept in. She finally said, "There's more?"

"We've decided to get married as soon as I graduate."

"Married!" Glenna no longer pretended to be calm and unaffected. "Married? What about college?"

"What about it? Married people can go to college. Dad did."

Chad's jaw became set in the stubborn line that was a replica of Jordan's.

"Your father was different. He had a job with his father after school, and I worked full-time. Even so we had to save every penny."

"Diana and I can do that, too."

"Chad, you and Diana haven't... I mean, you aren't..."

Chad laughed and shook his head. "She's not pregnant. We aren't stupid, Mom."

Glenna felt a wave of relief. "Good. That's good."

"We aren't going to have a baby until after I've graduated." A moment later, he added, "Like you and Dad did."

Glenna gave him a measured look. "You weren't born until two years after we married."

"I know that, but if Dad could go to college and have a family, so can I."

"It's not that easy!"

"If you and Dad had waited until he was out of college to marry, you would have had four less years together." He pushed his plate away and frowned. "Diana said you'd be like this."

"Like what? Concerned that you're rushing into responsibilities before you're ready?"

"She said you'd get mad."

"I'm not mad, just surprised. Chad, you've only had a few dates with this girl. Don't be so rash."

"I know what I'm doing. I'm old enough to decide these things for myself. Do you want me to be miserable?"

"Of course not."

"Well, Diana and I are going steady, and I'm not going to break up with her." He shoved back from the table and scrambled to his feet. Fixing his mother with a scowl, he said, "I'm going out."

"Out where?" she asked as he turned and walked away. When he didn't answer, she called after him. "Remember to be in early. It's a school night." Her only answer was a slamming door.

Because Jordan had always insisted that a good parent never lost his or her temper, Glenna repressed the twinge of anger Chad had evoked and quickly substituted concern for her son. As she slowly rose to her feet, she drew in a deep, calming breath, then began stacking the dirty dishes so she could carry them into the kitchen. Over the past few weeks Chad had become more and more belligerent, but this episode was worse than usual. She went over all she had said to him and could see no reason for him to get so defensive. She hadn't told him to break up with Diana or to date other girls as well. As had happened so often of late, Chad's anger seemed out of proportion to the situation. She decided his change in behavior had to be a function of his age, although she didn't remember going through anything such as this herself. Of course, everyone said that times had changed since then, and no one had ever said it was easy to be a teenager—or the parent of a teenager, especially on one's own.

A FEW BLOCKS AWAY, Beau Fletcher was putting the last of his family's dinner plates in the dishwasher. Dish washing was only one of a number of chores he shared with his two children. Since his divorce from Diedra a year and a half ago, he had found household chores to be more pleasant. The division of housework had been one of the problems of his marriage, since Diedra preferred watching TV all day to keeping house. Of course, had he known at the time what her other interests were, he would have encouraged her to watch even more television. Not until she left him for one of her lovers did he have any idea what had been going on behind his back for months. Once he got over the shock and embarrassment, he had almost been glad. Neither his son, Keith, nor his daughter, Kelly, had any knowledge of their mother's escapades, and by moving himself and his children to

Sweet Gum, he hoped they would never find out. Sweet Gum was nearly two hours east of Denton, where Diedra still lived, and Beau hoped the distance would make her visitations less stressful for the children.

Not that Keith was exactly a child anymore. He was a junior in high school and had made the football team easily. Kelly was in the eighth grade and was beginning to blossom from girlhood to young womanhood. Beau sometimes wished he could stop time and keep them small forever.

His first day of teaching at Monroe College had been a good one. His classes were full, and most of the students showed some degree of interest. As he dried a dish he had washed and put it away in the cabinet, Beau thought of his first-period class. One of the students had caught his eye at once. She was older than the others, he guessed in her mid-thirties, the same as he was. Her hair was red-gold and she wore it shoulder length. Her eyes had been light, probably blue, but he hadn't been able to tell for sure at that distance. Most of the class time she had kept her head down, taking notes. She was beautiful, but it was the kind of beauty that seemed friendly and approachable. Unfortunately she had worn a wedding ring. Not that he was surprised. No woman who looked as good as she did was likely to be single.

Beau finished by wiping clean the countertops and hanging the towel on the rack to dry. There was no point in wondering about her. He had his own rule against fraternizing with his students, which was much stricter than the nebulous one stated by the college. He liked Sweet Gum, and the college was a size he preferred. In time he would get his career tenure status, and he had no intention of trading that for a fling with a student.

Keith and Kelly were in the den. Keith was doing his homework, but Kelly was watching a sitcom on TV. Beau waited until the show was over, then pressed the remote control, turning off the set.

"Dad!" Kelly protested. "I'm watching that."

"The show is over. Do your homework."

"I don't have any." Her dark eyes didn't meet his.

"Good try. I saw your history book on the kitchen counter."

Kelly sighed and slumped lower in the chair, her dark hair ruffling against the back cushion. "I don't like this school as much as I did the one in Denton. The teachers are too mean."

"I know. That's why I wanted to move here," Beau said with a grin. "I asked around until I found the most boring town with the meanest teachers and I said, 'That's for us!' and we moved here in a flash. I had hoped to find a house with no electricity or running water, but we'll have to make do with this one."

Keith smothered a laugh, and Kelly smiled in spite of herself. "I met a new boy in school today. His name is Conan Hudson."

"Conan?" Keith said in amused amazement. "His parents actually named the kid Conan?"

Kelly indignantly tossed her head at him and turned to her father. "He's so cute. His hair is cut short in front and sort of long in the back, and he's taller than I am."

Beau nodded. In the eighth grade height was a serious concern among the feminine set. "Does he live around here?"

She nodded. "Over on Dorset Street. The big house with the tall glass windows in front. It has a pool inside."

"How do you know that?" Beau asked. At times Kelly was more status-conscious than he would have preferred.

"Conan told me so. He says I can swim in it if I want to."

"We'll see."

"You always say that when you mean no," Kelly complained. "I'll bet everybody in my class gets to swim in that pool except me."

"I didn't say no. I want to meet his parents first, and I don't want you to invite yourself over. Got it?"

"Yes, I have it." She pouted and looked straight ahead. "You want to ruin my social life."

"How much social life can you have at fourteen?" her brother put in. "You aren't even allowed to date yet."

"That's something else, Dad. I'm the only girl in the whole school who can't date. It's not fair!"

Beau regarded her thoughtfully. "I could agree to taking you on car dates."

"Car dates! With a parent driving? No way!"

"I'm not even going to consider letting you date anyone old enough to have a driver's license. It's car dates or nothing."

Kelly didn't look convinced.

Beau reached over and hugged her, and she hugged him back as she had when she was still a little girl. He said, "Come on. Let's clear out of here so Keith can do his homework. We'll go into the kitchen, and I'll help you get started on your history."

They went into the kitchen and Beau put Kelly's schoolbook and folder on the table. Kelly sat down, but she folded her arms across her chest and tapped her toe against the table leg. "I still don't see why you won't let me date," she said.

"Don't start that again. What homework do you have?" He sat beside her and opened her history folder.

"Cathy Compton dates. She goes steady with a boy in high school."

"That's between Cathy and her parents. You're too young to date, so get it out of your mind."

"Mom would let me, I'll bet. She loves me."

Beau sighed. This wasn't the first time he had heard this ploy. "I love you, too. You know that."

"No, I don't. I think you're just picking on me. Keith gets to date all the time."

"Keith is sixteen. He didn't date at fourteen. You can go out with boys next year or I'll drive you and your boyfriend wherever you want to go."

"I'd die if you did that!" Kelly exclaimed. "Nobody but nerds car date." She switched to her former tactic. "You don't want me to date just because you and Mom got a divorce."

"Kelly, that's plain silly."

"Go ahead! Call me names! You know I'm right. You just don't want to admit it."

Beau studied his daughter's rebellious face. He never knew what to say to her at times like this, and he had a feeling she was aware of it and had maneuvered him into a corner. "Let's do your homework."

"No. I'm going to flunk out of school so I can go live with Mom."

"Stop it, Kelly. You're acting like a spoiled brat." Beau felt his patience running thin. These were the same manipulative tactics that Diedra had used to get her way, and he was programmed to see red when he was talked to in this fashion. He drew a deep breath and opened the history book. "Is this the chapter?"

"You can do it if you want to, but I'm not." Kelly frowned at him sullenly. "I'd rather fail."

"No, you wouldn't. You enjoy summer vacation too much to want to spend it in school."

"I *enjoy* living with Mom. I don't know why you don't want me to go live with her. Just because you hate her doesn't mean I have to."

"I don't hate your mother," Beau said in a tired voice. "I don't hate anybody."

"You hate me or you'd let me live with Mom."

"That does it. I'm not going to sit here and argue with you. Do your homework and let me see it when you're through." Beau got up, poured himself a cup of coffee and went to the den.

He picked up a book and pretended to read it. The divorce had been hard on both his children. He had regretted having to put them through it, but he had had no choice. Keith seemed to have worked through his pain and accepted the situation, but Kelly was at an age where she was certain her parents should never be separated—no matter what—and sure that she could put things back the way they had been if she worked at it hard enough. Beau still suffered over some of the things Diedra had done, and Kelly's anger, predictable as it might be, opened old wounds.

Since they had moved to Sweet Gum, Diedra hadn't called to incite Kelly. In fact, she hadn't called at all. Her silence after a year and a half of irritation following the divorce made Beau suspicious and Kelly half-frantic. Although Kelly seldom voiced her fears, Beau was sure she was afraid her mother was forgetting her, and he was at a loss as to how to help her.

He noticed that Keith was looking at him, so he turned a page in his book and continued to feign reading. Marriage was not for him, he decided. Some people seemed to be cut out for marriage and some didn't. But having this notion surprised him in a way, because Beau enjoyed having a family, and he had never had trouble in relationships with women, except for the notable exception of Diedra. His marriage had never been peaceful, however, so he had decided not to try it again. His children gave him more than enough to do, and he had no time or energy left over to find and seriously court a woman. He glanced at Keith. If his family were really enough, and if he didn't want another long-term relationship, why was he so lonely so much of the time?

He put the book down and peered over his shoulder into the kitchen. Despite her denial that she had homework to do, Kelly was bent over her books. Beau watched her for a moment, then smiled. He loved his children, and their periodic outbursts of rebellion never altered that fact, just as he knew they loved him. Kelly wasn't cut from the same mold as her mother, he told himself. In time she would go back to being the sweet and loving daughter she had been before.

He hoped he was right.

As Beau turned, Keith looked up and asked, "Dad, can I talk to you a minute?"

"Sure. What's up?"

"I'm having some problems on the team. There's this guy named Chad King who seems to think he's God's gift to the world."

Beau nodded. "I've known people like that."

"He's the quarterback, and he keeps trying to make me look bad. He throws the ball just beyond my reach, and when he hands off to me, he makes sure the ball is hard to hold."

"Have you talked to him? Maybe it's because you're new to the team, and he's used to someone else running with the ball."

"I don't think that's it. And I haven't talked to him. You wouldn't believe how stuck-up he is. The high school is full of cliques and I'm an outsider. I think you have to be born here in order to fit in."

"I know it's been a difficult adjustment. Give it some time. School has only been going on a week and a half."

"You don't understand, Dad. It's pretty bad." Keith paused and added, "I'm even considering dropping out of football."

"But you've enjoyed playing football for years. You're good at it."

"It's not worth what this Chad guy is putting me through. I don't want to quit, but I'm afraid the coach will put me on the second string if I keep messing up."

"Maybe you should talk to the coach," Beau suggested, but when he saw the look on Keith's face he said, "No, I guess you couldn't do that."

"It would be the same as signing my death warrant," Keith said gloomily.

"I still think you ought to give it more time. The coach isn't blind. He may be aware of what Chad is doing and is giving it time to work itself out."

"I wish we had stayed in Denton. I miss Melanie. By now I'll bet she's going with someone else."

Beau went to Keith and put his hand on his son's shoulder. "I know it was hard for you to leave her." When Keith didn't answer, Beau asked, "Is there a girl here you'd like to date?"

"Sure. Want to guess who she goes with?"

"Not Chad King."

"The same."

"I think I see why he's giving you a hard time."

"I haven't said anything to her, but she winked at me in study hall."

"Why would she wink at you if she's Chad's girlfriend?"

"I've been wondering that, too."

Beau shook his head. "Son, you might as well learn now that women can be hard to figure out. Especially teenage women."

"Yeah. Tell me," Keith mumbled.

"Hang in there. Don't quit the team yet. Maybe this girl had something in her eye."

"If she did, it was still there during lunch break. Chad saw her wink at me, and he looked as if he wanted to tear me in half."

Beau grinned. "That might be hard to do. You aren't exactly a slouch in the muscle department. But you know I don't want you to fight, especially not at school. You could get suspended for that, and memories run long in small towns. You could be labeled as a troublemaker."

"I'll do my best, Dad, but I can't make any promises. If Chad comes after me, I won't just stand there."

"I know." Beau sighed and wished he had the wisdom to make growing up simpler for his children. "I know."

CHAPTER TWO

KEITH OPENED HIS LOCKER and took out his English book and put away his algebra and government texts. English had always been easier for him than math, and although he would never admit it to one of his peers, he enjoyed reading. The corridors were full of students, and lockers banged and books thudded one on top of another as the students prepared for their afternoon classes. Although no one spoke to him, Keith could hear snatches of conversation and laughter all around him. As always, the hall smelled of books and gym socks, but these were familiar smells and Keith would have noticed their absence more than he noted their presence.

As he was turning to go to class, he bumped into a soft and shapely body. "Sorry," he said and suddenly realized he was staring down into Diana Murdock's wide blue eyes.

Diana tossed her long flaxen hair from her face and smiled at him. "Why, Keith Fletcher, you practically flattened me."

"You know my name?" he asked inanely. He had never seen such blue eyes, and her hair was silvery gold and looked as soft as thistledown.

"Well, of course. Everybody knows you. We don't get many new students in Sweet Gum." She broadened her smile and rolled her shoulders flirtatiously. "Especially not new students who are as good-looking as you are."

As Keith felt the blush starting, he grinned and shoved his free hand into the back pocket of his jeans, hoping Diana wouldn't discover that he was shy when it came to compliments. "You're the head cheerleader, aren't you?"

"I sure am. Are you ready for the game Friday?"

"Yeah. I'm looking forward to it." He could hardly believe it but Diana was flirting with him. Her name started with an M so her locker was nowhere near the F lockers. Had she sought him out on purpose?

"Hey! What are you doing talking to my girl?" a harsh voice called out behind him.

Keith turned to see Chad King glaring at him. "We're just talking." He felt adrenaline pump into his veins.

"Nobody talks to Diana but me!"

"Maybe you'd better tell her that. She spoke to me first. And I don't see your name on her." When Keith didn't back down, the other students stepped away, forming a circle around the bristling adversaries.

"This *is* my name." Chad pointed to the letter jacket Diana wore. "Or can't you read?"

"I read just fine." Keith was getting angrier by the minute. "Maybe she just got tired of having to spell it out for you. Since you're so lousy at throwing a football, I don't imagine you have much in the way of brains, either."

Chad let out a roar and dived at Keith. The move caught Keith off guard and he fell, but he took Chad with him. He felt Chad's fist strike his belly, and Keith punched him as hard as he could as they rolled on the floor.

At once teachers came running. The biology teacher pulled them apart and wedged himself between them. Keith wanted to tear Chad apart with his bare hands, but he retained enough reason to know not to touch the teacher.

"What's going on here?" the teacher demanded. "What are you boys fighting about?"

"He's coming on to my girl!" Chad shouted.

"You shouldn't start something you can't finish," Keith retorted. "You're the one who started this."

"All right, that's enough," the teacher said. "Both of you, straight to the principal's office." When the boys stood their ground, continuing to glare at one another, the teacher grabbed an arm of each of them and propelled them on their way. "You heard me. Get going." To be sure the fight didn't resume, he escorted them to the office.

The secretary took one look at their angry faces and buzzed for the principal. Mr. West opened the door at once. "What's going on here?"

The biology teacher said, "They were fighting in the hall."

"Go on back to your class. I'll take care of this." To the boys he said, "Come in and have a seat."

The principal's office was stark. He had a small framed picture of his wife and one of his daughter and her two children on his desk beside a daggerlike letter opener and a paperweight shaped like an oil derrick. Behind his desk and swivel chair were built-in bookcases and a photo of some previous year's football team. Mr. West sat down, leaned back and regarded them sternly. "What do you boys have to fight about?"

"He was hitting on Diana," Chad said.

Mr. West frowned at Keith. "You hit Diana Murdock?"

"No, sir. He means we were talking. She said something to me and I answered."

"That doesn't sound like a reason to fight to me. What have you got to say for yourself, Chad?"

"They weren't just talking. He was coming on to her. He has no right to cut in on me."

To Keith Mr. West said, "Didn't you know Diana and Chad are going steady? Word spreads fast in this school. I knew it and so do all the teachers. Last I saw, she was wearing his letter jacket that half swallows her. I don't see how you could miss seeing that."

"I hope he didn't hurt my passing arm," Chad said as if to himself. He flexed his right arm as if it was sore.

Keith glared at him. He knew he hadn't hit Chad hard enough to damage him. His own ribs ached, however.

"I guess I had better call your parents," Mr. West said as he reached for the phone. "You boys know we take a dim view of roughhousing here at Sweet Gum High."

Keith knew he should have assumed it, even though no one had told him, but this sounded more serious than he had guessed. If he and Chad were both suspended—and nothing else would be fair—the football team was as good as beaten in the coming game. He wondered what his dad would say.

Mr. West dialed the college and sent a message for Beau Fletcher to come to the high school. Then he asked Chad for his home number and called Glenna. When she didn't answer after the sixth ring, he hung up. "I'll try Mrs. King later. You boys have a seat out in the office and wait for your parents."

Keith reached the door first and considered slamming it on Chad but thought better of it. He slouched in one of the metal folding chairs in the hall outside the principal's office, crossed his arms over his chest and glared at the floor. He wasn't to blame for starting this, but he had a feeling that wouldn't make any difference. Why had Diana spoken to him, anyway? he wondered. Then he remembered the K lockers were opposite his. She had come to meet Chad King. Keith felt like a fool. Why had he ever thought she might have been searching him out?

Beau got the message from Keith's principal during his free hour and drove straight to the high school. When he entered the administration office, he saw Keith and another boy sitting and staring at the floor. "Keith? Are you hurt? I got a message to come here."

The secretary gave Beau a wintry smile and buzzed the principal.

"I'm not hurt," Keith mumbled.

Mr. West opened the door and motioned for the boys and Beau to come in. As he shut the door, he said, "We had a fight here. Your boy hit Chad King."

"He hit me first," Keith objected.

Beau turned to Chad. The boy looked as if he might have come from Mount Olympus and could be a close kin to Adonis. This was the boy who was giving Keith all the trouble. "So you're Chad King," he said thoughtfully. "You wouldn't by any chance be Glenna King's son, would you?"

Chad nodded. His blue eyes were fearless, as if he knew no harm would come to him.

"I was unable to reach Mrs. King," Mr. West said. "I would have preferred to talk to both of you at once, but I can talk to her later." He leaned his forearms on his desk and interlaced his fingers. "We have a strict rule about fighting here. And these boys know they're in trouble. Usually a fight means automatic suspension. Because of mitigating circumstances, however, I'm going to let them off with a warning."

"Oh?" Beau glanced at Keith. "What mitigating circumstances?"

Mr. West gave him a parent-to-parent smile. "Well, there's a game coming up and we need both these boys on first string. I'm sure you will understand." Then he turned to Keith, and wagging his finger at the boy, he said, "Young man, you had better watch your step. I won't be so easy on you next time."

"Are you suggesting my son is the only one at fault in this?" Beau asked with a frown. "He said the other boy hit him first. And what's this about bending the rules because of a football game? It seems that whoever is at fault here ought to be punished."

The principal sat up straighter in his chair and pursed his lips. "Actually, it seems to have been your son's fault. He was apparently flirting with Chad's girlfriend, and Chad merely overreacted. We've never had any trouble with Chad before.''

"It wasn't my fault!" Keith exclaimed. "Diana and I were just talking, and I told you he hit me first.''

"He was goading me, Mr. West," Chad said earnestly. "I swear I wouldn't ever start a fight. I know better. He was bothering Diana and wouldn't leave her alone.''

Beau studied the boy. He could recognize blarney when he heard it. Apparently Mr. West couldn't.

"I know, Chad. I had to bring you in, too. You were part of the fight, you know. Now Keith, I want you to take warning from this. If you cause any more trouble, I will have to suspend you, team or no team.''

Beau could see that as a newcomer to the school, Keith wasn't going to be treated fairly by West and that the man didn't seem to be one with whom he could reason. Beau didn't want Keith to be punished for something he didn't do, but neither did he want his son to get the idea that the school's rules didn't apply to him because he was involved in athletics. Knowing West would not suspend the boys but hoping he could get his point across, Beau calmly said, "My son isn't a troublemaker, either. And since they were both breaking the rules by fighting, perhaps you should suspend both of them.''

"Dad!" Keith stared at him with as much astonishment as Chad.

Beau watched the reaction his words had on Mr. West, and the result was gratifying. The principal looked as if he had swallowed something fuzzy.

"Rules are rules," Beau added with a smile that would have done a gambler proud. "Wouldn't you have suspended boys that weren't on the team?"

"That's not the point," Mr. West said. Then he added quickly, "No, no, of course not. I'm not cutting Keith slack just because of the team."

"What about Chad? As you said, Keith wasn't fighting alone. He says Chad started it. Maybe Chad is the one you should suspend." He was almost enjoying himself. He never had believed sports should have any edge over scholarly pursuits. "Would you have cut him slack if he was a straight A student and didn't go out for football? And what about this Diana? She's the head cheerleader, isn't she? Seems like I saw her picture in the paper last week. Her father's on the school board, isn't he?"

"Mr. Fletcher, there's no reason for you to get all bent out of shape like that. Your boy did wrong but I'm willing to forget about it. Let's not blow this out of proportion."

"Out of proportion? I thought fighting was a serious offense. It must be if automatic suspension is the punishment. So let's make sure they never do it again. Let's suspend them both."

Mr. West stood, signaling that the interview was over. "I'm not going to suspend them this time. The matter is closed."

Beau smiled and stood. "You boys heard him. Next time you fight you're both out." He looked Chad straight in the eye. "Both of you."

Chad stared at him with his mouth hanging open. Keith was equally amazed.

"You boys get on back to class now." Mr. West waved his hand in dismissal.

When the boys were gone, Beau turned to him. "Are you still going to talk to Mr. and Mrs. King?"

"I don't see any need to do that. And there is no Mr. King. Not anymore. Mrs. King is a widow. I don't see any reason to trouble her with this."

"A widow? For how long?"

"Jordan has been gone about three years, nearly four."

Beau smiled again. "In that case, I'll talk to her. I believe parents should be kept informed about what their children are doing. Especially since I intend to be sure that if Chad and Keith fight again, both of them receive the same punishment." He nodded a goodbye and left the office.

Beau was inwardly furious. He knew the principal had intended to punish Keith and let Chad off with a verbal warning. Worse still, the boys also knew it. And this wouldn't be the end of it. He glanced at his watch. There was barely enough time to make it to class. He would have to talk to Glenna King in the morning or call her at home.

BEAU WAS UNABLE to reach Glenna that evening. Either Chad had expected him to call her and he was keeping the phone off the hook or someone was on the phone constantly. Beau decided he would have to talk to her in the morning after class.

The class was on Tennyson, Byron and Keats. Beau was as familiar with the lesson as he was with his own name. It gave him time to think. As he read *The Lady of Shalott,* Beau watched Glenna. She seemed to be hanging on every word, as if the poem was touching her personally. Of all his students, she was clearly the most interested. He thought it was a pity her son was a troublemaker.

As the class was being dismissed, he asked her to stay for a minute. Glenna paused as if she thought she must have misunderstood him, but she waited by his desk.

"Do you have a class next period?" he asked.

"No. This is all I'm signed up for." Her voice was lilting and somewhat expectant. He found himself wondering if her hair could possibly be as soft as it looked.

He brought his thoughts back to business. "I need to talk to you. Will you wait in the hall until I get the next class started?"

She nodded and left. The room was already half full with his next class. He went to the board and wrote the page numbers he intended to cover that hour. Under the number, he wrote, "Read them." To the groans of the students he went out of the room.

Glenna felt her pulse racing. About halfway through the class she had realized she had been staring at the instructor again, fascinated by the way he read poetry and, she had to admit, somewhat fascinated by the man himself. Apparently he had noticed and was going to reprimand her. But that made no sense. She hadn't disturbed anyone—except herself. Suddenly the thought occurred to her that he must have thought she was flirting with him and that he was going to ask her for a date. She wouldn't go, of course. She rarely dated, and then only friends who knew she wasn't interested in more than having an escort and someone to talk to.

She looked up expectantly when he came to join her. He was taller than she had thought he might be. Her head barely came up to his shoulder. His changeable eyes were dark green in this light. Even though she had already decided she would turn down his invitation, she was excited at his nearness.

"Our sons got in trouble in school yesterday," he surprised her by saying. "I guess Chad told you all about it, but I felt I should speak to you."

"Trouble?" Her head tilted to one side. She hadn't expected him to talk about Chad. "What kind of trouble? Who is your son?"

"Keith Fletcher. I suppose I'm not surprised that Chad didn't tell you. They were fighting. I gather Diana Murdock was the issue."

"Chad goes steady with Diana. He never told me he had a fight. Was your son hurt? Chad can be rough, I'm afraid." She was trying to think of a reason other than the obvious one that Chad wouldn't have told her this. She had thought she and Chad had no secrets from each other.

Beau frowned. "No, Keith wasn't hurt. I gather Chad wasn't, either? Keith is stronger than he thinks sometimes."

"Are we discussing whether my kid can beat up your kid? As long as neither was hurt, I see no reason to discuss it." She felt silly for having believed he was about to ask her for a date. She hoped he hadn't guessed the direction of her thoughts.

"Mr. West threatened to suspend them, but he let it drop because of the football team."

"I don't understand. Were they in P.E.? What does the team have to do with it?"

"It seems that the principal is more interested in winning the game Friday night than in reinforcing the concept that rules are set by authority and that there are consequences for disobeying them. I would rather have seen him punish them than give them the message that they are above the rules because they are athletes."

"You want your son to be suspended from school? That's dreadful! How can you say such a thing?" She stared at him in amazement. She had never heard a parent say such a thing.

"I don't want Keith suspended. The point is that football shouldn't be a reason for altering school policy. The emphasis should be on their studies and behavior, not extracurricular activities."

"Sweet Gum has an excellent team. We go to the state championships almost every year. School spirit runs high here." Glenna had always thought the same thing, but Jordan had told her she was wrong. She didn't know of anyone who had ever voiced such an opinion except herself.

"I want the boys to find another way to work out their differences. I've tried to teach Keith that fighting is wrong, but I can't tell him to stand there and be a punching bag for anyone who has different principles."

"What's that supposed to mean?" Glenna met Beau's eyes with an icy stare. "I've never encouraged Chad to fight."

"I didn't mean your son. I meant anyone who would rather fight than discuss a problem like an adult."

"You're saying Chad is childish? That he's somehow less civilized than your son? I've never had any trouble from my son. Can you say the same?" She was so angry her voice was shaking. No one had ever come to her with complaints about Chad before, and she was mortified—especially in light of Chad's recent behavioral changes. She couldn't admit to this man, however, that she had seen problems coming with Chad.

"Mr. West tried to call you but you weren't home. I tried to reach you last night but your line was busy. You don't seem to spend much time looking after your son."

Anger flushed her skin painfully as she said, "That's no business of yours, Mr. Fletcher. I'm a good mother, and I won't stand here and be insulted. I lead an active life in the community, and I was tied up yesterday afternoon. That doesn't mean I don't have time to spend with Chad!" She felt particularly guilty because she had been at a meeting of the City Beautification League, a club she attended to appease her mother-in-law. The group rarely did anything but complain that someone should do something and reiterate that no one except its members seemed to have any civic pride. Glenna couldn't point to a single thing the club had ever done to improve the town. "I suppose you're going to say next that you spend every waking moment with your children?''

"As a matter of fact, I do. Keith and Kelly are my prime concerns, and I always put them first.''

"Obviously that hasn't helped,'' Glenna said in her frostiest tone. "Keith is a troublemaker.''

"Chad started the fight.''

Glenna's mouth dropped open. "I don't believe that!''

"It's true. Not that I expect Chad or Mr. West to admit it. Keith was being blamed for the entire incident, and Mr. West was about to let Chad off scot-free.''

"Then he must have known that Chad wasn't to blame. I've known Mr. West for years. He's not the sort of principal to pick on students just for the fun of it.''

Beau's eyes darkened in anger. "I'm not lying about it.''

In her best imitation of her mother-in-law, Glenna lifted her chin and said, "I think we have nothing more to say, Mr. Fletcher. I trust this…unpleasantness won't be reflected in my grade.''

"Certainly not. What do you take me for?''

She smiled, but only with her lips. "I don't take you for anything at all. I wouldn't take you under any conditions.''

"What is that supposed to mean? I never offered—''

Glenna straightened so she would appear taller. "Good day, Mr. Fletcher.'' She turned on her heel and walked briskly away.

BEAU SWUNG HIS RACKET and connected with the tennis ball, slicing it over the net just out of reach of his opponent. This was the third game he had won in a row, and the other man threw up his arms in surrender.

"I give," Joe Tarrant said. "What's got you so upset? That last one nearly went through the back fence."

"One of my students." Beau took his towel off the bench and looped it around his neck. Joe was his next-door neighbor, and they had quickly become friends. "It seems her son and my son have it in for each other. I was trying to discuss the problem with her, and she flew at me like a wet hen."

"She sounds pretty bad. Do I know her?"

Beau shrugged. "Her name is Glenna King."

"Glenna King? Jordan King's wife?" Joe stared at him in disbelief.

"I thought he was dead. Yeah, I think that's his name."

Joe laughed. "Around here Jordan King may be dead, but he will never be forgotten. I can't imagine Glenna King losing her temper with anybody. What did you say to provoke her?"

"Nothing." Beau frowned at his friend. "At least not before she laid into me."

Joe shook his head. "I sure can't imagine that. I'd have said she didn't have a temper at all."

"You would have been dead wrong." Beau shoved his racket into the frame and tightened the screws at the corners. "What's so special about them anyway?

To hear Mr. West and Glenna King talk, you'd think her son is above reproach."

"To understand that, you'd have to have known Jordan King. He was a living legend around here. His athletic records have never been broken, and everything he touched seemed to turn to gold. He even gave up his life to save Glenna."

"That's the father. What does that have to do with the son?"

"Chad is just like him. It's like seeing Jordan when he was in high school. Even their voices are the same. The resemblance is remarkable."

"That's ridiculous. Chad is Chad, not Jordan."

"Maybe so, but around here, the King name is like royalty."

Beau shook his head. "Maybe everyone here is too near the forest to see the trees. The boy is good-looking and may be a star athlete, but if you ask me, he's too full of himself." He ran the towel over his face. "He could be a handful of trouble."

"I sure wouldn't say that too freely around town. Sweet Gum isn't too forgiving of outspoken newcomers."

"You were born here and you aren't overcome by the Kings."

"I was born here, but I lived elsewhere for a number of years. Sue Ann isn't from this area. I know it sounds archaic, but it makes a difference. You have to live in a small town like Sweet Gum to understand it, but the cliques and prejudices are there."

Beau became thoughtful. "One of my kids said almost the same thing to me just last night."

Joe said, "Take things slow. Especially when it comes to crossing swords with the Kings. The family is clannish. If you insult one, you've insulted them all."

"It's too bad Glenna King is like that. She's a beautiful woman. When I learned she was a widow, I thought I might ask her out. Fortunately she jumped at me before I had time. She nearly took my head off. My relationship with my kids may not be perfect, but at least I see them as they really are. She thinks Chad can do no wrong."

"As I said, that's a common perception in this town."

"She will have trouble with him if she isn't careful. I think the town may be in for some surprises if they expect him to be a carbon copy of Jordan the Magnificent."

"Come eat dinner with us and quit worrying about the Kings. There's plenty for you and the kids. Sue Ann made her chili, and she always makes enough to feed an army."

"I never turn down Sue Ann's chili," Beau said with a grin. "But shouldn't you check with her before you invite three hungry mouths for dinner?"

"She told me to invite you before I left the house. I wanted to see if I could beat you before telling you. Otherwise you might have let me win one."

Beau grinned. "You know better than that. I never let you win." He dodged Joe's punch. He still thought it was a shame that Glenna King was so difficult to get along with. She was hard to get out of a person's mind.

CHAPTER THREE

AS SHE WAITED FOR CHAD to come home from school, Glenna nervously paced the floor. She had always hated conflict, and the problems she was having with him had all the earmarks of becoming an all-out war. When she was eight her parents had decided to divorce, and she still remembered the arguments that had reverberated throughout the house. And the arguments hadn't stopped there. Before and after every visitation, her parents had fought. She couldn't recall either parent saying anything good about the other, and all their disparaging remarks had been directed to her or said in her presence. Then her mother had remarried, and because of Glenna's intense dislike for her stepfather, the arguments had continued. Marriage with Jordan had been like finding a safe harbor—but that had disappeared all too soon.

Her thoughts drifted to Beau Fletcher. His class had opened new vistas and had reawakened emotions that she had believed to have been buried with Jordan. Emotions that had caused her restless nights.

She recalled with a groan her embarrassment over assuming that her English instructor was intending to ask her out the day their discussion about their sons' fighting had turned into an argument. In the moments before he had started complaining about Chad, had she given him any clue as to what she was thinking? She certainly hoped not. It was bad enough that *she* knew what a fool she almost had made of herself.

Chad had been fighting. She couldn't imagine Jordan ever doing such a thing. Chad knew the school's rules about fighting as well as she did. As she paced she tried to think what Jordan would have done in this situation. What would he have said to Chad? Unfortunately she had no memories to supply this data. Chad had rarely needed discipline, and Jordan had left any necessary reprimands primarily up to her. That was as it should have been, she thought hastily. Jordan had been at the office all day while she stayed home. Discipline had been her responsibility, as were baking cookies for scout meetings and driving the car pool to school on Tuesdays.

She wondered if Beau Fletcher was a widower. It was unusual in her set of friends to find a husband with custody of the children after a divorce. She assumed the child he had referred to as Kelly was a girl, and surely a girl needed a mother to guide her. Glenna had always wanted a girl, someone she could teach to bake and sew and do all the other feminine things a daughter needed to learn. Of course, she had been glad Chad was a boy. Jordan had wanted a son to carry on after him. But she wished she had also had a daughter. She shook her head. This was no way for her to put the past and its regrets behind her.

The back door slammed, and a moment later she heard Chad's whistle as he came through the kitchen.

"Chad?" she called. "Come in here, please. I want to talk to you."

He strode into the den as if he owned the world. "What's up?"

"I hear you had a fight at school."

Chad frowned. "Did Old Man West call you? We got it all straightened out and he promised he wouldn't."

"*Mr.* West didn't call. So it's true?"

"Then it must have been Keith Fletcher's dad. I tell you, Mom, that man is nuts. He tried to get Mr. West to suspend us. Can you imagine that?" Chad shook his head as if he was still amazed. "No wonder Keith is so messed up."

"I'd like to hear your side of it."

"We were at our lockers at lunch break. Diana came to meet me there. Keith came on to her and I didn't like it." He shrugged as if he couldn't understand why she was concerned.

"So you did start it." Glenna stared at her son. He was so strange to her these days. The tone of his voice was one he would use to talk to a simpleton, not a parent, and his body stance was belligerent.

"He started it when he tried to hit on Diana. I finished it."

Glenna felt a prickle on the back of her neck. "I don't know who you are these days. It's not like you to pick fights. You weren't like this last year."

"So it's Diana's fault, right?" Chad scowled at her, his voice louder than necessary. "Go ahead and say it. Everything is Diana's fault."

"I didn't say that. I don't even know Diana, not really. You never bring her over."

"Yeah, right. Like you want me to bring my friends over to play. I'm not five years old, Mom."

"No, but you're acting like it. Fighting at school is a serious offense. You're lucky Mr. West *didn't* suspend you. That could have ruined your chances for the football scholarship you are hoping to get, not to mention your reputation."

"I'll let you worry about the King reputation," he retorted. "You and Grandmother are so good at it."

"Chad, that was uncalled-for."

"Right. I guess that was Diana's fault, too."

"Maybe it is. You didn't act like this before you started dating her. Does she talk to her parents this way?"

"'Bye, Mom. I'd really like to stay here and argue, but I have a date with Diana." He turned his back on her and strode out of the house.

"Chad! Chad, come back here!"

She heard him resume whistling as he crossed the kitchen, then slammed out the back door. Within minutes she heard the squeal of his tires as he peeled out of the driveway.

Glenna slumped into the nearest chair. Her thoughts were swimming. Chad had never talked to her like this! When her friends' children became teenagers and started causing problems, she had congratulated herself on having the perfect son. Chad had sailed peacefully through the dreaded early teens. Now that he was sixteen, however, all that had changed.

The back of her head hurt from the tension of her rigid posture, and she absently rubbed the nape of her neck. Chad hadn't even pretended the fight was a mistake, and he had as much as admitted that he had started it. As her headache worsened, she dialed the school and asked for Mr. West.

"Hello, Mr. West? This is Glenna King." She still felt a bit intimidated by the man. He had been principal during her high school years, too. "I hear Chad had some trouble at school yesterday."

Mr. West's voice sounded placating and grandfatherly. "Boys will be boys, Mrs. King. I think that new boy, Keith Fletcher, started it. I had to talk to Chad, too, in order not to seem prejudiced, but I wouldn't worry about it if I were you."

"Nevertheless, I am worried. Has Chad been a problem to any of his teachers? He seems to be going through a difficult stage these days." She tried to keep her tone light.

"Chad? Trouble? No way, Mrs. King. I wish I had a school full of boys like him."

Glenna drew in a deep breath. "I want you to do something for me, Mr. West. If there is any more trouble, please call me. It's difficult raising a boy alone, and I have to know when there's a need for discipline."

"Sure, I'll call you. I wouldn't hold my breath, though. As I said, Chad is no trouble."

"Thank you, Mr. West. Goodbye." She still wasn't satisfied. Could Chad be acting up at home and behaving like a model student at school? It seemed unlikely.

She reached for the phone and dialed another number. "Margo? Is it is okay if I run by for a minute? I need to talk to someone."

MARGO CLARK had been Glenna's best friend since high school. Glenna had always gone to Margo with her problems. Margo had been her maid of honor when she and Jordan wed, and Margo had been the first person she had told when she found out she was expecting Chad. Margo and her husband, Bob, had stayed by Glenna's side during the nightmare days after Jordan's death and her release from the hospital.

"It's Chad," Glenna said with no preamble. "He's driving me crazy."

"Chad?" Margo laughed at the idea. "You should have raised my Bobby and Mike! What one didn't think to do, the other did. Every gray hair on my head has either 'Bobby' or 'Mike' written on it."

"I'm serious. Something is going on with Chad and I can't figure out what it is." Glenna faltered and laced her fingers in her lap. "Do you think he may be using drugs?"

"Chad? Not in a million years. He doesn't even smoke."

"What else could make him act so... so odd? Sometimes I can hardly believe he's himself."

"All teenagers go through that. No, I don't think he is using drugs. For one thing he's still first-string quarterback and his grades haven't dropped. Have they?"

"No. He's still making straight A's."

"Then he's just going through an unpleasant phase. They all do it. Knowing Chad, it probably won't last a week."

"It's already been longer than that. Chad isn't the paragon you seem to think he is. Not anymore. Maybe it's his new girlfriend, Diana Murdock. Do you know her?"

"I've heard Mike talk about her and, of course, I know who she is by sight. They say she's pretty wild."

"I know. I've tried to talk to Chad about her, but I guess you know how it went."

"You worry too much. Chad will date her a few weeks, then they'll break up. You know how often Mike changes girlfriends. Bob and I hardly had time to learn one girl's name before he switched to another one."

"Chad thinks he's in love. He even says they'll get married."

Margo laughed. "He's pulling your chain to stir you up, see your reaction."

"I don't think so."

"Well, at sixteen he can't get married without your permission, so stop worrying. What has you so upset?"

"He was in a fight at school."

"He was? He must have had a good reason."

"Not really. Some other boy spoke to Chad's girlfriend. That's no reason to fight."

Margo finally became serious. "You're right. He could have been taken off the team for six weeks."

"It's more than that! I don't want Chad to think that the way to solve his problems is to hit someone. That's more important than the football team."

Margo nodded but she didn't look convinced. "Who's the other boy? Anyone I know?"

"I doubt it. He's new to Sweet Gum. Keith Fletcher is his name. I haven't met him, but his father teaches the English class I'm taking at the college."

"Fletcher. No, I don't think I've met them. What's his father like?"

Glenna laughed self-consciously. "When it comes to talking about kids, he's about as rude as they come. But when he reads poetry, I get shivers up and down my spine."

"What about his wife?"

"Apparently he doesn't have one. I don't know if he's divorced or widowed."

"His son sounds like a hoodlum."

"I haven't met the son. Mr. Fletcher told me about the fight, and we ended up arguing about whether or not Chad was to blame. Then I found out he was and that Mr. Fletcher was right. I'm so embarrassed."

"Maybe so, but don't admit it to Mr. Fletcher. Hold your ground." Margo went to the refrigerator and took out two diet drinks. She handed one to Glenna.

"I think I've come to rely too heavily on Chad. Since Jordan's death I've let Chad make too many decisions and be too responsible. Maybe that's why he's rebelling. Maybe he's looking for boundary lines that aren't there."

"Did you read that in some magazine? I wish my sons had been half as responsible. I would have fallen down in a dead faint if Bobby had carried out the garbage without being told or if Mike had ever made his bed. You don't know how lucky you are.''

"Am I? Lucky? I don't feel lucky. I feel lonely.''

Margo reached over and patted Glenna's hand. "I know. We all miss Jordan. There will never be another one like him, that's for sure. Unless, of course, it's Chad. Bob and I were talking just last night about how much Chad reminds us of Jordan. It's uncanny.''

"He reminded me more of Jordan before he started acting like a rebel without a cause. Jordan never talked to his parents the way Chad talks to me. What if he's acting like this in school?''

"I know his homeroom teacher quite well. You know Verna and I sing in the church choir together, and she always has something nice to say about Chad. Maybe it's all in your mind.''

"No, it's not. I know all kids need to rebel a little in order to untie the apron strings, but I feel as if I'm living with Dr. Jekyll and Mr. Hyde. If only Jordan were here to give me advice or to be a model for Chad. Maybe it's because Chad has no father figure to look up to.''

"I think you read too many magazines.''

Glenna had to smile. "Maybe so.''

"Take my advice and stop worrying. Chad will pass through this phase and be the wonderful person he always has been. You'll see.''

"I hope you're right. I wonder if I should apologize to Mr. Fletcher. I said some pretty rotten things to him.''

"Forget it. It's not likely your paths will cross again once you finish that class."

Glenna knew Margo was right, but nevertheless she felt guilty for having defended Chad when in fact Chad was in the wrong. Perhaps she would get an opportunity to apologize to him before the semester was over. But then, what did it really matter? As Margo had pointed out, they weren't likely to meet again after she finished her course.

BEAU COULDN'T GET Glenna King out of his mind. He tried calling her to apologize, but she wasn't home. Evidently she was seldom at home, and he wondered if that had adversely affected her son. He felt bad about the way their talk had gone, and he was hoping he could get her out of his thoughts if he spoke to her again. She seemed to haunt his mind. He had never seen hair that shade of red-gold, and her eyes were silver, not blue as he had first thought. Her skin was as creamy as ivory and looked smooth and soft. He found himself thinking that he had never heard her laugh. She had a pretty smile. He had seen it when he read Tennyson's *The Lady of Shalott*.

He knew he was being foolish. Glenna King wanted nothing to do with him, especially after the way he had argued with her in the hall after class. He rarely lost his temper, but she had a way of triggering his emotions. Last night he had dreamed about her. The memory of that dream put a smile on his lips before he remembered she was as inaccessible as a cloud.

He was still disturbed over the way Joe and Sue Ann Tarrant had insisted she was still as good as married to the late Jordan King. That didn't sound healthy to him, and he wasn't convinced Jordan or any man could have been as good and smart and wonderful as everyone remembered him. Beau suspected it was a case of reverence for the dead carried too far. How could she ever hope to get on with her life if she and everyone else still thought of her as Jordan's wife? He tried to tell himself that he didn't care one way or the other, but he knew he did. Glenna was too beautiful and too vibrant to mourn forever.

He knew he should mind his own business. Glenna had made it clear she wanted to have nothing to do with him. There had been a chill in her voice as well as anger, and Beau knew there was little hope for a relationship to develop. Still he touched the phone and considered calling her again. No, he decided. That would be a mistake. Resolutely he stood and went into the kitchen to start dinner. Glenna King was no problem of his. She would have to sink or swim on her own.

GLENNA POURED HERSELF another cup of coffee and went to the den. Despite her intentions not to, she glanced at the clock. The hands had only progressed five minutes since she had last looked. One-fifteen. She drew in a deep breath and sipped the coffee. She didn't need the caffeine to keep herself awake. Worry and anger were doing a fine job of that.

She turned the television to another channel as if some program would catch her interest. But all her thoughts were on Chad and where he could be at this hour.

Since their argument that afternoon, she had regretted her words. There was a good chance that Margo was right and Chad was only going through a phase. If so, he would probably pass through it faster if she didn't give extra attention to his misbehavior. She had decided to apologize to him, but he had been gone since that afternoon.

Had he been in a wreck? Surely if that were so, she would have been contacted by now. Because of Jordan's death she was unusually afraid of wrecks. She hadn't enjoyed riding in a car since that night, and it amazed her that Chad apparently could all but live in his.

Waiting alone at this hour was difficult. All the horrors her fertile brain could conjure up came alive in the darkness. It was at times like these that she most missed Jordan's courage and strength. Although he had never encountered such problems with Chad, he doubtless would have reassured her that Chad was an excellent driver and likely would have a good and valid reason for being so late.

Perhaps Chad did have a reasonable excuse, but whatever comfort it might have been that he was a good driver was erased forever the night Jordan, an excellent driver himself, was taken from her because of an unavoidable accident. Shuddering, Glenna shifted her thoughts to how she would deal with Chad when he finally came in.

Chad had never been so late before, at least, not that she was aware of. She had trusted him so completely that she didn't wait up for him. Now that she thought about it, she always turned off the den light when she went to bed and left the hall light on downstairs for Chad. The windows of the den could be seen from the street.

A suspicion crept in. If Chad wanted to be out past his eleven o'clock curfew, it would be possible for him to drive by and determine whether his mother was waiting up for him or had gone to bed. Maybe now he was not coming in because he knew she was waiting for him and he didn't want to be confronted. Glenna got up and turned off the light. Because of the angle of the TV, its light didn't reflect on the window and the room would appear to be completely dark. She pulled her feet under her and waited.

Thirty minutes later she heard the purr of Chad's car. He cut the engine at the end of the drive and let it coast to a stop at the garage. Glenna put her coffee cup on the end table and clicked off the TV. As Chad slipped through the door, she said, "Where have you been?"

Chad jumped and wheeled to face her. "Mom? You scared me half to death! What are you doing standing there in the dark?"

"Waiting for you, of course." She went to the light switch and turned the light on. Chad flinched and squinted. "You didn't answer me. Where were you?"

"I had a date with Diana."

"Until nearly two in the morning?"

"We went to the late show, okay?" His voice again had the surly overtones she had come to dread.

"No, it's not okay. The show closes at eleven."

"Keith Fletcher was there, and he was trying to cause more trouble. I had to get Diana away before there was another fight. He tried to follow me, so I drove out to the Old Mill Road and turned off my lights so he couldn't find us."

"Why not just drop Diana off and come home? There was no reason for you to go out there. I know as well as you do that Old Mill Road is a favorite parking spot for teenagers."

"Did you want me to fight Keith again? Diana could have gotten hurt."

Chad was trying to look as if the thought truly concerned him, but Glenna could see through it. She stepped nearer her son. Chad's face looked as if he had been kissing for hours; his hair was tousled, his shirttail coming out of his jeans. The smell of beer was easy to detect at this distance. "You've been drinking!" she exclaimed.

"I have not! You know I don't drink. Besides, I'm in training."

"Don't lie to me, Chad. I can smell it."

"Oh, hell! You never believe me." He turned and stomped toward the stairs. "Believe whatever you want to."

Glenna remained where she was and watched the stranger who was her son go up the stairs. Her eyes were stinging, but it wasn't until she felt the dampness on her cheeks that she realized she was crying. Slowly she wiped the tears away. She had to be strong and to somehow figure out what to do.

After a moment to gather her thoughts, she went upstairs and knocked on Chad's bedroom door. After her second knock he growled, "Come in."

She crossed to his bed and sat beside him as he took off his shoes and socks. "Won't Diana's parents have been worried? I started to call them but—"

"It's a good thing you didn't. They don't wait up for Diana as if she was a baby."

Glenna put her hand on Chad's shoulder. "Don't be like that. I'm trying to say that I was worried and that I'm glad you're safe."

Chad looked at her warily but he didn't answer.

"It's not easy to raise a child all alone," she tried to explain. "You didn't come with an instruction booklet, you know. If your father were here, maybe he would know what to say to you, how to talk to you without putting you on the defensive, but I've never been a teenage boy and I don't know what to do with you."

Chad sighed and wadded his socks into a ball and threw them into the corner. Glenna watched without comment. "Mom, if you'd just get off my back and give me some slack... I feel like you're watching me all the time."

"It's because you haven't been acting like yourself. I'm worried. Chad—" she paused "—you aren't taking drugs, are you?"

First he stared at her, then he laughed. "I can't believe you asked me that! Wait until Diana hears this one."

Glenna recoiled. "I don't think it's amusing."

"I do. No, Mom, I'm not doing drugs." He mimicked her voice. "I'm not robbing stores or stealing hubcaps, either, in case you're wondering. Neither is Diana."

"That brings up something else I've been wondering about," she said in a level voice. "How about sex?"

This time Chad didn't laugh. He locked his eyes with his mother's and stared at her for several seconds, then ground out between his clenched teeth, "Get out of my room. You heard me, get out of here! I don't have to answer a question like that."

Glenna's stomach knotted. Chad hadn't denied it and he looked guilty. She was at a loss as to what to say next. She knew she should somehow convince him not to have sex with his girlfriend, and she had arguments from AIDS to pregnancy to back up her objections, but she knew he wouldn't listen. She had rarely felt so helpless.

"Well? What are you going to do? Sit there while I undress?"

Glenna stood but she felt shaky. "We'll talk about this in the morning. Both of us are too upset to discuss it now."

She heard him mumble something behind her back but she pretended she had not. At two o'clock in the morning no issues could get resolved. She closed the door behind her and walked slowly down the hall.

Her bedroom seemed too big and empty. She stared at the side of the bed Jordan had slept on and wondered again what he would have said to Chad. Certainly Chad wouldn't have been allowed to talk to her the way he had if Jordan were alive. Jordan would have seen to it that Chad grew up with respect for her and the rules.

Glenna sat on the bed and picked up Jordan's silver-framed photo from the bedside table. He looked so alive and young. She tried to divine how he would have handled this crisis, but she received no answer. Awash in a sea of confusion, she put Jordan's picture in its place. After turning off her bedroom light, she removed her robe and slipped between the cool and empty sheets. As she lay in the darkness, her headache returned with a vengeance. A tear rolled down her cheek, and this time it had nothing to do with Chad.

She was so lonely she ached.

CHAPTER FOUR

"KELLY, IF YOU'RE too sick to go to school, you're too sick to talk to your boyfriend." Suspicion dawned on Beau. "Is he home sick, too?"

"It's something that's going around, Dad. A lot of people have it."

"Hmm," Beau said in disbelief. "You don't sound that sick to me. When I left for work this morning you seemed to be on your last legs."

"I thought you'd be happy I'm feeling better," Kelly protested with teenage logic. "Now about this camping trip. Conan and his parents are going to Huntsville State Park and will be gone just for the weekend. I wouldn't miss any school. They rented one of the shelters, so I wouldn't be sleeping on the ground. Please, Dad?"

"No, Kelly. I've never met the Hudsons, and if they wanted you to go, Mr. or Mrs. Hudson would have called me."

"Conan asked them and they said it was all right. Please?"

"I've got to finish this paperwork before my next class. The answer is no, and I'll talk to you when I get home."

"But that's not fair! You let Keith go camping when he was fourteen."

"Keith went with a scout troop, not strangers. Go drink some orange juice and watch TV."

"I don't want any orange juice and there's nothing on that I want to watch." Kelly's voice was petulant.

"Kelly, I'm busy. We'll talk when I come home." Beau was running out of patience fast. He couldn't stand to be nagged.

"Mom would have let me."

"I'm not your mother. Goodbye." He hung up before Kelly could switch the argument to how mistreated she was because of the divorce.

He rubbed his eyes and tried to remember what paper he had been reading before Kelly's phone call. Conan was also at home. With a sinking feeling he wondered if the boy was actually with Kelly. She had said the Hudsons lived nearby. Beau glanced at his watch. There wasn't time before class to run home and check on Kelly.

He had almost collected his thoughts when there was a knock on the door. "Come in," he growled.

Glenna stepped in hesitantly. "Am I disturbing you?"

"The entire world seems determined to disturb me today, Mrs. King." He hoped his brusque tone would conceal the fact that his heart had skipped a beat when he had seen her. "What can I do for you?"

"I have to talk to you, and since this is your free period I thought... But I can come back another time."

"No, no. What is it that you wanted to say?" He motioned for her to sit in the chair opposite the desk in the conference room.

"It's about our sons," she began.

"They haven't been fighting again, have they? Keith said he wouldn't."

"No, at least not that I've heard of. Actually I've come to apologize."

"Oh?" He looked up, and as he frankly stared at her, she moved uneasily.

"I was rude to you when you told me there had been trouble between the boys. I thought Keith must have started the fight and that you were being pigheaded." She paused as if to let the barb sink in, but just as he was beginning to doubt the sincerity of her apology, she contritely admitted, "As it turns out, Chad was to blame."

"He admitted it?"

"Not in so many words, but I know he's been up to something when he's being evasive." She hesitated. "Was Keith at the late movie last night, by any chance?"

"No. He isn't allowed to be out that late on a school night."

"I thought not. Well, I've taken up enough of your time. Thank you for talking to me."

"Not so fast." Beau was having to struggle hard to keep his voice businesslike. His impulse was to take her into his arms. She seemed so vulnerable, and he could see worry in her eyes. "Was there a problem last night?"

"Nothing you need be concerned about." Her silver eyes met his as she asked, "Are you certain our argument won't affect my grade?"

Beau's brows knitted. He wasn't sure whether he was disappointed at this turn in the conversation, or insulted. "I've already told you that it won't. Is that why you came in to apologize?"

"Well, I—"

Feeling his disappointment winning out and not wanting her to know it, he angrily retorted, "Because if you think I'm such an unethical teacher, you should switch to another class. In fact, maybe it would be better if you did that anyway. We don't seem to be able to get along even for five minutes."

"That's not my fault. You jumped down my throat as I came through the door. Are you this hard to get along with all the time or do you just have it in for me?"

This was too close to the truth, so Beau shot back, "It's just you, Mrs. King. Everyone else seems to think I'm easy to be around. Some people even seek out my company on a regular basis."

"Amazing. Do you know a large number of masochists?" she asked with feigned sweetness.

Beau tightened the muscles in his jaw to keep from roaring at her. "Was there anything else or is your rather unique apology finished?"

"It's finished. I can't think why I bothered to talk to you at all. You're the most thickheaded, obstinate man I've ever had the displeasure of meeting."

"Apology accepted. Goodbye." He frowned at her until she slammed the door in her wake.

He drew in a ragged breath. How did that woman manage to get under his skin so easily? Was he really being thickheaded and obstinate?

Glenna opened the door again and stuck her head in. "There's something else. I've decided to drop your class."

"Good!" he retorted as the door slammed again. "And good riddance," he added under his breath. He tried to ignore the loss he felt over her words. His class would seem barren without her.

GLENNA WAS SEETHING as she strode down the hall from Beau's office. She hadn't intended to say she was going to drop his class. It had spilled out of her mouth by accident. She had only wanted him to know how angry she was. Now she had put her foot in her mouth and was going to have to drop a class she really enjoyed.

She walked around the campus twice before she calmed down enough to see what a dilemma she was in. As infuriating as he was, Beau Fletcher was a good teacher. In the few days she had been in his class, he had taught her more about British authors than she had learned in four years of high school. Beau had a talent for making learning seem fun.

On the other hand, she couldn't pretend their argument had never happened. He had sorely provoked her, and she had said she would drop the class. Why had she ever said such a thing? She was rarely given to impulses like that.

Glenna looked at her watch. It was almost three o'clock. She was due at the garden club at three.

Muttering under her breath, she hurried toward the administration building.

"I have to drop a class," she told the woman behind the desk.

"Is there a schedule conflict?" the woman asked as she went to a computer. "Name?"

"King. Glenna King. No, there's no conflict with another class. I'm only dropping it."

"I see. You know there will be a charge for doing that?"

"Yes, I know." Glenna wanted to get it over with. She was weakening and would stay in the class if she didn't move quickly.

The woman called Glenna's name up on the computer. "You want to drop it, you say? Most of the other students are trying to find an opening in one of Mr. Fletcher's classes."

"Is there a form I should fill out? I'm really in a bit of a hurry."

All too easily it was done. Glenna walked out of the administration building and looked around the campus. Her college career had been remarkably short. She grimaced. It was too late to sign up for another class this semester, but she would register again next spring. Once she decided to do something, she didn't let obstacles stand in her way.

She got into her car and frowned at the student sticker she had put on her windshield only a few days before. Now she would have to scrape it off.

As she drove through the quiet streets of Sweet Gum trying to calm herself, her thoughts kept returning darkly to Beau Fletcher and all the trouble he was causing in her life. It hadn't been easy for her to go to his class in the first place, and now, because he had made her lose her temper, she had been forced to drop his course. It just wasn't fair. Again she reminded herself that it wouldn't do for her to arrive at the garden club in a temper. No member of that prestigious group ever admitted to having had a bad day or a less-than-perfect life.

The garden club met at a small brick building bought specifically for that purpose. The building sat on the edge of the rose gardens owned by the garden club. The club met every month to discuss various plants and its own worth to society. The paved parking lot was already full of cars.

Glenna parked across the street and hurried to the building. She hated to be late for anything, especially for anything that Jordan's mother attended. It was Arlene King who had urged her to join the club, and she was sure it was because of Arlene King that she had been accepted into the exclusive fold. The club's roster was made up of ladies who were the blue blood of Sweet Gum, not merely of women who wanted to learn more about flowers.

The speaker was already in full voice when Glenna reached the front door. Glenna crept in and tried to close the door noiselessly behind her, but failed. All the women's eyes turned to her. The group was prepared, she was sure, to chastise whoever it was for her tardiness, but when they recognized her as Arlene King's daughter-in-law and Jordan's wife, their faces changed. Almost in unison they smiled and nodded, then turned their attention back to the speaker.

"Sorry," she whispered as she slid into a chair at the back.

The discussion was on the symbology of flowers, a topic that Glenna had thought would be interesting. She had, however, failed to take into account the talents of the speaker. Harriet Knelford, who was the club's current president, was giving the talk, and Harriet, who meant well, wasn't blessed with a gift for public speaking.

Glenna listened to the woman drone on about rosemary and Shakespeare, but her attention began to wander. Soon Beau Fletcher would know she had dropped his class. Would he care? She hoped he did. She had always thought truly good teachers cared if a student learned or not, and she was sure that he was unusually good at what he did.

She found herself remembering how his voice sounded when he read poetry. Unlike Harriet Knelford's monotone, his words rose and fell in caressing waves. His baritone voice was mellow, and it touched her in ways she thought it best not to question. He had made poetry seem fresh and romantic and as alive as it must have been to the men and women who had penned it. Like all good teachers, he had made her think—not just about the poem, but about the person who had composed it and about what had brought about the poem's creation.

Glenna shifted in her chair and tried to look attentive. Would he call her and ask her to change her mind about taking his class? No, that was most unlikely. He would probably go out and celebrate instead. They had been at odds with each other from the very start.

Harriet shifted from herbs to flowers and began comparing pansies to shyness and spring and offering a few other similes that seemed less well conceived. Glenna looked around the room. As usual there was a good attendance. None of these women worked, and they all considered functions such as the garden club to be part of their routine existence. She was surprised to see that Arlene King wasn't in the room, then remembered she had said something about having a beauty shop appointment at an odd hour this week. The beauty shop was another ritual of Arlene's life and was considered on a par with her club activities.

As Harriet showed them watercolors of various flowers and drew parallels between such things as devotion and true love, Glenna began wishing she were somewhere else. Why *was* she here? She didn't have a green thumb, and her yard and garden were cared for by the son of the man who tended the rose gardens outside the building in which she now was sitting. She had joined the club because Arlene had encouraged her to and because Jordan had been pleased at her becoming as much like his family as possible.

Glenna tried to shake off the urge to bolt out the door. The garden club might not do any actual gardening, but it contributed generously to many charities in which she believed. More than one fund-raising goal had been met because Harriet Knelford had rallied her ladies to the cause. Glenna felt guilty for wishing she hadn't agreed to continue in the club after Jordan's death. As Arlene had said, she was still in the family, mother of their only grandchild, and she had nothing else to do. It was remarkable, Glenna thought, how Arlene and her friends were able to fill their time so thoroughly and never really do much of anything.

She tried to concentrate on Harriet and what she was saying. Soon the talk would come to an end, and she wanted to be able to converse with the others on its merits. As she tried to think about daisies and innocence, however, her mind filled again with thoughts of Beau Fletcher.

DIANA MURDOCK popped a second stick of gum in her mouth and headed for the hall that led to the biology lab. From careful observation she knew that Keith would have that class next. As she had hoped, she saw him standing under the hall clock. With a smile on her face and a swing to her hips, she went to him. "Hi, Keith. What are you doing?"

Keith's surprise was written on his face. "Just waiting for class to start. Why aren't you with Chad?"

Diana shrugged and let her pale hair sway flirtatiously. "Chad King doesn't own me."

"That's news to me. Have you told him that?"

Diana feigned a pout. "We've been having some arguments lately. Chad can be so possessive."

"Yeah, I've noticed. So are you breaking up or what?"

"We might." She lowered her eyelashes the way she had seen seductive women do on television. "I might break up with him if I thought anyone else cared for me."

Keith took the hint. "As pretty and as popular as you are? Half the boys in this school would break their necks trying to date you."

"They would?" she asked innocently. "Does that include you, Keith?"

He grinned. "Maybe."

"Well, I'm not going to break up with Chad on a maybe. Not with Homecoming less than a month from now."

"Okay, then, yes. If you were to break up with Chad, I'd date you."

"Would you date me this coming Saturday? There's a show on that I'm just dying to see." She waited for him to swallow the bait.

"Sure. We'll go out on Saturday. Friday, too, if you want."

"Thank you, Keith. Well, I'll see you." She gave him a wink and hurried away.

Diana loved to flirt. It was the only thing she was really good at other than being a cheerleader. She had discovered at an early age that the combination of blond hair and blue eyes could be used to gain an advantage over almost any boy. To see the boys dance to the tunes she played gave her a heady sense of power, and Diana loved power.

She saw Chad leaning against her locker, waiting for her. Diana's heart beat faster with the thrill of the game she was playing. "Hi, Chad."

"What took you so long? It's almost time for the bell. Where were you?"

Her eyes widened and she looked away, guilt written all over her face. "Oh, nowhere."

Chad's eyes narrowed. "What's that supposed to mean? You had to be somewhere."

"I went to the girls' room to put on lipstick, and half the school was in there, so I went down to the one by the biology lab." She paused for effect. "Keith Fletcher was there. I didn't know he had lab this period. Really I didn't."

"So? Did he say anything to you?"

Diana bit her lip as if she were reluctant to say. "No. Of course not. Chad, I don't want to talk about it."

"Then he did. Didn't he learn his lesson the other day? I'll break him in half this time."

She put a restraining hand on Chad's muscled arm. Feeling the primitive urges pulsating through him excited her beyond reason. "Okay. He spoke to me. Big deal."

"What did he say to you? Don't look away like that, Diana. What did he say?"

Affecting reluctance, she said, "He asked me out. For Saturday. And Friday." She looked up at Chad with wide eyes. "Please don't say anything to him. I don't want any trouble on my account."

A growl erupted from Chad. He glared around him as if he hoped Keith would walk by. "I'll get him for this. I'll show him that he can't try to take you away from me! I'm going to tell him to meet me tonight behind the stadium, and I'm going to tear him apart!"

Diana hid her smile behind the fall of her hair. "Just walk me to class, Chad. I feel so safe when you're beside me."

As they walked down the hall, the bell calling them to their next class rang. She smiled and gloried in her power.

GLENNA COULDN'T SLEEP. Her emotions had been on a roller coaster since she had spoken with Beau Fletcher earlier that week and backed herself into a corner. She loved to learn, and Beau was an excellent teacher. Much better than the local college usually attracted. At least that's the reason she gave herself for the empty feeling inside her now that she would no longer be attending his class.

She had been trying to read, but she had pored over the same paragraph several times and still couldn't have said what it was about. With a sigh she closed the book and stared at the wall, thinking again that perhaps she should get a portable television for her bedroom. She had resisted the urge before because she already had trouble sleeping and thought it might make going to sleep even harder. Now, though, since it was apparent that she was likely to be awake all night anyway, she wished she had something to distract her.

The nights had become long and trying since Jordan's death. She missed him lying beside her. Even after three years without him, she hadn't become accustomed to how lonely a bedroom could be with only one person in a king-size bed. *King*-size. She and Jordan used to laugh about that.

To get her mind off Jordan she replayed the unpleasant scene with Beau Fletcher. He was the most arrogant man she had ever met, and she couldn't imagine any woman wanting to spend her life with such a man. His voice might remind her of firelight and velvet, and he might be handsome, but his abrasive personality negated all that. She wished now that she hadn't gone back to the school to apologize. She especially wished she had not taken the time to put on her prettiest dress and to redo her makeup. The man was a cretin!

Unwittingly, her thoughts turned to his appearance and the striking contrast between the pale color of his shirt collar and his tanned neck, and she wondered if he was involved in some sport that kept him so tanned and trim. His body wasn't thick with bunched muscles as Jordan's had been. Rather he seemed to have the long muscles usually associated with swimmers.

The last time she had seen him, his eyes were as green as the moss that grew on riverbanks. She wondered if they turned that color when he was angry or if it had been a trick of the light. Since he had been angry every time she had been close enough to see their color, she wasn't sure.

Glenna gave herself a mental shake. Thinking about Beau Fletcher was even less conducive to sleep than thinking about Jordan. After a glance at the clock, she let her head fall back onto the pillow. Nearly midnight. The night was ticking away.

Since she was obviously not going to sleep anytime soon, she swung her legs out of bed, intending to go downstairs to watch television. Sometimes at this time of night there were classic black-and-white movies on, and Glenna loved old movies.

From the hall she heard a rustling sound and froze. Chad had gone to his room at the usual time. She had locked all the doors herself. Was it possible for a burglar to have broken a back window and come upstairs without her hearing him until now? A chill ran down her spine. Her hand rested on the telephone beside her bed.

Again she heard noise. With a mother's instinct, her mind darted to Chad. At times like this, she was positive he was still three years old and in need of her protection. She tiptoed to the door and put her cheek against the wood.

The hall was silent. Cautiously Glenna opened the door and peered out. The hall was dark, but a skylight at the far end let in enough moonlight over the stairs for her to see that there was no one in the hall. She frowned. Surely it couldn't be her imagination. She was familiar with all the house's sounds, and she wasn't one to manufacture noises to frighten herself in the middle of the night.

With a glance at the phone, she decided not to call the police until she knew she had a genuine need. She grabbed her robe from the foot of the bed and slipped into it. Moving slowly, she went into the hall.

The house was quiet. No lights were on downstairs, and when she checked, she found that the doors were still locked. Then she made another round to be sure none of the windows had been broken. Everything was as it should be. Glenna was baffled. She was positive she had heard something.

She went back upstairs and silently opened Chad's door. The room was dark and quiet. As she pulled the door shut again, a suspicious notion entered her head. She opened the door again and said, "Chad?"

There was no answer. Not even the sound of him breathing. "Chad?" she said again. She turned on the light and saw his bed was empty. "Chad!"

The bathroom door was open, and she could tell at a glance he wasn't in there. Her heart began to pound. "Chad!"

She hurried downstairs, turning on lights as she went. The house was empty, and when she looked out, so was the driveway where Chad always parked his car. "Damn!" she muttered.

Her first inclination was to call Diana's parents, but she paused and forced herself to think rationally. Chad wasn't likely to slip out to meet Diana, whom he had seen only a couple of hours before. It was far more likely he was going to meet someone else, such as Keith Fletcher.

She went to the phone and looked up the Fletchers' number. On the fourth ring Beau picked up the phone.

"Do you know what time it is!" he demanded instead of saying hello.

"Yes, I do. This is Glenna King."

Beau groaned. "That figures."

"Is Keith there?"

There was a pause as if Beau was trying to wake up enough to make sense of her question. "It's nearly midnight. Of course, he's here."

"Would you mind going to check?"

"What is this, a prank call? You're not supposed to give your name. You just hang up when the victim wakes up."

"Mr. Fletcher, I'm in no mood for games. Please go see if Keith is at home."

"Why would you think he might not be?"

"Because Chad is gone."

Beau paused again. Finally he said, "Wait a minute." He dropped the receiver on the end table and it clattered in Glenna's ear.

In a couple of minutes he was back. "Hello? You're right. Keith is gone." This time he sounded far more awake than he had earlier.

"I was afraid of that. They must have gone somewhere to fight." Glenna bit her lower lip anxiously. "Has Keith said anything to you about a fight?"

"No, but then he wouldn't. He knows I don't condone that sort of thing."

"Neither do I, Mr. Fletcher."

"Look, let's call a truce long enough to find the boys. Do you have any idea where they might have gone?"

"They could be in any of a dozen places. East Texas is riddled with roads through the oil field. Some of them aren't even marked on the map."

"I think I should go and look for them."

"I believe we should."

"We?" His voice was wary.

"There's no point in you going alone. You don't know the oil field."

"And I suppose you do?"

"Yes, I do. I've lived in Sweet Gum all my life. Come by and pick me up. We live at 618 North Saratoga, three blocks west of Compton's hardware store on South Main. The house number beneath the gaslight is easy to read."

"Yes, ma'am," he said sarcastically.

"I thought we were declaring a truce until we find the boys."

"I'll be there in ten minutes."

"I'll wait for you out front."

Glenna hung up and hurried to her closet. She pulled on the first outfit she found, a pair of jeans and a sweatshirt, and quickly brushed her hair. As she ran down the stairs, she remembered she had on no makeup, but she had neither the time nor the inclination to do anything about it. When she reached the curb Beau was pulling up.

"You're ready. I figured I'd have to wait."

Glenna almost snapped at him in anger because of her frayed nerves but noticed he had a smile on his face and realized he had intended his words as a compliment. Smiling back, she said, "When I say ten minutes, I mean ten minutes." She slipped into the seat next to him and pointed down the street. "Turn left at the corner." Perhaps his abruptness on the phone had only been the result of having been awakened at this hour with such bad news. At a time like this it was important that they work together, and apparently he felt the same way.

Beau was a careful driver, and he followed her directions without question. Glenna thought the most likely place for a midnight fight was the oil road the boys of Sweet Gum had always used as a drag strip. Chad, like his father before him, assumed none of the parents knew this road lay straight enough for a track and had seen more than one perilous race.

"I don't see anyone," Beau said as they turned onto the road.

"Neither do I. Drive to the far end." She leaned forward as if that would make it easier to see Keith.

When the road proved to be deserted, she directed him to turn north. There was an abandoned shack at the bottom of the next hill. "There! In the woods. Slow down." She pointed at the deserted shack. "They may be in there."

Beau stopped the car and they walked to the gaping doorway. There was no need to go in to see it was empty. "Do you come here often?" he asked as he looked at the sagging roof.

"Jordan told me boys come out here sometimes to smoke and drink and try to scare themselves. It's supposed to be haunted."

"Obviously by a ghost with no taste."

Glenna rubbed her head. "Where can they be? It's not like Chad to do something like this."

"Well, it's not like Keith, either. He never slipped out in Denton."

"I wasn't trying to start an argument. I was just worrying aloud." She hurried to the car. "Maybe they've gone to the lake."

For the next hour they drove around the small lake at the edge of town. They found several parked cars, but neither of their sons. Glenna was becoming frantic.

"Calm down. They aren't trying to kill each other."

"Drive by my house again. Maybe he's back."

Beau did as she said, but the driveway was still empty. He looked at her for the next suggestion.

Glenna rubbed her forehead, where a headache was beginning to pound. "Jordan once said the lot behind Wilson's grocery store is a meeting place."

"You often refer to him. Your husband, I mean. How long has it been?"

"Three years, but at times it feels as if he's been gone forever. Other times it's as if it happened yesterday. If only Jordan were here. He would know what to do."

"I don't know how anyone could do more than we have. We've been driving for two hours."

"I know. Do you need coffee? I feel terrible about this."

"The truck stop café will still be open." He paused as if he expected her to object.

"Yes. Let's go there."

They parked between two eighteen-wheelers and went into the neon brightness of the restaurant. Glenna slid into a booth in the no-smoking section, then said, "Is this okay?"

"I don't smoke."

"I didn't think so. I'm so allergic to cigarette smoke that I can usually smell it all the way across a room."

Beau studied her face as they waited for the waitress to bring their coffee. "You didn't put on any makeup."

Glenna touched her face self-consciously. "There wasn't time. I was too worried about Chad to care. I must look terrible."

"On the contrary, I was thinking how young you look."

Her heart did a flip-flop. "As opposed to how old I usually look, you mean?"

"You're the only person I know who can have an argument with yourself. No, that's not what I meant."

"Oh. Thank you." She glanced at him warily. Jordan had always said she looked far better in makeup and had preferred her to wear it even when she wasn't planning to leave the house.

She looked at Beau across the table. His hair wasn't dark enough for him to have a heavy beard, and he looked as well shaven as he usually did. His wavy hair lay close to his head, as if he had just combed it. She found this surprising since Jordan's hair always had stuck out in all directions after he had been asleep.

Realizing she was staring, she dropped her eyes to the cup of coffee the waitress placed in front of her. "I want to thank you for helping me look for Chad."

"What did you expect me to do? Roll over and go back to sleep? I'm not that unfeeling."

The vision of him in bed flustered her. "I couldn't sleep. That's how I knew Chad was missing. I thought I heard a prowler, but when I went to check, the house was still locked. Evidently what I heard was Chad leaving." She added, "Don't you have two children? Where's the other one?"

"Kelly was fast asleep. An earthquake wouldn't wake her up. I left a note on my door to tell her where I've gone, just in case."

Glenna sipped her coffee, musing about his thoughtfulness. Maybe he was a better father than she had assumed.

"What did you think?" he asked with a teasing smile. "That I have her chained to a rafter?"

Glenna looked away, feeling ill at ease under his gaze. "So you have a boy and a girl. I thought so." She hesitated. "I always wanted a girl."

"It's still not too late. You have a few good years left."

She smiled. "Jordan is gone. Unless a star rises in the east, there's not much chance of me having another baby."

"So it's true that you don't date." He made it a statement, not a question.

"Who told you that? Have you been talking about me to somebody?"

"Sweet Gum is a small town. Word gets around."

She wondered if he was evading a more direct answer. "I date occasionally. I'm not looking for anyone to marry, if that's what you mean."

"Neither am I. Once was enough for me." He signaled for the waitress to bring a refill.

"So you're divorced and not widowed."

"Were you wondering? Why?"

Her cheeks burned with her blush. "I wasn't wondering. The thought simply passed through my mind." Hope made her lean forward. "Maybe your ex-wife knows where Keith is."

Beau laughed. "Diedra? She never paid much attention to Keith and Kelly when we were married. Why would she know where he is tonight?"

"Sometimes boys confide in their mothers. Maybe we should call her."

"Not me. We divorced so we wouldn't have to talk. I'm not going to wake her up. Besides, I can guarantee she won't know where Keith is. When a boy is going out to fight, he doesn't clear it with his mother, especially if she lives two hours away."

Glenna slumped in her seat. "I guess you're right. But I still think that if Jordan were here, he would know what to do. He always knew what to do."

"He would probably say to go home and get some sleep," Beau said, unable to mask his irritation.

"That doesn't sound like Jordan."

"Look, I never knew the man, but no one can be as perfect as everyone seems to think he was. It's impossible."

"No, it isn't. Besides, how do you know what people think about him? You *must* have been asking questions about me or my family."

"Come on, let's go. Maybe the boys have gone home while we were here."

Glenna followed him to the cash register and waited while he paid for their coffee. "It's on me," he said as he steered her out the door.

Glenna protested. "I don't like people to pay my way. Let me reimburse you."

"Forget it. Call it a truce gift."

She smiled. "Thanks for the coffee."

He gazed at her. "Did I mention you look damned good in jeans?" Before she could answer, he went around to his side of the car.

As they drove through the quiet streets, Glenna felt a subtle difference between them. There was still tension in the air, but it was more exciting than irritating. Beau rolled to a smooth stop at her curb. Chad's car was indeed in the drive.

"I guess he's home. Do you think they're all right?"

Beau opened his door. "I'll come in with you before I go home."

"You needn't do that."

He ignored her protest and went with her up the front walk. Glenna could feel him beside her, and every fiber of her body called to his. She unlocked the door and opened it to the dark house. "He's here. The hall light is off, and I left it on." She turned to him. "I'll be all right. Thank you for your help."

Beau's eyes, darker than before, met hers, and from his expression she felt as if he were suppressing an unwelcome emotion. Involuntarily, she swayed toward him, and for a moment she thought he was about to kiss her. Then the woman who delivered the morning newspaper drove by and threw the paper onto the walk. Beau raised his head, his gaze following the car, and Glenna had the impression he regretted the interruption.

When he turned back to her, the moment had passed. He nodded as he stepped away. "Good night."

"Good night," she said softly. Then she realized she was still longing for him to kiss her, so she hurriedly shut the front door and locked it. She wanted to savor the tender feelings he had awakened in her, but she had other matters she had to tend to first.

Not bothering to be quiet, she went upstairs and into Chad's room, snapping on the lights as she went. Chad sat up in bed, and when she saw the condition of his eye, she gasped. "Where have you been?" she demanded, although it was obvious.

Chad looked as if he were considering a lie, then shrugged. "I met Keith behind the football stadium and knocked some sense into him."

She had never considered looking there. "Have you decided to just throw all our rules and agreements out the window or are you simply trying to see how far you can push me?"

"The whole world doesn't revolve around you, Mom," Chad observed in a particularly surly tone.

Glenna's temper snapped. "That does it. You're grounded. I've been as lenient with you as I can be, but there's a limit to what I'll put up with. If you have a date for this weekend, you'll have to break it, because you aren't going anywhere."

"You can't stop me!" His swollen eye somehow made his words seem even more threatening.

Glenna straightened and glared at him. "Yes, I can."

She left the room and slammed the door behind her. Because she knew she wouldn't sleep anyway, she went downstairs and got her flashlight and went outside. Glenna knew very little about cars, but she disconnected enough wires under Chad's hood to be certain he wouldn't be able to drive it. Then she went to bed.

CHAPTER FIVE

GLENNA CURLED HER FEET under her and sipped another cup of Margo's scalding hot mocha, trying to relax and let go of the tension that plagued her from her confrontation with her son the night before. "You should see Chad's eye today. It's almost swollen shut. His knuckles are bruised and cut. He looks as if he's been kicked by a mule."

"I'm sure Chad gave at least as good as he got," Margo said.

"That's not the point. I don't want Chad to hurt anyone, either. Can you even imagine Jordan in a fight?"

"Maybe Jordan never ran across someone as troublesome as Keith Fletcher. But then, if he had, Jordan would probably have made friends with him rather than fight. He always was a peacemaker."

Glenna nodded, cupping her hands around her mug to warm them. Always when she was upset, her hands became icy cold. "I grounded Chad, of course. He's terribly upset over it."

"I don't blame him. All he did was defend himself."

"I'm not sure that's true." Glenna stared into the cup. "From what I gather from Beau—Mr. Fletcher—Keith isn't prone to trouble."

"Naturally he would say that. What did you expect him to do? Admit his own son is at fault?"

"You haven't been around Chad lately. I'm telling you, he's changed."

Margo laughed teasingly. "You aren't still hung up on the idea of him taking drugs, are you?"

"No." Glenna didn't meet Margo's eyes. After Chad left for school, she had gone through his room in search of anything that might give a clue as to why he was changing. All she had found were a few dog-eared copies of a popular magazine featuring nude girls. She wasn't happy to see that Chad was developing a taste for that sort of thing, but she thought this was probably normal for a sixteen-year-old boy.

"Trust me. Treat Chad the way you always have and he'll shape up."

"You never had to go out in the middle of the night to hunt for Bobby and Mike."

"You did? Alone? You should have called. Bob would have gone with you."

"I wasn't alone. Beau Fletcher went with me."

"Beau Fletcher? I thought you two hated each other." Margo leaned forward to hear more.

"I don't hate anyone. I really don't. He and I have had some differences of opinion, but that doesn't have anything to do with who he is." She stopped short of mentioning his flirtation the last time she had been with him. She wasn't sure what he had meant by it or even how she felt about it. Until she did, she thought it best to keep it to herself.

"More mocha?"

"No, thanks." Going to a safer subject, Glenna said, "Margo, I'm having a lot of trouble disciplining Chad. He looks and sounds so much like Jordan that I confuse him with his father. Mike looks like Bob. Did you have that problem?"

"No, but then Mike was into everything when he was in high school. For that matter, Bob was, too. Unlike Jordan and Chad." Margo shook her head thoughtfully. "It's hard to imagine Jordan doing anything that would require discipline."

"He wasn't a saint, for heaven's sake." Glenna laughed but felt sure the sound was unconvincing. "Jordan wasn't perfect."

"He was the closest thing to it. As far as Sweet Gum is concerned, he could do no wrong. I can't drive by the King Shelter for the Homeless or sit in the King Memorial Football Stadium without remembering Jordan. I used to feel like crying every time I saw the word 'Memorial' above the entrance."

"It was nice of the school to change the name in his honor."

"No one else deserved it so much."

Glenna glanced at her watch. "It's later than I thought. I told Mrs. King I would come over and help her decide on a theme for the fund-raising concert. I'd better run."

Margo walked Glenna to the door. "Take my advice. Relax and stop worrying so much. I'm telling you, Chad is just going through a phase."

Although she was unconvinced, Glenna nodded. She wasn't at all sure Margo was right.

Arlene King was waiting for Glenna, her table spread with an assortment of colored paper, pencils and pens. "There you are! I was about to send George out to look for you."

"I'm sorry I'm late. I went to see Margo this morning and time got away from me." She waved at George King, who was reading the newspaper in the other room. Even after all these years she had never called either of them by their first names, not that either had encouraged her to do so.

"I think I have everything we need," Mrs. King said with a gesture at the table.

Glenna sat in the nearest chair and shuffled through the papers. "Where is the list of music?" As usual her mother-in-law had bought far more materials than they would use and had probably misplaced the ones they needed.

"I must have left it in the study. I'll go find it."

Glenna rested her chin on her palm and looked around the sun room. She could hear the maid working in the kitchen, but otherwise the house was, as always, as silent as a museum. The color scheme throughout was pale peach and cream, which lent an austere beauty but wasn't welcoming. She couldn't imagine Jordan running and playing in this house, although he had lived here all his life until their marriage.

"Here it is," Mrs. King said as she returned with the list of the musical arrangements. "I had left it by the phone."

Glenna glanced over the titles. "These are good selections."

"I can't take credit for it. Marie Murdock put them together. I'm to do the theme and design the program."

Glenna suppressed a smile. She knew Mrs. King would do no more than watch while her daughter-in-law did the designing.

"How is Chad doing?" Mrs. King asked unexpectedly.

"Chad? Why do you ask?"

"He hasn't been over to see us in days. He isn't ill, is he?"

"No. As a matter of fact, I've been wanting to talk to you about him. I need some advice."

Arlene King sat down and characteristically adjusted her silk skirt so it would fall in graceful lines around her legs. "What sort of advice?"

"I've been having..." Glenna found herself reluctant to discuss Chad now that the subject had been broached. "Well, I've been having some problems with Chad."

"Problems? With Chad?" Her mother-in-law's expression was one of humorous surprise.

"What's that?" George King asked from the other room. "What did she say?"

"She says she's having some problems with Chad." The woman turned to Glenna. "What sort of problems?"

"He's become so rebellious. He seems angry all the time."

"He's what?" George called out. "Who is she talking about?"

"For heaven's sake, George!" his wife exclaimed. "If you want to be in on this conversation, come in here." She turned to Glenna. "I can't imagine Chad being a problem."

Mr. King came into the room and lowered his bulk into one of the chairs. "Chad? A problem?"

Glenna wished she hadn't brought up the subject. "I don't know what to do with Chad these days. Every time I say anything to him he tries to take my head off. He has stopped doing his chores almost altogether."

"I never thought he should have chores." Mrs. King shook her head decisively. "I never insisted that Jordan do chores when he was a boy."

"But I think it's good for Chad to learn how to run a house and to know garbage doesn't take itself out and that dishes don't automatically clean themselves."

"You haven't let your maid go, have you? She came with such good recommendations, and it's almost impossible to find a good one these days." Mrs. King's face was filled with genuine concern.

"I still have her. But Chad is expected to do his share. What did you do when Jordan misbehaved?"

Mrs. King frowned and looked at her husband, who seemed puzzled. "Why, I don't recall Jordan ever misbehaving at all," she said. George nodded in agreement. They both turned their eyes on Glenna.

"Never? Jordan never acted up or talked back to you?" she asked in disbelief.

"Not that I recall. George, do you recall having to correct Jordan?"

"No." He shook his head as if he were racking his brain to remember an occasion when Jordan hadn't been perfect. "No, I can't say that I do."

Glenna stared at them in amazement. "But that's impossible! I mean, I know Jordan was never a problem child, but *all* children misbehave at one time or another." She waited for his parents to recant.

"Jordan was never anything but a joy to us." Mrs. King's eyes grew shiny with unshed tears. "I don't think I'll ever get over him being gone."

"I know. I feel the same way." Glenna pursed her lips thoughtfully, unexpectedly aware that this was the first time she had seen Jordan's mother become tearful over her son's memory without tearing up herself. Forcing her mind to the problem at hand, she said, "That still doesn't tell me what to do about Chad, however."

"Just love him," Mrs. King counseled. "The rest will take care of itself." She touched the corners of her eyes with a fingertip to keep the tears from marring her makeup. To her husband she added, "Watch your arm, George. You're messing up our work."

George straightened up. "What's the boy done?"

"He got into a fight at school. Last night he slipped out to fight with the boy again."

Mrs. King's eyes widened. "Chad wasn't hurt, was he? We should call the police and report the hoodlum!"

"No, no. It's not like that. Chad is at least as much to blame as the other boy. Keith Fletcher is new in town and evidently didn't realize that Chad and Diana Murdock are going steady. I gather the fights were over her."

"Chad and Diana are going steady?" Her mother-in-law smiled, then sobered. "No one ever tells us a thing. I spoke to Marie Murdock not an hour ago, and she never mentioned a word of it."

Carefully Glenna probed. "Do you know much about Diana? I haven't been around her lately, and I'm wondering if she may not be the reason Chad has become so belligerent since they started dating."

"Certainly Diana Murdock couldn't be a bad influence!" Mrs. King exclaimed. "I've known Marie for years. We often serve on committees together."

"I play golf with Caleb Murdock," Mr. King put in. "I can vouch for that family."

Glenna wasn't convinced. A parent's behavior wasn't always indicative of his child's. But she wasn't about to debate that with the Kings. "I've grounded Chad, but I'm afraid I won't be able to enforce it. Mr. King, will you talk to him and see if you can reason with him?"

"Sure, I'll talk to the boy, but are you sure it's a good idea to ground him?"

"We never had to ground Jordan," Mrs. King added. "Not once."

"What else can I do?" Glenna asked.

Mrs. King continued. "A boy's childhood is so important. He shouldn't have to miss a single golden hour."

Glenna mentally chastised herself for asking them for help. She should have known better. "I'll take that

into consideration.'' The sooner she finished designing the program, the quicker she could be on her way.
Discussing Chad with the Kings would be fruitless.
She was pretty sure they wouldn't stop arguing until
they won out.

In record time she had roughed out a program and
selected a color scheme for the musical evening. Mrs.
King was full of praise for Glenna's talent and thanked
her as graciously as if she were as royal as her name.

Glenna was glad to get away from the stiff formality of the King house and into her car. As she drove
home, she wondered if Jordan could really have been
as well behaved as his parents seemed to think. It certainly seemed impossible.

What would Jordan have done about Chad? She
had asked herself that so many times the words were
losing their meaning. Suddenly the answer came. He
would have done nothing. In all the years Chad was
small, she couldn't recall Jordan ever raising his voice
or correcting the boy. Not that Chad hadn't needed it.
Discipline had always been her job. Glenna finally
understood. Just because the Kings had never
grounded Jordan or punished him hadn't meant he
never deserved it. Jordan had happened to grow up to
be an exemplary person, but his parents weren't responsible for that.

Now that she thought about it, she and Jordan had
had their rare arguments over how to raise Chad. Jordan had been in favor of letting him do as he pleased;
she was adamant that a boy needed to be taught right
from wrong. Ruefully, she recalled that as she was
leaving, her mother-in-law had insinuated that Chad's

behavior might be due to Glenna's rules rather than to the boy himself.

She wished she had made some excuse to skip going to see the Kings. She always felt insecure and inadequate whenever she spent more than a few minutes in their company. If only, she thought, Chad still had a strong male role model. Jordan had been wonderful, but now he was gone. The thought was automatic, and as it formed, she realized Jordan hadn't really been all that perfect. If he were still alive, she might have an even larger problem with Chad. Certainly Jordan wouldn't have wanted to punish the boy at all, and that might have made matters worse. This time when she felt the guilt that inevitably followed that sort of thinking, she pushed the guilt, not the thought, aside.

BEAU BOUNCED the tennis ball and caught it effortlessly. He and Joe Tarrant had just finished their usual Saturday tennis game and were walking the several blocks home. "I had to tell Kelly she couldn't go camping with her boyfriend and his parents this weekend. She's not speaking to me."

Joe grinned. "That can be a blessing at times. I sometimes wish my kids would stop speaking to me, especially when I'm trying to watch TV."

"Kelly seems to be growing up so fast. Keith wasn't interested in girls this early. Kelly has been after me to let her date since she was twelve."

"At fourteen she's probably old enough." Joe examined the grip on his racket and ran his hand over the smooth wood. "We let Jody start dating at that age. I dread Kay Lynn getting old enough. At times I want to keep them little girls all their lives.''

"I know the feeling. I guess what really bothers me is that I see a lot of her mother in Kelly. That's enough to turn any parent's hair white.''

"Oh?'' Joe glanced at his friend. "In what way?''

"Diedra always had an eye for the men. I don't know how many affairs she had during our marriage. That was the reason we broke up and why I have custody of the kids. She's too busy jumping from man to man to care about them.''

"That's really rough. I've been lucky to have a wife like Sue Ann. Neither of us has had any problems with fidelity.''

"I wish I could say the same. At times I wonder if I'll ever start trusting women again.''

"Don't let one bad experience ruin the rest of your life. Not all wives are like Diedra.''

"I just hope I'm wrong about Kelly. I don't know what to tell her about relationships. Obviously I'm not a sterling example of how to make a workable marriage.''

"All girls like to play at being grown-up. Kelly is probably just learning how to flirt and how to exert her power over a male.'' Joe grinned. "How else will she ever be able to bring her future husband to heel?'' He swung the racket at an imaginary ball. "How's Keith?''

"I had to ground him for the weekend. He had another fight with the King boy. This time he slipped out in the middle of the night to do it.''

"That happens." Joe whirled his tennis racket in the palms of his hands. "At least with two daughters I've been spared that."

"He has a bruised cheek and some scraped knuckles. He said Chad looks worse. I never had this problem with Keith in Denton. Do you know if this King boy is usually so ready to fight?"

"It's news to me. I don't know him well, but I knew his father."

"Didn't everyone? He's all I've heard about since we moved here."

"He was really something. Jordan was influential in the Jaycees and was a deacon on the church board. He built that indoor pool for the YMCA and founded the shelter for the homeless here."

"I'm surprised he hasn't been canonized by now," Beau said wryly.

"I guess he does sound too good to be true, but I swear he was all you've heard and probably more. I'm told he even made most of his donations anonymously."

"If so, how would anyone know that?"

"Good point."

"Besides, my problem is with the son, not the father. I don't want Keith learning that fights are the way to work through difficulties."

"Have you tried to talk to Glenna again?"

"Sure. I drove her all over the county a couple of nights ago when we were looking for our sons. They came home while we were scouring the back roads in the oil field. If you ask me, everyone would be better off if the Kings forgot to revere Jordan and came down to earth."

"I imagine it's hard for her to raise Chad alone. If he doesn't turn out to be the image of Jordan, some people will blame Glenna."

"That's ridiculous."

"That's Sweet Gum."

Beau thought for a minute. "We had a lot of time to talk that night. She was too worried about her son to stay mad at me, and I finally got to see her without her guard up."

"You did?"

"I might ask her out."

"She won't go."

Beau looked at his friend for a sign he was joking. "How do you know?"

"She never dates. Not a real date, that is. I've seen her out with family friends, but that's it. She keeps to herself."

"A woman her age shouldn't retire from living just because her husband died."

"She hasn't retired from anything. I don't see how she has enough time to do half she does. The society page of the paper is full of clubs she belongs to and charities she's working for and so forth. She's very influential in this town."

"That's not the same as having a life of her own. You make it sound as if she's carrying on under Jordan King's banner. Doesn't she ever have fun?"

"Maybe clubs and charity work are fun for her. I don't know. Sue Ann would rather see a movie or play a game, but who's to say she gets more enjoyment out of life than Glenna King?''

"I think I'll call and ask her out."

Joe grinned. "I'll bet she says no."

"You're on."

AS GLENNA GRABBED for her ringing phone, she dropped her grocery bag onto the countertop, tearing the sack and sending cans and spice bottles spilling into the sink. "Hello?" she said as she rescued one of the spices from the dampness under the faucet.

"Hi. This is Beau Fletcher."

"Oh." She paused as dread filled her. What had Chad done now?

"You sound underjoyed."

"Is there another problem?" She bent to retrieve a can that had rolled to the floor.

"No, I can use the phone for other reasons, too. What are you doing? You sound out of breath."

Glenna straightened. "I'm chasing cans across the kitchen. I was in such a hurry to reach the phone my grocery sack split."

"If I had known you enjoy answering the phone so much I'd have called more often."

With a frown, Glenna said, "Are Chad and Keith fighting again? If so, I—"

"No, not that I know of. Keith is grounded for the weekend and is holed up in the den with two days' worth of videotapes."

"I grounded Chad, too." She didn't admit that he was evidently not at home since the TV was silent. "He was pretty upset about it."

"Keith took it in stride. He knows he earned it."

"Did you call just to let me know that?"

"Nope. I called to ask you to go to the movies with me."

"The movies?" She couldn't keep the surprise out of her voice. "With you?"

"Right. Or we can crash Keith's marathon movie trash-out. He checked out some good ones."

"I don't think I'm free tonight." She had never been good at lying, and she knew he didn't believe her.

"When will you know?"

"Well, I know now. I have another engagement for tonight."

"Did I say tonight? How about tomorrow?"

"Mr. Fletcher, I don't—"

"Beau. I think we're past the 'Mr. Fletcher' stage. After all, you did drop my class."

Glenna felt herself blushing. She felt childish for having done that in a spurt of anger. "Whatever I call you, the answer is no. Thank you," she added.

"You're welcome. How about next weekend?"

"Mr.—Beau, I'm afraid my calendar is booked until the middle of 1995. Perhaps if you call me then." She tried to keep her voice cool.

"Great. Pencil me in, say, in June of '95. We can decide where to go in a year or two."

Glenna set aside the can of green beans she had picked up and leaned against the counter. It had been a long time since anyone had tried this hard to date her. She found she rather liked it. "On the other hand, I may have some cancellations. Maybe you could try me again in, say, autumn of '94?"

"I'll have to check my calendar, but I'll keep it in mind. See you then." He hung up.

Glenna held the phone as if she were reluctant to hang up, then, as a smile crept across her face, she gently replaced the receiver on its cradle. He would call again. At least she hoped he would.

She looked toward the door that led into the rest of the house. "Chad? Come help me bring in the groceries." She waited. "Chad? Are you in there?"

Silence was her answer. Chad had disobeyed her again. All the soft warmth she had felt from Beau's phone call dissipated. She sank into a kitchen chair and tried not to feel as if all was lost. If she couldn't control Chad even to this extent, how could she ever hope to teach him the principles and discernment he would need to be an asset to society? Glenna wondered how Beau had managed to do what she obviously could not.

CHAPTER SIX

"YES, MOM," Glenna said as she cradled the receiver between her cheek and shoulder. "Chad is handsome in his school picture. They turned out better than usual this year." She turned to see the clock on the kitchen wall and motioned for Chad to hurry and finish his breakfast.

Chad pretended not to see her and continued chewing slowly.

Glenna turned her back on him to restrain her temper. Correcting Chad when her mother was on the phone was never a good idea. They spoke so seldom she always tried to keep the conversations on a congenial level. "How is Max?"

"His asthma is better now that he has acclimatized to Arizona. The move was good for him."

"That's good." Glenna had never liked her stepfather but she tried to pretend to her mother that she did. "Maybe if he quit smoking he would feel even better."

"Now don't start on that. Max is a grown man and he's smoked since he was a teenager. He knows how to make these decisions for himself."

Glenna wrapped the phone cord around her hand. "You're right. I suppose it's up to him. After all, it's not as if he has never heard that smoking leads to heart disease, lung problems, cancer and death." At once she regretted her words.

"I had hoped you would be more pleasant about Max. I know you two never became close, but he has been a father to you most of your life."

"I know, Mom. I'm sorry. It's just that I feel strongly about smoking."

"That's fine for you to say, but think how it makes me feel when you go on and on about cancer and heart attacks and unpleasant things like that. You can't know how that tears my heart out."

"I'm sorry." Glenna closed her eyes and tried to keep her voice light. "I'm glad Max is feeling better. Really I am."

"Well, you'd never know it. I mean, we haven't talked in weeks, and practically the first thing out of your mouth is complaints about your stepfather."

Glenna could sense her mother was getting started on her usual diatribe about ungrateful stepchildren, so she said, "Chad is on his way to school, Mom. I'll let you say goodbye to him and I'll talk to you soon." She thrust the phone at her son.

Chad swallowed a mouthful of toast and said hello to his grandmother.

There was a knock on the back door, and through the window Glenna saw Margo waving at her. She made a motion for her to come in. Quickly, she whisked away Chad's empty plate, put it in the sink and handed him his schoolbooks as he told her mother goodbye then hung up.

"Go straight to school or you'll be late again," she instructed as she propelled him toward the door.

"Mom, I know how to go to school." He barely nodded a greeting to Margo as he passed her.

Glenna took down another cup and poured coffee for her friend. "It just occurred to me that Chad seems to feel as hemmed in by me as I did by my mother."

"I guess there's nothing new under the sun." Margo sat at the table and picked up her cup. "I hear most things repeat from generation to generation. Behavior patterns, genes, all sort of things."

"That was my mother on the phone. Can you believe it? We only talked for ten minutes and we were already becoming upset with each other."

"I have an aunt like that. I love her, but I love her more when we aren't together."

"I love Mom," Glenna said quickly. "The problem is Max. You know how he is. There is no subject on which he isn't an authority, even if he's never heard of it before. They moved all the way to Arizona because of his lung problems and he still won't stop smoking."

"Speaking of problems, how's it going with Chad?"

"About the same. I decided to ease up about him being grounded." She didn't meet Margo's eyes. "He came in at reasonable hours all weekend."

"See? I told you there was nothing to worry about. Can I have a piece of toast?"

"Sure." Glenna dropped a slice of bread into the toaster and leaned against the cabinet as she waited for it to pop up.

"I'm walking to lose weight, but it makes me hungry."

Glenna smiled. "You don't need to lose weight. You can still wear the same size you always have."

"I want to keep on wearing that size, too. Where's the butter?"

"In the tray in the refrigerator." The phone rang and Glenna sighed. "You don't suppose that's Mom calling to continue telling me how ungrateful I am, do you?"

"Probably not." Margo opened the refrigerator door and peered in. "Cantaloupe!"

"Help yourself." Glenna gingerly picked up the phone. "Hello?"

"Hi. It's Beau."

Glenna found herself smiling. "Well, hello. I didn't expect to hear from you until 1994."

"I guess my calendar is fast. Listen, there's something we need to talk about."

"Not again!" Glenna covered the mouthpiece and said to Margo, "I think Chad has been fighting again!"

Margo rolled her eyes and pushed the refrigerator door shut with her hip as she ate a slice of cantaloupe.

"No, not fighting this time," Beau said. "Now Keith wants to quit the football team."

"Why would he want to do that in the middle of the season?"

"He says Chad is pressuring him to quit. This far into the semester I don't think it's a good idea to re-arrange his schedule, but Keith is pretty upset."

"I'm sorry to hear that."

Margo whispered, "Who is that?"

Glenna mouthed his name to her. "I don't know what I can do about it, Beau. I could try to talk to Chad, but he may not realize he has caused any difficulty."

"I think it would be a good idea if we talked. Say, tomorrow night? I have to grade test papers tonight."

"Is this really necessary?" She felt her excitement build at the prospect of seeing Beau again, and she tried to quell her interest. "What can we possibly discuss in person that we can't say over the phone?"

"If you tell Chad to lay off Keith, will he do it?" Beau asked bluntly.

Glenna sighed. "Probably not. They dislike each other a lot."

"That's what I thought. How about if I pick you up at seven and we go to Becket's for dinner?"

"Becket's?" she asked doubtfully. That was the best restaurant in Sweet Gum, and his offer sounded suspiciously like a date.

"I was trying to find neutral ground. I know the truck stop is 'our place' but Becket's is quieter and the pie isn't greasy."

She smiled and coiled the phone cord around one finger. "I guess Becket's would be all right."

Margo swallowed a mouthful of cantaloupe. "Is he asking you for a date?" she whispered.

Glenna covered the mouthpiece and shook her head at her friend. "Seven o'clock is fine. Maybe I should meet you there."

"No, I'll pick you up. I have to drive by your house to get there anyway."

"I thought you lived on Amherst. North Saratoga isn't between there and Becket's."

"I always take the long way around wherever I go. It's an eccentricity."

"Or a clever ploy. Okay. Pick me up at seven tomorrow." She smiled as she said goodbye.

"That sounded like a date to me." Margo studied her in disbelief.

"Well, it's not. We are only going to meet to discuss the trouble between Chad and Keith."

"At Becket's? That sounds pretty steep for a teacher's salary."

"He's a professor, not a schoolteacher, and Becket's was his idea, not mine."

"I don't see why you have to sit face-to-face in order to discuss the boys. Why not do it by phone?"

"He has a class in five minutes. You're sounding more like my mother every minute." The toast popped up and she handed it to Margo.

As Margo buttered it, she said, "If you ask me, he's using that as an excuse. It's a date, believe me."

"So? What if it is? Beau is single and Becket's isn't a secluded spot by anyone's reckoning."

Margo put down the butter knife and stared at Glenna. "What would Jordan say?"

Glenna paused, then poured herself some more coffee. "Jordan is dead, remember? I'm single, too."

When Margo was uncharacteristically quiet, Glenna said, "What?"

"Nothing."

"Don't do that to me. Why shouldn't I go out with Beau?"

"I didn't want to tell you, but there's gossip about you two already."

Glenna couldn't help but laugh. "Gossip? About Beau and me? That's impossible." She looked speculatively at Margo. "What have you heard?"

"Marie Murdock told my mother that you're having an affair."

"Marie— Why on earth would she say a thing like that? I barely know Marie Murdock."

"As I understand it, Marie's cousin's wife works at the newspaper office, and she heard it from the woman who delivers your paper."

"Whoa. You've lost me. I don't even know the woman who delivers my newspaper. How could she know anything about me? Especially something that isn't true," she added.

Margo leaned forward. "The story is that she was throwing papers at three o'clock in the morning not too long ago and saw Beau Fletcher coming out of your house."

"At three..." Realization dawned on her. "That must have been the night we drove all over creation and back looking for Chad and Keith. She has quite a nerve spreading rumors about me!" Glenna frowned at Margo. "I think I'll call and confront her."

"I wouldn't do that. If you make too big a thing of it, people will think there's some truth in it."

"But there isn't! I told you why Beau was here at that hour."

"Knowing Marie Murdock, it's all over town by now. She was particularly upset since her only daughter is dating Chad."

Glenna's mouth dropped open in outrage. "I'm going to call Marie right this minute!"

"No, don't. You'd have to say where you heard it, and I promised Mother I wouldn't tell."

"I don't want someone going all over town and saying I'm having an affair when I'm not! How would you feel? I'm amazed you didn't come straight to me with this. When did you hear it?"

"Last Thursday. If I had known you'd be this upset, I wouldn't have told you at all."

"Margo!"

"Sometimes friends have to shield each other from unpleasantness. That's what I was trying to do. Now you can see why I don't think you should meet Beau Fletcher at a public place. It will only add fuel to the fire."

"There's no fire to begin with! We aren't having an affair. And even if we were, it would be nobody's business but our own."

"In Sweet Gum? Nothing is private here."

"Obviously. Not even something that hasn't happened."

"Why not call him and say you'd rather talk over the phone? I think that would be easier than denying you're seeing each other when you'll probably see half of Sweet Gum at Becket's."

"I don't care if people say Beau and I are dating. I just don't want them to accuse me of having an affair. And I especially don't like Marie Murdock's suggestion that we were doing anything immoral with my son under the same roof."

"Mother may have exaggerated that part. You know she does that occasionally. The point is, as Jordan's wife you can't let anyone think ill of you."

Glenna's expression grew dark as her friend's comment hit an increasingly sensitive nerve. In carefully controlled tones, Glenna said, "You make it sound as if Jordan is still alive and well. I'm not his wife anymore. I haven't been for the past three years."

"Not technically, maybe, but everybody thinks of you that way."

"I'm not so sure I like that." Glenna's feelings ran deeper than her words expressed, but she intentionally moderated her response. Slowly she sat opposite Margo and ran her finger around the warm rim of her coffee cup. "I don't like to be put into storage like that. Who really cares if I date Beau?"

"Jordan's parents for one. Two, I should say. Mr. and Mrs. King are good friends with Mother, you know. They would be very upset if they thought there were rumors about you and another man."

"It's none of their business," Glenna retorted more sharply than she intended. She didn't want to be reminded of what the Kings thought about how she conducted her life, for she knew all too well. She still considered herself a part of the King family, primarily because she had worked so hard to fit into it in the first place, but also because of Chad. Yet now she wondered if she should have made an effort to start a life of her own, despite what her in-laws felt was best. She was a bit embarrassed that she also had continued to behave as if she was still Jordan's wife. At the time it had been the easiest solution.

"In Sweet Gum everything is everybody's business. Especially when it involves the Kings. It's not as if you haven't benefited from having your name linked with theirs. When you wanted that loan to repair your roof last winter, the bank put the loan through right away without the usual mountain of paperwork. Right?"

"They would have done the same for any long-term customer," Glenna responded defensively. At the time she'd taken out the loan, she hadn't questioned the speedy approval, but what Margo was saying was beginning to make her think.

"Not without putting up collateral, they wouldn't."

"But I have my savings account with them. We've always used that bank." Immediately she realized what she had said and she amended it to, "I mean I've always used them."

"These days loans aren't that easy to get. And what about the time Chad's car was stuck in that ditch and Harold Bitterwater pulled it out for free? Do you think wreckers operate that way? It was because George King asked him to do it as a favor."

Glenna had a dreadful feeling that Margo was right. "Naturally they consider me to still be a part of the family. Chad is their only grandson."

"Exactly. And that's why they won't be pleased if you go out with Beau Fletcher."

"That's not fair. I don't have to ask their permission. I'm thirty-six years old and have a son who's practically grown."

"Maybe *you* are. I've started subtracting a year on my birthdays. I'm down to thirty now."

"Be serious, Margo. I'm upset over all this."

Margo finished off the toast and coffee. "No need to be. Just refuse to see Beau and let the gossip die a natural death. If no one ever sees the two of you together, they will assume the paper-delivery woman was wrong and feel guilty for having thought ill of you. I've got to run."

Glenna nodded, but her thoughts were far away. She had never considered how much she had allowed everyone to continue to see her as Jordan's wife. Now that Margo had pointed it out, she could think of numerous incidents where the King name had opened doors and paved a path for her, especially in the early days of her widowhood when she had scarcely been able to function. But that had been three years ago and she had continued to allow it, even perhaps subconsciously encourage it.

Even the clubs she belonged to had been chosen by Arlene King.

She picked up the phone and dialed a number. "Hello, Harriet? This is Glenna King. I'm calling about the garden club meeting next month. I was to give the program, but I'm afraid I'll have to back out."

She waited patiently for Harriet to finish protesting. "Yes, I know the history of tulips is important and that we can't know enough about them at this time of year when we ought to be planning spring gardens, but I can't do it.'' She took a deep breath. "The fact is I'm going to have to become inactive. At least for a while.''

Harriet raised her voice in protest, but Glenna held her ground. "I appreciate your kind words, but the truth is, I'm not fond of gardening. Yes, I like the flowers, but there are others who truly enjoy planting them, and I feel it's not fair to them for me to take up space.'' In a sudden inspiration she added, "Think of it as weeding out the straggler.''

When Harriet finished assuring Glenna that no one thought of her as a straggler, Glenna said, "I may become active again at a future time, but for now I need to pull back. No, nothing is wrong. I just need the time to get to know myself a little better.''

When she hung up she felt surprisingly happy. Until that minute she hadn't realized how much she had been dreading having to research the history of tulips. Before her momentum had a chance to wane, she dialed the presidents of all the other clubs her mother-in-law had insisted over the years Glenna belong to. When she was done, she called Mrs. King to tell her what she had done.

"You did what?'' Arlene King was too shocked to keep her voice modulated.

"I've resigned from all my clubs. I think I need to spend more time with Chad. Maybe his rebellion is a bid for more attention. He'll be grown so soon and out on his own. I want to enjoy these last two years. Besides, you enjoy those clubs more than I do.''

"That's not true. You enjoy them, too, I know you do. Did someone say something to upset you? I'll bet it was Harriet Knelford. She was always a busybody, even in high school."

"Harriet didn't upset me. No one did." This wasn't strictly true. She was still distressed that she was the subject of gossip, but she certainly couldn't tell her mother-in-law about that.

Mrs. King sounded doubtful when she said, "I certainly can't fault you for wanting to spend more time with your son. Jordan was all the world to me when he was growing up. I nearly died when he left home." Hastily she added, "Of course, we were thrilled at having you for a daughter-in-law. George and I tell everyone that you are as much a part of our family as Jordan."

Glenna noticed that Mrs. King, like Margo, spoke of Jordan as if he were only on an extended trip and not gone forever. "I appreciate your being so understanding. I couldn't have come this far without you and Mr. King."

Sounding as if she was smiling, Mrs. King said, "It's hard on a daughter when her mother moves away like yours did. Thank goodness my mother was always here in town for me. Of course, she never divorced."

"I have to go," Glenna said. "I have a dozen things I need to do, and I want time to cook a special dinner for Chad tonight." Most of that was true. She really did intend to spend more time with Chad. Otherwise she was afraid she might lose him altogether.

CHAD WAS THERE at the dinner table, but he might as well not have been. He ate silently, his eyes on the plate. Glenna tried to draw him into conversation, but he answered mostly in monosyllables.

"How did school go today?" she tried again.

"Same as always."

"Did you get your grade back on that test in math?"

"Mom, why do you always give me the third degree every time you see me? Yes, I got my test back. Okay?"

"What was your grade?" Glenna made an effort to keep her voice even and not accusatory. At one time Chad would have volunteered all this information.

"I got a D. The teacher lied about what was going to be on the test. Half the class failed."

"I doubt the teacher would trick you into making a bad grade. That doesn't make sense. Can you do extra work to bring the grade average up?"

"No. I'm not going to bust my rear over math. A hundred years from now what difference will it make?"

"None. But five or ten years from now it could mean a great deal."

"I'm not kissing up to the teacher. Either I do well or I don't." He shoveled a forkful of peas into his mouth. "Did you make a dessert?"

"No, I didn't. You're in training. The coach says sweets are bad for you."

"What does he know? All the other moms make desserts for their sons."

"Do they? Who, for instance?" She was tired of being unfavorably compared to unnamed parents. "I'd like to know their names so I can call and ask them for myself."

"There you go again—trying to start a fight." Chad glared at her.

Glenna felt cold all over. If she had this relationship with a husband, her marriage would be in serious danger. How long had Chad looked at her with such disdain in his eyes? What could she possibly do about it? This was going beyond the usual problems that teenagers created, no matter what Margo thought. "I'm not trying to do anything except have a conversation with you. We never talk anymore, Chad. You never bring your friends over. We never do anything together."

"I'm a little too old to need my mommy," her son retorted. "As for my friends, we have other things to do." He stood up and tossed his napkin onto the table.

Glenna made no comment. She didn't know what to say. After a few moments she heard him slam out the back door, and soon his car engine roared to life. She heard him leave rubber in the street when he drove away, but still she sat there. She knew her relationship with her son was headed for trouble.

Mechanically, she cleared the table, put the dishes in the dishwasher, added detergent and turned it on, then went to the den. What was she going to do about Chad? Her first inclination was to talk to Beau about it, but she hesitated because Beau had never seen the Chad she knew. Chad had never been anything but difficult, if not downright surly, whenever Beau had been around. No, she had to figure this out on her own.

She picked up the newspaper and thumbed through it absentmindedly. Chad was so much in her thoughts that she was unaware of the words on the page until a headline leapt up at her. "Parents Anonymous Conducts Parenting Workshop."

Curious, Glenna sat and read the entire article. She was familiar with Parents Anonymous as a group organized to help prevent child abuse and had never considered that they might be able to help her with her problems with Chad. But the article clearly stated that anyone who was having difficulty with parenting could benefit from attending the workshop and by participating in their weekly chapter meetings.

For a minute she considered the possibility. Should she do it? She had never been involved with a group of this type, though it had seemed to her that it was certainly more useful than the organizations Arlene had insisted she join. Arlene had discouraged her from participating in anything outside their own social circle, and Glenna had followed the path of least resistance. Now things were different.

She dialed the number of the group's president and asked when and where the workshop would be. Reid Judson was friendly, and after he had answered all her questions about the workshop, he put his wife on the phone and she told Glenna all about their weekly chapter meetings. Before the conversation was over, Glenna had volunteered to help the group in any way she could.

After she hung up, Glenna was still a bit surprised that she had done this, but she was filled with a growing sense of fulfillment. At last she was going to use her time working with an organization that she felt would truly benefit the community, and she hoped she would get some helpful pointers on better ways to deal with Chad. For the first time in a long time, she felt in control of her home and child.

WHEN GLENNA AND BEAU walked into Becket's restaurant she was uncomfortably aware of the interest they aroused. At that hour the restaurant was full. She glimpsed Marie and Caleb Murdock across the room, but she pretended not to see them.

After they were settled at a table near the fountain, she studied Beau as she pretended to be reading the menu. The dark blue suit he was wearing was stylish and well tailored, and his claret tie was a perfect accent. He was as at ease here in Becket's formality as he had been at the truck stop. Of course, she had been aware from the first time she saw him in class that he was handsome, but in this setting he appeared even more virile than she remembered. Perhaps, she thought, her new awareness of his masculinity was due to the fact that she had consciously decided to give more importance to her own feelings and thoughts and less to what she thought others expected of her.

"I recommend the curried chicken," he said. "I almost always order that here."

"You've been here before?" she asked, not intending to sound so surprised. His comment had unexpectedly broken her reverie and caught her off guard.

"As incredible as it may seem, yes. But I promise I've never taken another woman to the truck stop. That place will always remind me of you."

Glenna smiled, thankful that he not only wasn't offended by her faux pas, but had countered with a light but genuine compliment. "Why, thank you. I hadn't been there since high school. It was always open when everything else was closed."

"Then I'm not the first? I'm shattered."

Glenna enjoyed his teasing banter and the sparkle in his eyes, eyes as deep green and as mysterious as a forest pool—and equally mesmerizing. For a long moment she savored the intimacy, then her insecurity returned and she felt compelled to know where his thoughts were. Hesitantly, she said, "I thought you wanted to talk about Keith and Chad?"

"I do. I also want to talk about you."

Glenna swallowed the lump in her throat. She was almost afraid to continue exploring this new sense of connection with him, but felt compelled to do so. "I'm afraid there isn't much to say about me. I've lived in Sweet Gum all my life. I've traveled some, but not recently. I don't have a college education, but I would like to have a degree someday."

Without taking his eyes from hers, he said, "That's hard to do when you drop the only class you're registered to take."

"How did you know I wasn't registered for any other classes?"

"I checked."

At one time she would have reprimanded him for prying into her business, but the truth was she was flattered. Before she could respond, the waiter arrived. After they made their dinner selections, Beau suggested a wine he thought would complement their meals and waited for her nod of approval before ordering it.

Once the waiter was gone, Beau surprised Glenna by saying, "Keith says he still intends to quit the football team."

At first Glenna was disappointed at the abrupt change of subject, but she quickly felt relief as she realized she had been responding strictly to her feelings, all logic and reasoning left behind. Talking about their children was much safer. "Chad mentioned that. I tried to talk to him about it, but I didn't get very far. I made his favorite casserole last night so he would stay put long enough for a conversation, but he simply wouldn't discuss it." Actually Chad had expressed pleasure at the thought that Keith might quit, but Glenna saw no reason to be so frank and give Beau even more reason to dislike him. "I tried to appeal to his team spirit, but he said the team got along fine without Keith before and they can win without him now."

"That's not quite the way the coach sees it."

"You talked to Jack Hevener?"

"Of course. As I told you on the phone, I don't want Keith to rearrange his schedule in the middle of a semester. He might lose more grade points than he can afford to, to graduate on time. Jack said Keith is an important part of the team, especially since Mike Clark graduated last year."

"Yes, Mike was a good player. I'm friends with his mother."

"Jack seems to think losing Keith could cost the school some wins. He wants to see Sweet Gum take the championship this year."

"He wants that every year. He would still have Chad."

Beau smiled without amusement. "As incredible as it seems, Jack doesn't think Chad can win all the games alone. He appears to think there should be ten other players. Amazing, isn't it?"

"There's no need to be sarcastic. I wasn't implying that Chad was the only important player on the team."

"No? Anyway, I don't want Keith to quit. Not that I'm as rabid about football as most fathers seem to be, but I think it's a bad idea for him to abandon ship just because the going is rough right now."

"I agree."

"You do?"

"I'm not nearly as obtuse as you seem to assume. I want to see the team win, but I also think it's good for the boys to learn the kind of give and take they will be faced with in the corporate world."

"Not all of them will be white-collar professionals. A few might even become lowly teachers."

"Why did you insist I come with you if you are going to spend the evening sniping at me?"

"If we were talking on the phone, you might hang up."

"You've got that right." She attacked her salad as if she wished she were sticking her fork into him instead.

"And believe it or not, I'm not trying to be unpleasant."

"No?"

"I have every reason to expect you to defend your son, and I'm preparing for the battle."

"Perhaps you haven't noticed, but I left my cannons at home. This started off being a very pleasant dinner, and I was beginning to think we might even be able to discuss our respective sons in a civil manner."

Beau looked thoughtful. "I never thought of it that way. Civil. Maybe. It has potential."

Glenna glanced at him in puzzled exasperation. "I can't tell when you're serious and when you aren't."

"Just then I was being a little of both. Okay, let's talk about the boys. I have to admit that I only hear the worst of Chad. I'm sure the same is true at your house regarding Keith."

"Yes, that's true."

"Therefore, I believe it's safe to assume that neither version is entirely accurate nor completely inaccurate."

"Correct again."

"So I propose we start from there and try to figure out some way of preventing our sons from murdering each other."

Glenna was relieved that the chance of war between them seemed to be diminishing. Lightening her tone, she quipped, "We sound like Adam and Eve."

He grinned. "I knew you had a sense of humor. I always suspected it."

"Of course, I do. You've just never seen me under pleasant circumstances. I even have friends."

"I guess I should start by explaining that my divorce was hard on the kids. I thought Keith had taken it better than Kelly, but now I'm not so sure. I see an anger in him that wasn't there before."

"Divorce can be extremely difficult on children. My parents are divorced, so I know that firsthand. It's equally hard when a parent dies, and that's what Chad is struggling with. He's become more difficult lately, but I expect that's because he has more pressure on him to be a carbon copy of his father than I had assumed. I had a conversation lately that opened my eyes about how Sweet Gum views us."

"Kelly is a handful, too. She's fourteen going on twenty and is positive she is the only girl in Sweet Gum who can't come and go as she pleases."

"I'd like to meet her. For that matter, I'd like to meet Keith."

"You would? Why?"

"To get to know them, of course. How can we reach a workable decision as to how to handle our sons if I never meet Keith?"

"True. I met Chad in the principal's office, but you could hardly call it a meeting. We barely spoke."

"It certainly would have been under awkward conditions," she agreed.

"What do you suggest? We can hardly take the little tykes out to the park together."

"Why don't you come for dinner one evening, and I'll come over to your house on some excuse or other?"

He smiled. "I'd like that."

"To talk about the boys, I mean."

"That's what I meant, too."

The meal was over too soon. Glenna wondered if Beau was oblivious of the stares they were receiving or if he was simply ignoring them. She felt like something under a microscope.

As Beau drove through town, she found herself unaccountably quiet. She hadn't had an attack of shyness since high school, but she seemed to be unable to think of anything to say. At the same time she wanted to say too much. This evening she had thought Beau had decided to postpone the discussion of their children so they could have time to get to know one another better, but then he had turned the conversation to the boys and the intimate mood had been broken. Until she knew whether Beau was interested in her for herself or if he was simply trying to make peace between the boys, she was afraid to give too much of herself away.

"You're awfully quiet," he said as if he had been listening to her thoughts. "What are you thinking?"

"I was wondering if you only asked me out because of our sons."

"Not entirely."

"No?"

"We could have talked that out over the phone or let the boys work it out the hard way. But I wanted to see you."

"Why?"

He laughed. "You cut right through to the heart of matters, don't you? I honestly don't know. I don't want to start a new relationship of any kind. I don't have the time or energy it takes, and after my divorce I'm not sure I want a relationship at all.''

"That's honest enough. As a matter of fact, I feel the same way.''

"You do?''

"I recently found out the town sees me as something I'm not. At least that I'm not anymore. I want to try my wings at last and see if I turned out to be a butterfly or a moth.''

"You're a butterfly. Trust me on this.''

Glenna gazed at him in the dark. The instrument panel lights and streetlights gave off enough glow for her to see his features, but not clearly. She decided she shouldn't pursue what he meant by that. "Since neither of us wants commitments, maybe we could be friends.'' She added, "I'm very good at being a friend. You can ask Margo Clark for references. We've been friends since grade school.''

"Friends? I could handle that. I guess you've heard the gossip about us?''

Glenna's heart sank. "What gossip?''

"There's a rumor that we're having an affair. The dean asked me about it. He didn't realize you had dropped my class, and the college has rules forbidding fraternization.''

"I hope you set him straight!''

"I did. Had you heard about it?''

"Yes, but it was so ridiculous I never gave it a second thought,'' she lied. "Sweet Gum is like any other small town when it comes to gossip.''

Beau parked in front of her house. "I still don't know how such a rumor got started,'' he commented.

"I'm sure I have no idea, and I really don't want to talk about it." She reached to open her door. When she got out she saw Beau coming around the car to walk her to the door. "There's no need to see me in. We're just friends, remember?"

"I'd feel better knowing that you're safe inside. Call it a holdover from having lived in and near a city too long."

Glenna fitted her key into the lock and opened the front door. The hall light was on in welcome. She hated to return to a dark house. She turned to Beau. "Thank you for dinner. I feel we've at least begun to accomplish a peacemaking."

"Anytime." He leaned forward and his eyes met hers.

Glenna couldn't have looked away if she'd tried. It was as if time were suspended between them. Beau's eyes were dark and intent as though he was silently wondering whether she would push him away. Glenna knew she should. She couldn't make herself do it.

His lips covered hers and she swayed toward him. Her pulse was racing so fast she thought he must be able to hear it. Every nerve in her body sprang to life at his nearness. Her breasts molded against his chest, and she felt the length of their bodies match. Beau's arms tightened around her and he kissed her as she hadn't been kissed in too many years. Her heart skipped, and she realized her arms were around him, too, holding him close.

When he at last released her, she felt as if her knees had turned to jelly. She knew she should reprimand him, to tell him she wasn't ready or willing for that kind of relationship. The words wouldn't form. Her lips felt soft and her cheeks warm. Finally, she was able to say, "I thought we were just going to be friends."

He grinned. "There are all kinds of friendship."

Before she could reply, he was leaving. Glenna went inside and shut her door, but she leaned against it with a smile.

CHAPTER SEVEN

WHEN THE KNOCK SOUNDED on her door, Glenna thought it must be one of Chad's friends. Chad was sprawled on the couch, watching TV, and gave no sign of having heard the bell, so she went to answer it.

Beau Fletcher stood on her doorstep. "Hi. Want to go see a movie?"

Glenna was so surprised she couldn't think of an answer. The sight of him triggered a fresh recollection of the passionate kiss they had shared on her doorstep. "I didn't expect to see you tonight."

"I know. I was out walking and thought I'd drop by. That new movie with Jane Seymour is playing now."

"It is?" Glenna had seen the film advertised on television. "I *had* planned to see it."

"If you're like me, you hate seeing a movie alone. All my married friends want to see it with their wives, and a threesome at a romantic movie is definitely not appealing."

Glenna glanced over her shoulder. "I think Chad has plans for tonight. I guess I could go."

"Just throw all caution to the wind and come on. The next show starts at seven."

She looked at her watch. "We have time to make it." She felt her resolve weakening. "What about us being seen together?"

"I'm not ashamed of you, and as far as I know, you're not ashamed of me. What do you care what gossip mongers say?"

"You obviously haven't lived in Sweet Gum or any other small town for long. Gossip makes the wheels go around."

"So let's give them something to whisper about."

"Okay, I'll do it." She lifted her chin decisively. "Come in while I tell Chad where I'm going."

Beau followed Glenna into the den. "Chad, I'm going to the show. What are your plans for the evening?"

"I'm going over to Diana's. Who was at the door?" He didn't bother to look around.

"Me," Beau said. "Your mother and I are going to see that Jane Seymour movie."

Chad turned so quickly he almost fell off the couch. His expression was comical in its amazement. "You! And my Mom? A date?"

"You heard him. Would you and Diana like to meet us there?"

"No way. I mean, we don't . . . I didn't really think you two . . . Oh, forget it."

Glenna smiled. She was enjoying Chad's discomposure. "Beau and I met because of you. Remember? You and Keith, that is. I'll be in before you, probably."

"Probably?" Chad frowned at his mother as if he were the parent and she a teenager going out on her first date with a boy.

"Or maybe not," Beau said with a wink at Glenna.

She laughed and hurried to get her coat and purse. When she returned, Chad was gone and Beau was turning off the television. "Where's Chad?"

"He went tearing out of here as if he were heading for a fire. I imagine he went to Diana's house."

"I shouldn't have sprung you on him like that. He doesn't know we've become friends, and he knows I never date. It must have shocked him."

"Shock is good for teenagers. It gives them practice at keeping their balance in an ever-changing world." Beau opened the door for her and waited while she checked to be sure it locked behind them. "I can't wait for you to meet Keith and Kelly. They both think I'm in the dinosaur set."

"It seems to go with the territory."

He matched his steps to hers as they walked downtown. "I like to walk," he said conversationally. "You don't see as much when you're in a car. It all goes by too fast. I walk to school when the weather is nice and when I get an early enough start to make it on time. But that's not very often."

"You like to sleep late? I wouldn't have guessed that."

"And you'd be right. I get up early to read my day's lesson. I'm a morning person and I do my best thinking then."

"I'm sorry now that I dropped your class," she admitted. "I've never heard anyone read poetry the way you do. I have to admit I wasn't looking forward to the poetry part of the class. Literature is my favorite."

"Mine, too, actually. I'm sorry you dropped out, too. Maybe you could sign up again next year. The poetry semester is a prerequisite for the prose semester."

"I may do that."

"Of course, then we couldn't shock your neighbors like this. The college frowns on fraternization. We'd have to be content with passing lurid notes in class."

Glenna laughed. "I like being with you. I really do."

"Amazing, isn't it? I like you, too."

Glenna glanced at him. "I guess we just got started off on the wrong foot."

"An understatement if I ever heard one. You came on like Dragon Lady."

"You needn't elaborate. We proclaimed a truce, remember?"

Beau took her hand and held it as they walked. "Fighting with you is the last thing on my mind."

"Oh? What's the first thing?"

"Do you really want to know?"

"No." She looked away quickly. Her hand felt small and secure in his, and she discovered she really didn't care if anyone saw them walking along hand in hand. In her new resolution to be her own person, holding hands with Beau Fletcher might rank high in importance.

The movie was as good as she had expected it would be. Beau bought a huge container of popcorn with butter, and they sipped their soft drinks contentedly.

When the credits rolled at the end, Glenna was sorry the show was over.

As they walked home beneath the orange glow of the streetlights, her hand was again nestled in his, this time at her own instigation. In a nearby yard a dog barked, and as they passed an elderly couple, they exchanged a nodded greeting. Glenna didn't know the couple, but she assumed they would think she and Beau were a married couple taking a break between dinner and bedtime. The intimacy of the thought startled her and she withdrew her hand.

"What's wrong? Afraid they'll tell our parents?" he teased. "Maybe they're out courting, too."

That possibility hadn't occurred to Glenna. Then she realized the impact of what Beau had said. "Is that what we're doing? Courting?"

"I don't think it's still called that, but yes." He added thoughtfully, "What do they call it these days? We seem to have let a perfectly good word become archaic without coining another to take its place. I'll have to ask Keith. Or better yet, Kelly. She seems to be the romance expert."

"Is she still upset over not going camping with her boyfriend?"

"Yes, she says her life is ruined and it's all my fault. But I ask you, could you let your daughter go camping with a family who would name their only son Conan? They probably wear animal hides and eat raw meat."

Glenna laughed. "As a matter of fact, they aren't so bad. I know the Hudsons. Their primary flaw lies in the naming of their children. Conan's sisters are named Storm and Tempest.''

''You've got to be kidding.''

''I swear. Storm is in Chad's class. She's one of the band twirlers this year.''

He looked at her as if his thoughts were far from the subject of their conversation. ''I'm glad you went with me tonight. I was half-afraid that you wouldn't.''

''Were you? I can't imagine you being insecure about anything.''

''Good. My mask is working. No, I have as many doubts as anyone else.''

''Jordan never seemed to have any doubts,'' she said thoughtfully. ''Not a single one.''

''I forgot. He was perfect.'' Beau looked away.

''Actually, I was thinking what a flaw that was.''

Beau turned to her with a look of surprise.

''Do you have any idea how hard it is to be with someone who never has clay feet or makes a bad decision? It can be very intimidating.''

''I can imagine. I can't imagine, however, anyone being of such sterling quality in real life.''

''Lately, I can't either.'' Glenna shook her head. ''I don't mean to be finding fault with Jordan.''

''It's okay with me.'' Beau tucked her hand into his.

''Would you like to go to the football game on Friday?'' she asked suddenly. ''I'll understand if you don't want to.''

''Sure I would. What could be more fun than watching our sons charge at someone other than themselves for a change?''

Glenna smiled. ''Well put.''

"Besides, I think it'll drive them crazy if they see us dating each other."

"That's a distinct possibility. Chad was certainly tipped off balance." She found she was enjoying the prospect of being in the lead in the struggle with her son. "Let Chad wonder what I'm doing and where I am for a change."

"Parent power. We should all band together and have a sign or a password."

"We do. It's called gray hair. You and I just haven't been in the club long enough to have earned ours."

"I'm afraid you're right."

Glenna breathed in the cool night air and let herself become fully aware of how much she was enjoying walking beside this man. Beau was special, and this time in her life could be special, if only she could hang on to it.

"WHAT DO YOU MEAN you're going to the game with Keith Fletcher's dad?" Chad demanded.

"What don't you understand? He's going to pick me up in his car. We'll sit together in the bleachers. Afterward we'll probably go somewhere for coffee and then come home. A date."

"He asked you for another date?"

"No, I asked him." Glenna pretended to be mulling over a thought. "Maybe I should pick him up. What do you kids do in a situation like this?"

"This isn't funny, Mom." Chad glowered at her, his head lowered and his hands on his hips.

"I wasn't trying to be funny. I have a date with Beau Fletcher, and I don't see any humor in that. Do you think he'll like this sweater I'm wearing? It's supposed to turn cold tonight." She held out her arms and looked at her fisherman-knit sweater. Beneath the cream-colored sweater, she was wearing a red blouse, and she had donned her best jeans. "Maybe I should dress up more and take a chance on freezing."

"Don't change the subject. I don't want you to go with him again."

Her eyes widened in surprise. "I didn't ask your permission. You seem to forget that I don't have to do that."

"You're doing this to get back at me, right? Okay, so I'm upset. Call Mr. Fletcher and tell him you aren't going."

Glenna reached up and patted her son's cheek. "When you glare like that, you remind me of when you were a little boy. You dad used to say he hoped your face wouldn't freeze like that."

A growl rumbled from Chad's throat as he reached for his coat. "I can't stand around here. I have to pick up Diana and go to the field house."

"All right, son. Return with your shield, or on it, or whatever it was that those Spartan mothers used to say. Knock 'em dead."

He shook his head and left. Glenna put her fingers to her mouth to hide her smile in case he looked back. She was enjoying putting Chad on the defensive.

A glance at her watch told her she had a while yet before Beau would be there, so she went into the den and curled up in her recliner. She picked up the book she had been reading earlier, but she couldn't get interested in the words. As she raised her head and looked across the room, a picture of Jordan and herself caught her attention. The photo had been taken on a vacation and they looked relaxed, healthy and happy—like a toothpaste commercial, she had told him when she had framed the picture.

Glenna got up and went to the photo. There were others on the shelf, all of Jordan and Chad. Until now she hadn't realized how few there were of her. The reason, of course, was that she was usually the one taking the pictures, and she had always been more prone to frame photos of them than of herself. She now wondered, however, why Jordan hadn't taken pictures of her more often and why he never thought to display the ones that he had taken. Had she always been no more than a satellite to him? And to Chad? The idea wasn't a pleasant one, but she had to admit its truth. Until she'd started dating Beau, she had rarely done anything that would make waves in the King pond.

But now she had caused a few ripples, and, she decided, it was time for more. Resolutely she gathered up the pictures of Jordan and herself and of Jordan alone and took them to the kitchen table. Soon she had relegated them to the photo album in which she kept the studio portraits and the more important photos of her family.

Next she began rearranging what Jordan had called the "sit-arounds" so the room would be balanced again. As she placed a heavy crystal swan on the shelf where Jordan's largest picture had stood, she let her fingers trail over the glassy surface. Her life was changing, and she hoped that when she completed her metamorphosis, she would prove to be a swan in her own right and no longer merely the reflection of one.

She stepped back to assess the new arrangement. The room now was subtly her own. For a moment she felt a twinge of sadness that the changes had been necessary, then she heard the doorbell and the sadness disappeared as she hurried to greet Beau.

As they drove to the game, their conversation was light and animated. After they exchanged pleasantries about the days since their movie date, Glenna related her favorite story about the peacocks her grandmother tried to raise when Glenna was a child. Beau shared several humorous anecdotes from his first teaching job. Glenna was keenly aware that Beau was keeping his eyes on the road and his attention on his driving, and for the first time since the accident that killed Jordan, she felt safe and secure riding in a car. But it wasn't just her confidence in Beau's good driving habits that was helping ease her fear, it was something about the man himself, the same intangible something that had sparked the courage she needed to throw off the shackles that had kept her from being herself. She still wasn't sure who she really was or what she wanted to be, but the more time she spent with him, the more she liked who she was becoming.

As she studied Beau's profile, now freely comparing him to Jordan and finding that comparison surprisingly in Beau's favor, she thought he looked *accessible*. That was an odd trait to ascribe to someone, but for Beau it was true. No one would ever be tempted to put Beau Fletcher on a pedestal, and even if anyone did, he was the type to climb down again. He was outspoken but not opinionated, and she never felt he was trying to intimidate her or force his beliefs on her. His intelligence was the sort to feed her own, not overwhelm it. He had his vulnerabilities, but he was not afraid of them, or of his emotions. When he was angry, he expressed it. When he was happy, he laughed. And the passion of his kisses—

"What are you smiling about?" he asked.

She realized she had been staring and she turned away, still smiling. Feeling suddenly shy, she answered, "I was just trying to picture you on a pedestal."

Beau laughed. "I would never fit. Does that disappoint you?"

"On the contrary. It pleases me."

"There's a seminar on British writers in Dallas next weekend. Would you like to go?" His hand covered hers.

She wasn't sure, but she had an idea he was offering more than a chance to hear about British writers. "Next weekend?" she hedged.

"Last year they featured contemporary American writers. I went and I enjoyed it. There will be several workshops and it will last all day on Saturday."

"Chad is at such a difficult age. At sixteen he's too old for a baby-sitter, and I'm not sure he wouldn't have Diana over or host a weekend-long party the minute I pass the city limits." She wanted to go, and she was fully aware that the reason had nothing to do with British writers.

"I asked my neighbors to look in on Keith and Kelly."

"I suppose I could ask Mrs. King to check on Chad."

"Of course, Keith doesn't have a steady girl, and he doesn't know enough people yet to have a really all-out wild party."

"Mrs. King would probably relish the chance to see Chad alone."

"And Kelly's boyfriend is too young to drive a car yet, thank goodness."

"If Mrs. King is tied up that weekend, I could ask Margo."

"But I understand if you feel you shouldn't go. After all, there is the matter of the gossip we seem to have stirred up. Maybe Chad shouldn't be tempted by too much freedom."

"I'll have to think about it. Do I have to tell you right now? Because if I do, I'll have to say no." She paused and found herself hoping he would give her some leeway. "I could let you know tomorrow or the next day. Tomorrow. I could tell you tomorrow."

"That would be fine."

"Okay. I'll go. You're right. I shouldn't hover over Chad like a mother hen. If I can't trust him to behave for a weekend, I can't trust him, period."

Beau smiled. "Did I say all that?"

"Maybe I shouldn't go. Mrs. King and Margo would be up in arms if they thought we were going away together for a weekend." She blushed. "Not that I think you meant anything, well, intimate by your invitation. Don't get me wrong. I'm not trying to put words into your mouth. But Mrs. King and Margo don't understand that we're just friends. They wouldn't understand at all."

"Is your answer yes or no? I can't keep up with you."

"It's no. Yes, it's definitely no." She frowned. She wanted to go. Being able to see him for an entire weekend was very appealing. "On the other hand, why should I have to ask their permission? That's what it really boils down to, isn't it? It's high time I made such decisions for myself. Yes, I'll go."

"When you finish arguing with yourself, tell me the final score."

"It's yes. I'll go to Dallas with you. And forget what I said about it sounding too intimate. I was out of line to even think such a thing. I'm sorry."

"Are you through? The answer is yes, you'll go?"

Glenna nodded. "Yes. Thank you for asking me."

"You're welcome. And thank you for the mental tap dance. I don't think I've ever seen anything like that before. Is this how you make all your decisions?"

"I rarely have any decisions to make. Not like this, at any rate. My biggest decisions lately have been whether to cook pot roast and what blouse to wear."

"And whether to drop my English class."

"I made the wrong decision there, as I said. At the time I didn't feel I had a choice."

"By the way, you weren't putting words in my mouth about us going away together for a weekend. Not necessarily. I'm leaving that up to you."

Glenna looked at him for a long time without speaking. At last she said, "I don't know how to make that decision. As I told you, I've rarely dated since Jordan died, and I sure haven't been doing anything else." She felt herself blushing brightly. "I guess I'll never pass as a *Cosmo* woman."

"I have to admit that I've wondered. Not even once?"

"Not even nearly."

He smiled. "I like that. It's certainly a refreshing change from my ex-wife."

Glenna shook her head. "It's not that I'm frigid or anything like that. It's just that a person would have to mean something to me for me to go to bed with him."

"I feel the same way. Do I mean something to you?"

She drew her hand away from his and punched him in the arm. "Don't ask me that! Not at a time like this."

"Ouch. All I meant was should I reserve one room or two?"

She thought for a moment. "Reserve two. I'm not sure I'm ready for anything else." She drew a deep breath. "Does that alter your wanting me to go with you?"

"Not at all. I never had anything else in mind but to go to the seminar. I don't want to rush you into anything."

She wondered if that meant he eventually intended to lead up to that. To her surprise she hoped he would. "You confuse me," she said. "I think I know what I want and then I find myself thinking exactly the opposite. Meeting you has turned my whole world upside down. I quit all the clubs Mrs. King convinced me to join. I've been teasing Chad just to watch him stew. Margo thinks I've taken complete leave of my senses. You're a bad influence on me."

"Am I? Or am I just an overdue one?"

"And you ask questions that are too hard to answer. Do you have this effect on everyone?"

"No, just the ones who want to get out of the rut they're in."

"Is that how you see me? In a rut?"

"Not anymore."

"Mrs. King was upset over my rebellion. I was to give a talk on the history of tulips at the garden club's next meeting."

"The history of tulips? Now there's a thrilling subject. I've always wanted to know, but I was hesitant to ask."

"Don't tease me. It really is interesting to some people, just not to me. I don't like to garden. I've never liked getting my hands dirty, and gloves make me too clumsy."

"I don't like it, either. I've always said that if I could afford help, I would hire a gardener. I don't even like to mow the yard. Does Chad mow your yard?"

"Theoretically. I usually end up paying a neighborhood boy to do it, or I do it myself and complain the rest of the day."

"Keith and Kelly take turns. I try to rotate chores so neither feels as if I have it in for him. Being teenagers, they usually feel that way anyway, but at least I can tell myself I tried."

"Being a teenager is so difficult. I remember how it was for me. My stepfather and I were always arguing. I don't think we ever agreed on anything."

"That must have been rough on all of you."

"It seemed to be at the time. Looking back on it, however, I can see that most of the things I thought of as life-or-death issues then weren't all that important. That's the teenager's curse, I suppose. Everything seems to be top priority and there's no room for negotiation."

"I think you're right. Naturally I was perfect as a teenager, but my sister was a pill."

Glenna laughed. "Right."

"It's a shame I didn't know you then," he said.

"I was going steady with Jordan all the way through school."

"I might have given him a run for his money."

Glenna smiled. "You might have at that," she said softly as they pulled into the stadium parking lot.

Football had never particularly interested Glenna. She liked the bands at halftime and watching the people parading up and down on their way to the concession stand. She watched for Chad's number, and whenever he did anything that seemed remarkable, she cheered and clapped her hands.

"You aren't even watching the game, are you?" Beau accused.

"Sure I am. What are you talking about?" She had been watching a group of teenage girls with their hair sprayed red and blue, the school colors.

"We just lost the ball and you clapped."

"So did those people over there."

"They're rooting for the other team."

"Oh." She had tried to be interested in football, but she had never found the game to be logical, much less exciting. "Did you see those girls with the wild-colored hair?"

"Yes. I could hardly miss them."

She glanced at the scoreboard. "Only one minute left, and we're ahead. It's been a good game." She knew by experience that this was a safe observation.

Beau grinned. "Look, Chad is about to hand off to Keith."

"How can you tell? Oh, look! He did!" She rose with the crowd and clapped loudly as Keith ran for another touchdown.

"Would you like to go now and miss some of the traffic? The other team can't possibly catch up with us before the game is over."

"If you'd like."

Beau helped her down the bleachers, and as they passed the concession stand, he waved at three girls and two boys standing in line. One of the girls waved back, did a double take and frankly stared.

"Who is that?"

"My daughter, Kelly. I'd introduce you, but she made me swear I would pretend not to know her. I gather all the others have parents who are too cool to speak to their kids in public. She's wondering who you are."

"You didn't tell them you had a date tonight?"

"Yes, but not that it was with the most beautiful woman in town."

"I'm not. Don't say that." She always felt uneasy when anyone complimented her appearance. People usually did it in such a way that it praised Jordan and his choice of her.

"You have that look on your face again."

"No, I don't. What look?"

"The one that says I've stepped over another boundary. Why can't I say you're beautiful? You are, you know."

"I don't believe it, that's why. I don't need to hear that kind of compliment. It's not necessary."

"I really meant it."

Glenna shook her head. "Can't we talk about something else?"

"Does it embarrass you? Why should it?"

"I don't know! Okay?"

Beau shrugged. "Okay, but if you ask me, you should have become accustomed to getting compliments by now. If I were married to you, I'd have told you so often you would have believed me."

Glenna refused to look at him. She knew he had divined the reason compliments had always seemed false to her. Compared to Jordan she was plainer, less co-ordinated, less talented at almost everything. Compliments had been his right, not hers. She wondered how Beau had ever figured that out when she hadn't known it herself.

CHAPTER EIGHT

"ARE YOU SURE this is a good idea?" Glenna whispered as Kelly walked ahead of them in the mall.

"Kelly loves to shop. She misses having her mother take her to the mall. This is the perfect place for you two to get acquainted."

Glenna was not convinced, but she kept it to herself. Since Beau had picked her up, Kelly had sat slumped in the back seat. Now she was walking several yards ahead of them as if she didn't want anyone to know they were together. She had yet to speak a word to Glenna.

"She's pretty. Her hair is darker than I expected. I'll bet yours was blond as a child."

"It was. Kelly looks more like her mother."

Glenna fell silent. She knew Beau wasn't on friendly terms with his ex-wife, and she wasn't sure he liked being reminded that his daughter resembled the woman. Glenna wondered if the resemblance was only in her coloring. Kelly didn't look at all like Beau. "Do Kelly and Keith resemble each other?"

"I forgot you've never seen Keith up close. Yes, they do. They both have curly dark hair and brown eyes. I asked Keith to come with us, but he had other plans."

"So did Chad. At least, he said he did. He thinks he's too old to go shopping with his mother."

"It's hard to be a teenager." Beau's eyes were on his daughter. "Kelly is a child one minute and an adult the next. I never know what to expect."

Kelly glanced over her shoulder to be sure her father was watching her, then she headed into a dress shop. Beau and Glenna followed. Glenna was familiar with the shop. It carried expensive dresses that she would have assumed were out of Beau's price range.

As if she were rummaging through her own closet, Kelly slid clothing along the racks until she found a cranberry sweater she liked. She held it in front of her and peered into the mirror.

"That's a nice one," Glenna said. "You would look so pretty in that color."

Kelly looked at Glenna as if the words had come from a complete stranger. Without responding, she put the sweater back and went to look at dresses.

"How about this one?" Beau asked as he pulled an apricot dress from the rack.

"Oh, Dad." Kelly sighed with amusement. "I could never wear that."

"Apricot is a good color this year," Glenna said. "Perhaps if you tried it on you'd like it."

"I hate orange." Kelly moved to the jeans.

Glenna caught a glimpse of the price tag on the pair of jeans Kelly held up and hoped Beau would read it before he gave the girl permission to buy them. Glenna wouldn't have paid half that for her own clothes, let alone for school clothes for a girl who was still growing. "There are some nice ones in Twain's. Maybe we should try it. I always find just what I'm looking for there."

Kelly sighed and didn't look at her. "I detest Twain's. All my friends' mothers shop there. They don't have any clothes that I would like."

Beau frowned at his daughter. "Behave, Kelly. You remember what I told you."

Glenna was reasonably sure she could guess what the instructions had been. She had issued her share of edicts to Chad when company was coming, especially when she knew Chad didn't particularly like one of them. Beau hadn't mentioned that Kelly had decided to dislike his new lady friend even before meeting her, but it was evident Kelly had done just that. Nevertheless, Glenna was determined to win the girl over. She went to the jewelry counter and picked up a necklace made of blue and silver beads. "Look, Kelly. This would be pretty with the blouse you're wearing."

Kelly rolled her eyes and looked at her father. Beau's glare at his daughter spoke volumes. Shaking her head, Kelly went to Glenna and looped the beads over her finger. "Nope. Too short."

"There's a longer one here." As Glenna was fishing out the necklace from behind the others on the plastic rack, the rack tilted and would have spilled onto the floor had Beau not caught it. The saleslady behind the counter gave them a reprimanding glance, but Beau and Glenna's eyes met and they smiled at the near disaster.

Kelly caught the intimate exchange and flounced away without looking at the necklace. Glenna suppressed a sigh of frustration.

The girl went back to the sweaters and once more fingered the cranberry one. Glenna could see she really wanted it. An inspiration came to her, and she beckoned the saleslady. "We would like that sweater, please."

Kelly's eyes darted toward her, and for a moment Glenna saw the little girl in her. Then Kelly straightened and pushed the sweater back on the rack. "I don't want it."

The saleslady turned to Glenna for instructions. Glenna shrugged. "Maybe your daughter would like that same sweater in blue," the woman suggested.

Kelly gave the clerk a frigid glare, then turned and strode out of the store, leaving the adults staring after her.

Glenna took the sweater off the rack and handed it to the clerk. "I know she wants this one." She handed the woman a charge card.

"Let me pay for that," Beau objected.

"No, really. I want to do this. I think it may help Kelly see me as something other than an interloper if I give her a present."

"Maybe. I'm sorry she's acting like this. I had no idea she would be such a pain in the neck."

"She's not being any such thing," Glenna said with more conviction than she felt. "She just doesn't know me."

"That's no excuse for rudeness."

Glenna took the sack containing the sweater from the clerk and went with Beau to where Kelly stood waiting in the center of the mall's walkway. "Here. I got the sweater for you."

Kelly seemed about to waver, but instead she shook her head. "I told you, I don't want it. I don't know why you didn't listen to me."

"Take the sweater," Beau said in a threatening voice. "And say thank you."

Kelly glared at him but took the sack. "Thank you," she muttered.

"You're welcome," Glenna answered automatically. She could see now that she had made a mistake in buying the sweater. Kelly would assume Glenna had done it in an effort to buy her affection. Uncomfortably, Glenna realized that it was true.

"You need some new sneakers," Beau said. "Let's get some while we're here. Glenna, Kelly was telling me that all the girls are wearing pastel ones this year. Maybe you could help her pick out a pair."

"I'd be glad to help," Glenna said a bit too quickly. "What colors do you wear, Kelly?"

"Blue," she said, holding her shirt collar between two fingers. "I wear blue. And cranberry," she added darkly.

"Blue," Glenna repeated tactfully. She thought the girl needed a spanking more than she needed new shoes, but she kept her opinion to herself.

The shoe store carried blue in shades from aqua to baby blue to almost violet. Glenna pointed to the pale blue ones. "Those go best with your blouse."

"I can pick out my own shoes. I'm not a baby." Kelly refused to meet Beau's eyes and missed his visual reprimand.

"Maybe you don't need shoes after all," Beau said threateningly.

Glenna put her hand on his arm to keep him from saying more. Kelly frowned at Glenna's hand until Glenna stepped away from Beau. "I like these." Kelly pointed to the near-violet ones.

Glenna looked doubtfully at them. They were a color that wouldn't go with many others. "Are you sure? These baby-blue ones are more versatile."

By now a sales clerk had come to wait on them. "Your mother's right," she said helpfully.

Kelly turned on the woman and ground out, "She's not my mother."

"That does it," Beau said. "No more shopping today." He stepped back and motioned for Kelly to precede him out of the store. She did as he indicated, but her cheeks were blazing with anger.

Glenna had rarely felt so uncomfortable. She supported Beau's decision not to reward Kelly's bad behavior, but she knew the girl would blame her. Helplessly she walked with Beau to the car. Kelly had outdistanced them immediately.

"I apologize for my daughter's behavior," Beau said stiffly. "She isn't usually like this."

"I'm sure she isn't. She just doesn't want me to take her mother's place. Not even on a shopping trip. I can understand that."

"So can I, but I don't condone it."

"I told Chad I'm going to be out of town next weekend. He was upset when I told him that I'm going with you."

"Maybe you shouldn't have been so direct."

"Why not? We aren't planning an illicit weekend. It's a seminar. Besides, I was afraid you were going to tell Keith and that he might say something to Chad. I wanted to be open with him.''

"That's probably best. I told Keith and Kelly that we're riding to Dallas together. I guess word could have gotten back to Chad.''

"Maybe that's why Kelly is so upset with me,'' Glenna suggested.

"I hadn't thought she was before today, but you're evidently right. There's no other reason for her to act like a spoiled brat.''

"No, no. She's not spoiled. I don't blame her for trying to stake out what she considers to be her territory.'' She thought for a minute. "Does this mean you don't bring women to shop with Kelly on a regular basis?''

Beau laughed and reached for her hand. "You're the first.'' He looked at her in a way that melted Glenna's heart. "It's important for Kelly and Keith to get to know you.''

"Why? Why is it important?'' She suddenly felt out of breath and weak in the knees as she waited for his answer.

"Because you have become very important to me.'' His voice was low and caressing, almost intimate, and he seemed to be oblivious to the fact that they were walking through a crowded mall.

Glenna felt as if she were full of smiles. "You're important to me, too. It scares me a little, but you are.''

"Yeah.'' Beau tucked her hand more firmly into his. "It scares me a little, too.''

BEAU WASN'T SURE he wanted Glenna to know why he had invited her to the British writers seminar in Dallas. He was hardly able to admit it to himself. For days, weeks, she had rarely been out of his mind. He found himself wondering what she was doing and what she would think of this or that. Things a lover would wonder.

The words scared him. Love. It was such a short word to have such a big meaning. Beau had been sure he was in love with Diedra when he married her, but now, in the face of his new knowledge, he wasn't at all certain. What he felt for Glenna was far different from what he had felt for Diedra, even in the early days of their marriage. As different as a shower from a hurricane.

He glanced at Glenna, who was seated next to him in the packed lecture hall. She was leaning forward, trying to absorb all the speaker was saying about the contrasts and similarities between Jane Austen and the Brontës. Beau was far more interested in Glenna's contrasts. At times, like now, she could be silently intent and appear to be totally confident. At others, she seemed so unsure of herself that he wanted to protect her. She was naively complex. Beau smiled. She was a paradox, and he was fascinated by all her facets.

Glenna apparently felt his gaze on her, because she turned to look at him, and he found himself becoming lost in her silver eyes. She wore her hair in a sleek pageboy style that brushed her shoulders. He had noticed her hair first, that day he had found her in the front row of his class. Her hair was thick, and its red-gold hue was remarkable. He had wanted to touch it from the very first.

After a long moment, he realized they were staring at each other, and he made an effort to focus his attention on the lecturer. Glenna did the same, but now he sensed her lack of interest in the speech. She was as aware of him as he was of her. Beau wasn't sure how he knew this, but he was positive.

When the lecture was over, Beau stepped into the aisle between the tables that were serving as desks and held a place in the exiting crowd for Glenna. She smiled as she stepped in front of him. He caught a trace of her perfume and had to restrain himself from pulling her to him and burying his face in her hair.

"That's the last lecture," he said as he consulted the sheet of paper they had been given on registration. "We're free until the banquet tonight. Dr. Quincey Pilzner."

"Did you read Pilzner's latest book?"

"*The Last Georgian*? I read it but I didn't agree with his premise. Some of the writers he referenced were really early Victorian writers, not Georgian."

"I tried to read it when I heard he was going to be here, but I couldn't get interested in it."

In a whisper for her ears only, Beau said, "That's because his style is as dry as sawdust. He has a lot to say, but it's hard to stay awake until he makes his point."

Glenna smiled and whispered, "Do you suppose he speaks the way he writes?"

"I don't doubt it." Beau studied her profile. "Are you suggesting we might skip the banquet?"

"It's up to you." She seemed to be avoiding looking at him.

"I wouldn't mind if we did."

"Neither would I."

"We could spend the time discussing the conference."

"We could do that."

"Or we could talk about our kids and what to do with them."

She wrinkled her nose. "Not that. I need a break from thinking about Chad and what to do with him."

"You know, we ought to combine forces." He walked her to the elevator and held the door as she went in. "United we stand, that sort of thing."

"It has a nice ring to it. United in what way?"

Beau wasn't sure himself. He thought he had sworn off commitments. That was before Glenna, however. "Keith and Kelly need a woman's hand, and I suspect Chad could use a father figure. In a manner of speaking, we could form a sort of parent co-op."

"I don't believe I've ever heard of one of those."

"I just made it up a second ago. Think about it. We could offer each other the parental part that's missing. I'm sure the kids would benefit from it."

"How would this proposed co-op work, exactly?"

She looked up at him and he saw the amusement in her eyes.

"I'm not sure. We might have to spend a great deal of time together planning it."

She pretended to be serious. "I could do that. For the kids' sake, I mean. No sacrifice is too great for a parent."

"Exactly. We may find a method of child raising that will revolutionize parenthood."

"And even if we don't, we'll have someone else to talk to about it."

"Yes." He grinned at her. "Would you like to come to my room for our first planning session?"

"A planning session?"

"Or whatever."

Glenna nodded slowly. "I don't really want to go to my own room this early. Not if we aren't going to the banquet."

"I don't want to be alone, either," Beau confessed. "It seems as if I've been alone for too long already."

Glenna wondered if he could possibly mean that as intimately as it had seemed. She could seldom tell when he was teasing and when he was serious because of his unique way of combining the two, but she had discovered she enjoyed trying to figure him out. The challenge was refreshing after having had Jordan spell everything out to her for so long. Immediately she was aware that the thought had not triggered even the slightest twinge of guilt. With relief she was aware that she no longer thought of herself as Jordan's wife.

Beau put his key into the lock of the room next to hers. "We could open the door between the rooms and not have to come back through the hall."

"Good idea." She opened her door and unlocked her side of the connecting door. When Beau opened it from his side, she stood still for a minute, trying to decide if this was really what she wanted.

Beau also seemed to be making a decision, because he simply stood there gazing at her. Glenna knew they were at a turning point in their relationship. "I thought I didn't want any more commitments," she said in the stillness. "I never intended to have anyone else in my life but Chad."

"I felt the same. It turns out that kids can't fill all the empty spaces. At least not for me."

"I feel that way, too. At times I feel guilty that Chad isn't enough. I've tried to tell myself that he should be."

"Sundays are the worst." Beau ran his fingers through his hair as if he, too, were trying to decide if this was all right. "Sundays and holidays."

"And evenings. Dinnertime is terrible. That's when families are usually together or at least touching base with each other." She paused. "And bedtime."

"Yes, bedtime," he agreed softly. "But it's not a gap that can be filled with just any warm body. Sometimes you're more alone with someone else than you would be if you had no one at all."

The pain in his eyes touched her soul, and Glenna stepped forward. As if this was the signal he had been waiting for, Beau took her in his arms. For a long moment he gazed at her as if he was trying to memorize every detail of her face. Then he ran his fingers through her hair, and she pressed her face against the firm wall of his chest.

Drawing in a deep breath, she closed her eyes. She felt heady with the fragrance of him—his after-shave, the laundry-clean smell of his shirt, and beneath it all, the scent of his warm skin. Her arms tightened around him and she ran her hands over the broad planes of his back. Her fingers dipped in at his spine, then caressed the swell of muscles on either side. He was as lean and as firm as if he spent his days as a laborer.

Beau tilted her head and lowered his lips to hers. Glenna tasted the warmth of his mouth and opened her lips beneath his. His tongue tempted hers, and she felt as if the room rocked beneath her feet.

The kiss seemed to last an eternity, and in that span of time, Glenna made her final decision. When he released her, she walked with him to the bed. Beau sat beside her and they kissed again. Glenna lay back, drawing him with her. Their bodies touched. Glenna was certain they were wearing far too many clothes. She stroked her hand along the column of his neck, pausing to feel his pulse beating as quickly as her own, then moved her hand to the top button of his shirt.

Beau drew back, still poised over her, his hand entwined in her hair. "Glenna, be sure before we go any further. I don't want just one night with you."

She stroked his smoothly shaven cheek. "I wasn't offering just one night. Maybe you're the one who should be sure."

He gazed at her. "I love you, Glenna."

Her breath seemed to catch in her throat. "Don't say that unless you mean it, Beau."

"It's not something I could say lightly. I do love you. I've tried not to. The last thing I wanted was to fall in love with you or anyone else. I don't even know how you feel. I've tried to figure you out, but you're a mystery to me. I know I'm taking a chance telling you. I'm afraid you'll run from me now, but I had to tell you. I want to make love with you, and I don't want you to think I'm doing it merely because we're out of town or because I just want to see if I can get you into bed. I love you, Glenna."

She felt tears sting her eyes, but they were tears of happiness. "I love you, too, Beau. Don't you already know that? I feel as if our souls are together even when we are not."

"You feel it, too?" His eyes were soft. A lover's smile was on his lips. "It's as if I'm a part of you."

"I know. I feel it." She hesitated. "I don't know if I'm ready for marriage or not. I think you should know that."

Beau nodded. "I understand."

"I don't think you do. I have so many ghosts to bury first. I can't rush into anything. I have to be certain."

"So do I."

She smiled at him. "Can I just love you without any strings attached? Without any ties or promises?"

"Is there any other kind of love? I don't want to rush you into more of a commitment than you feel comfortable with. I'm not ready for marriage, either."

"Do you really love me?" She wanted to hear him say it again. The miracle was still so new.

"Yes, Glenna. I do love you." He smiled at her tenderly, and as he traced his fingertips over her lips, he said, "How could I know you and not love you?"

She unbuttoned the top button of his shirt. She no longer had any doubts. Beau was here with her, and he wanted her as much as she wanted him. Knowing he would expect no more from her than she was willing to give freed her to love him without restraints.

Beau pulled her blouse out of her skirt waistband and began unbuttoning it. The air felt cool on her hot skin. The touch of his fingers as they grazed the skin between her breasts excited her more than she would have said was possible. She kicked off her shoes and heard him do the same.

His chest was smooth and corded with muscle. Glenna ran her hand under his open shirt and marveled at how good he felt to her. Every inch of her was crying out for his touch, and he seemed to know it. She shifted so he could reach the buttons down the side of her skirt, and he accommodated her without a word being said.

Beau rolled her over so that she lay flat on her back. Kneeling over her, he slid the skirt over her hips along with her half-slip. His hand glided up the outside of her leg to her waist, then he slipped two fingers under the elastic at the top of her panty hose. Glenna was eager for him and tried to help him remove her clothing, but with a smile he kissed her hands and put them on his shoulders.

"Let me," he murmured. "I've thought about this a lot."

She smiled. There was no shyness with Beau. It was as if they had been lovers for an eternity. At the same time, Glenna felt as if each action was new. Beau slowly drew off her panty hose and let them drift over the side of the bed. He caressed her hips and buttocks and ran his fingers along the top of her bikini panties.

Glenna's breath felt ragged in her throat. She wanted to draw out each moment, savor each touch, but the gnawing need within her begged to be quickly met. She saw Beau's eyes darken as if he knew exactly what she was feeling and was equally affected by their mutual longing.

She unbuttoned the rest of his shirt and pulled it away from his shoulders. His torso was as perfect as she had thought it might be. Hard muscles rippled under her questing fingers, and his skin was taut and smooth. Her hands played across his chest and down his ridged belly and up his ribs. "You feel so good!" she sighed. "I love the way your skin feels."

Beau eased away from her, but only long enough to remove the rest of his clothing. Glenna gazed at him in open admiration. "Your body reminds me of Michelangelo's David. Only warmer."

"Definitely warmer," he said with a grin.

He helped her remove her blouse and unfasten her bra. Glenna felt more naked than she had in a long time, and she studied his face to see if he was disappointed in her. By the expression in his eyes and the smile on his lips, she knew he was not. Her momentary shyness was replaced with urgency.

"Beau, I want you," she whispered. She drew him to her so that their skin teased, then touched. He caught his breath, and she knew he had felt the electric charge just as she had. She had never been so eager for fulfillment in her life.

As Beau slipped her panties down, she arched her back, lifting her hips to help him. The full length of their bodies kissed as she buried her face in the warm curve of his neck and held him tightly.

He rolled so that she lay beside him, her head cradled on his shoulder. Gently, he touched her waist, then let his hand drift up to cup her breast. Glenna's heart pounded and she felt light-headed, almost floating in his embrace. Soon his fingers became more bold and he rolled her nipple to a bead that throbbed for his touch. When he lowered his head and bathed the pouting bud with his hot tongue, she laced her fingers in his hair and arched her back to offer herself to him. Beau's arm slipped under her, and he lifted her toward his lips and seeking tongue. Glenna heard a sibilant moan escape her lips.

The tip of his tongue traced her open lips, and as their lips met and his tongue began probing her mouth, she rolled her hips against his loins. Her body was tingling all over from wanting more of him, and she could tell he felt the same.

Beau was a consummate lover, teasing and pleasing her until she cried out for him in her need. Only then did he ease between her thighs and become one with her. Glenna called his name as he filled her, and she wrapped her legs around him, pulling him deeper into her. As he began to move within her moist recesses, her body answered his as if she were the instrument and he the musician.

Almost at once she felt the rushing headiness that meant her climax was near. Beau moved more surely, and Glenna gasped as her body was rocked with the force of her culmination. Beau's body continued playing its rhythmic song of love, gradually slowing the tempo, and soon she became aware that he was holding back on his own ultimate pleasure, letting her enjoy every last moment of her own. When she opened her eyes, she found him smiling down at her.

Glenna couldn't put the love she felt for him into words, for it was too grand for such meager expression. A moment later, he started to move again, and she was amazed as her body gladly responded. She had never experienced anything like this before, and she opened her mouth to tell him so, but the ecstasy of the moment was too great and she could only murmur his name. She held fiercely to him as her blood turned to lava and her body answered the primitive call of his. This time when her world exploded into prisms of light and pleasure, he rode with her. His arms tightened reflexively and she heard him call her name as he pressed into her.

For an endless time they drifted in the ethereal mist of contented lovers. Glenna touched his face in wonder; he drew his fingers through her hair. She smiled and saw the same smile reflected on his face. He nuzzled the erogenous spot behind her ear and she put butterfly kisses on the pulse in his throat.

"If I hadn't already been in love with you," he said at last, "I would love you now."

"I've never—" She stopped herself. This moment was too precious to let any memories crowd in. He had given her pleasures she had never known were possible. "I love you," she said instead.

"You remind me of firesides and flowery meadows and sunshine when you look at me this way," he whispered.

"I feel like firesides and flowery meadows and sunshine. I'm glowing inside."

"I know. I can feel it."

She rubbed her forehead against his cheek and into the curve of his neck and shoulder. "Let's stay right here forever," she said softly. "I never want to go back into the world."

"I wish we could." He held her securely, as if he was determined to keep the world at bay. His mouth tilted in a grin. "I'm glad now that you dropped my class. What would Dean Winston say?"

Glenna laughed and put her arm across his chest so she could explore the long muscle in his arm. "For that matter, what will everyone say?"

The thought sobered her. She shrugged it away and put it out of her mind.

CHAPTER NINE

"MOM?" KELLY LEANED forward eagerly at the sound of her mother's voice over the phone.

"Why, hello, Kelly. I didn't expect to hear from you."

"What's wrong? Are you crying?"

Diedra sniffed. "No, baby. At least not very much."

"What's happened? Are you sick? I could come take care of you."

"No, no. I'm not sick. It's just that Ted and I broke up." She sniffed again. "I guess I'm just feeling blue."

Kelly frowned. "I hate it when you're unhappy." It was true. She felt as if her stomach were tying itself in knots. "Are you sure you don't want me to come to Denton and look after you? I could cheer you up."

For a moment Diedra was quiet, as if she was giving the suggestion consideration, and Kelly's hopes began to rise. But then she said, "No, you can't do that. Your daddy would never allow it. You know how he is about me."

Kelly had a sudden inspiration. "No, he's changed. He talks about you all the time."

"He does?" Diedra sounded more cheerful already. "What does he say about me?"

"All sorts of things." Kelly prevaricated, making things up on the fly. "Maybe if you came for a visit, you two could patch things up."

"You think so?"

"I know so. Gosh, Mom, you can't imagine what Sweet Gum is like. No one but dweebs live here. Except for my boyfriend, of course."

"You have a boyfriend? You're growing up!" Her mother made it sound like an unexpected calamity.

"His name is Conan Hudson and he's real neat. His hair is below his shoulders, and his parents let him get his ear pierced."

"Your boyfriend is named Conan? Does he have an older brother?"

Kelly didn't understand why her mother would ask such a question, so she ignored it. "Mom, they are just now starting to wear Minnette earrings here." She touched her earrings as she imparted this evidence of Sweet Gum's backwardness. In Denton all her friends had worn Minnettes, a new style in which one's earrings didn't quite match each other. "Sweet Gum is still in the Stone Age. And I don't mean stoned."

Diedra laughed. "Kelly! You're so bad!"

Kelly smiled. She liked it when her mother treated her like a grown-up and laughed at things that would have drawn a questioning frown from her father. She had never had anything to do with drugs, either here or in Denton, but she sometimes hinted to her mother that she might have. For a moment she felt a bit uneasy that her mother never questioned her about that. Her stomach began to knot again, so she put the worry from her mind. "I'm glad you don't treat me like a baby. Dad won't even let me date unless a parent is driving."

"You're kidding! I wouldn't do you that way."

Kelly slid lower in her chair and rested the receiver between her cheek and her shoulder. "Can I come live with you?" she asked.

"You know your daddy wouldn't let you."

"Then you come here. If you lived in Sweet Gum, Keith and I could at least see you more often."

"Honey, think about it. What would I do in a place as dead as Sweet Gum? I'd die of boredom in a week."

"What about me, Mom? Don't I count? I can't see you in Denton."

"That's not my fault, you know."

Kelly sighed. "Maybe if you sent me money for a bus ticket, Dad would let me come for a weekend."

"Sorry, hon. I don't have any money."

"You don't? What are you living on?"

Diedra's voice grew mournful again. "I'm making do. I'll be all right."

"I could send you my allowance. I have nearly twenty dollars saved up."

"I can't take your money. I'm not that hard up yet."

"Will you let me know if you are? I can mail it to you."

"Sure, babe."

"Mom, do you ever wish you and Dad never got a divorce?"

Diedra laughed. "Sure I do. I never knew how good I had it. You should see the rags I'm wearing now."

Kelly's active imagination supplied a picture of her mother clothed in rags and living on the streets of Denton. She felt she had to do something, so she told another lie. "Mom, I'm really calling because Dad asked me to."

"Oh?" Diedra's voice became wary. "Then why didn't he call me himself?"

"I guess he was afraid you might yell at him." Kelly was frightened when her mother shouted at her, and she assumed that her father might feel the same way. "We miss you and he wants to make up with you."

"He said that?"

Kelly hated to lie, but she would for a good cause. Years from now she was sure her parents would thank her for it. Besides, she had to do something or her dad might find someone else. Someone like Chad King's mother. "Yes, he did. So I was thinking, Homecoming is next week and he's supposed to be one of the chaperons for the dance. If you just happened to be in town and happened to drop by the Community Hut, he would be there. You could wear a pretty dress and fix your hair shaggy like I saw it last, and he couldn't say no to you."

"He really said he wants me back?" Her mother sounded hopeful.

"Yep." Kelly felt a stab of guilt, so she didn't elaborate. She reminded herself that this was for her dad's own good.

"It's this coming Friday? I don't have anything planned for that night." After a hesitation Diedra said, "I might just do that. What about my red dress? You know, the one that's cut low, the one Ted liked?"

"Perfect. Dad likes red."

"I thought blue was his favorite color. Oh, well, you would be more likely to know that than I would. So the red dress it is. I'll have to get a permanent."

Kelly again thought of her mother in rags and wondered how she would ever be able to afford a permanent, but she knew how resourceful adults could be. "The game starts at seven if you want to see it."

"Football games aren't my gig."

"The dance will be afterward. I guess it'll start about ten."

"Okay. I'll see you at the dance. You will be there, won't you?"

"Sure. I'm going to meet Conan there. I can't wait for you to meet him." She smiled to think how glad her father would be to see her mother coming toward him across the dance floor. It would be just like in a movie she had seen once. They might rush into each other's arms and kiss right then and there. At the very least, they would talk, and somehow a miracle might happen and they would decide to remarry. "I have to go now, Mom. I have homework to do."

Kelly was grinning as she hung up. From the sound of her mother's voice, Kelly was sure she was already deciding what jewelry and shoes she would wear with the dress.

THE NIGHT of Sweet Gum High School's homecoming dance, Glenna was wearing a silver-gray dress that made Beau's hands itch to touch her. The dress was of lightweight wool that clung to Glenna's shapely upper torso, then floated away, promising more than it revealed. As they danced, her bright hair swung toward her face whenever she bent her head, then swept away again when she looked at him. Beau had never seen a more provocative woman. "That dress reminds me of Dallas."

"Don't look at me that way," she said with a smile to belie her words. "Everyone in here will guess what you're thinking."

"All the men are probably thinking it already. You're beautiful, and when you smile like that, you seem to glow from the inside out. Your hair makes a man want to tangle his hands in it. Your lips—"

"If you plan to stay here and chaperon this dance, you had better not finish that thought. We are supposed to be setting a good example for the kids."

Beau pretended to pull a long face. "Is this better?"

Glenna laughed and shook her head. "You're impossible. Look, there's Kelly. Is that Conan Hudson she's dancing with? Goodness, but he's grown tall."

"That's Conan, all right. I drove them here, and you would have thought Kelly was being sentenced to death. I let them out in front and then parked so they could at least walk in alone."

Glenna nodded. "I remember when Chad first started to date. We went through the same sort of thing."

Beau leaned nearer and whirled her to the music. "Have I told you that I love you in the past five minutes?"

"That you love me in the past five minutes? No, I don't think you tied it down that specifically."

"An English teacher with a misplaced preposi-
tional phrase. You would probably have made an A in
my class."

"Probably. I have an in with the teacher."

"I enjoy the way you play with me. At first I
thought you had no sense of humor."

"There was nothing to laugh about then. I feel as if
I've come alive this past week. Was it only seven days
ago that we were in Dallas?"

His eyes sparkled. "I want to tell everyone we're in
love. I have this wild urge to write it on my blackboard at school and take out an ad on a billboard."

"Now, Beau, we agreed it would be best to ease the
children into this. We can't just spring it on them. Not
with them all feeling the way they do about us. If you
want proof, look over there at Chad. He's glowering
at us over Diana's head. Keith is doing the same on the
other side of the room."

"It may not be only because we're together. The
coach taking Chad out of the game and putting Keith
in instead may have had something to do with it."

"Chad's game was off tonight. He kept looking
over at Diana instead of paying attention to what he
was doing."

"I noticed that. I also noticed Keith talking to Diana after halftime. She was smiling at him on the
bench. Chad probably noticed it, too."

"Probably. He has radar where that girl is concerned." A look of concern replaced Glenna's smile.
In a lower voice she added, "I don't like that girl."

Beau looked at Chad and Diana. She was turned so
he could see her face, and as he watched she smiled

and winked at Keith, then buried her face in Chad's neck. "I don't like her, either. She's a troublemaker."

"Those are her parents over there by the soft-drink machine. The blond woman and the heavyset man."

"I thought that might be them. Do you think it would do any good for me to talk to them?"

"And say what? That their daughter is provoking fights between our sons and would they please make her behave? No, I don't think we would get very far that way. Why do the boys fall all over themselves for her? She's not the only tall, thin blonde in school."

"No, but she's probably the only one who is arranged in exactly those proportions."

Glenna shook her head. "I still think of her as she was when she was in elementary school. She was a crossing guard but she never could figure out which side of her sign to show to the cars. That should have told me something."

Beau led her into an intricate dance step that made her skirt swirl around her legs. "You're a good dancer."

"You can thank my childhood in Sweet Gum for that. All the girls in my class took dance lessons. It's one of the traditions here. What about you? Not everyone knows how to lead."

Beau grinned. "I figured out in high school that I could put my arms around a girl if I knew how to dance, so I learned how."

"Somehow I can't see you having to rely on dancing for that."

"Believe it or not, I was shy. I would get tongue-tied if a girl so much as looked at me. Fortunately, I outgrew it while I was in college."

"I'd say that was an understatement."

"You bring out the romantic in me." He gazed at her and wished the dance would end soon so he could get her away from the crowd. "I've wanted to kiss you all evening," he whispered.

"I know. I've been thinking the same thing."

"You have that look on your face again. People are beginning to stare."

Glenna looked around. "They're staring because the music has stopped." She stepped away from Beau and they laughed together. "If we keep this up, we won't have to tell anyone."

Beau was about to answer when he saw a flash of red in the doorway. Several heads turned to look in that direction, and he heard a speculative whisper. When he turned to take a closer look, he saw his ex-wife standing there in a flame-colored dress that left nothing to the imagination. Her black hair was tousled as if she had just climbed out of bed, though he knew from experience that she never looked that good in the morning. Her face was painted as if she anticipated a photography session at any moment. Her eyes met his, and she smiled in the sultry way he had once found so enticing.

"Damn!" he muttered.

"What?" Glenna stood on tiptoe to see over the crowd, but she was a full head shorter than he was and couldn't see the doorway.

Diedra came toward him, her eyes predatory, her hips swaying. The dress was made of a glittering fabric that seemed to have been sprayed on her. Beau wondered if there was an exit behind them.

Before he could escape, she was standing in front of him. "Hello, Beau," she purred.

"Diedra. What are you doing here?"

She smiled, drawing her lips up but keeping her teeth hidden. "I came to see you."

Glenna stared from one to the other. It only took her a moment to figure out who this woman was.

Beau turned toward Glenna. She tried to read the expression in his eyes, but for the first time since they had met, she couldn't. "Glenna, this is my ex-wife, Diedra." To the other woman he said, "Glenna King."

Diedra glanced at Glenna, assessed her and dismissed her. "I saw Kelly by the jukebox. Why don't we go over and talk to her?" Just then the music started and Diedra began to sway with it, snapping her fingers. The red dress shimmered and flirted with her movements.

Glenna felt as if her mouth were filled with sawdust. This was Beau's ex-wife? She could never compete with a woman who seemed to ooze sex from every pore. Her pearly-gray dress suddenly seemed dowdy and felt too short. "Beau, I know you must have things to talk about. I could—"

Before Beau could answer, Kelly launched herself at her mother. "Mom! You came! You look great. Conan, this is my mom."

Conan seemed to be as speechless as Glenna.

"Easy, babe. Don't pull on my dress," Diedra said. She put her arm around Kelly's shoulders but she kept a distance between them. "My goodness. You've grown up. Hasn't she, Beau? We made a beauty."

Beau didn't answer. To Glenna, he looked terribly uncomfortable, and he hadn't said enough for her to know what he was feeling. He obviously hadn't expected Diedra to be here tonight, but that was all she was certain of. She was losing self-confidence by the second. Was he so uneasy because he couldn't figure out how to gracefully rid himself of his new friend so he could spend time with his ex-wife?

"Doesn't she look great, Dad?" Kelly asked.

"Sure." Beau didn't elaborate.

Glenna didn't agree. The dress was all wrong for a homecoming dance. Glenna didn't think she would have had the nerve to wear it even if she was going to a nightclub. On the other hand, she didn't have the curves Diedra did, or she at least didn't have them in such abundance. She was aware of the interest Diedra was creating, and she wished she could sink through the floor. She saw Keith making his way toward them. From his expression she couldn't tell if he was glad to see his mother and her red dress or not.

"What are you doing here in Sweet Gum?" Beau asked Diedra.

"You already asked that. I came to see you. I drove all this way just to see you." Her black eyes dared him and promised him at the same time.

Glenna wasn't sure her eyes could ever sparkle that way or express such an obvious invitation to bed. Her old shyness was back in full force, and she felt as awkward as a schoolgirl.

"You should have let me know. I would have told you this is a bad time. Keith and Kelly both have dates and they won't want to leave the homecoming dance to visit with you."

Diedra patted Kelly's head as if she were a puppy. "I didn't come just to see our kids. I came to see you, as well. Kelly says you've been missing me lately."

Glenna felt as if she couldn't get air into her lungs. She began glancing around for an escape. Across the room she caught a glimpse of Chad coming toward them. She had never been happier to see him.

"Kelly said that?" Beau gave his daughter a piercing glance. Kelly shifted uneasily.

Keith arrived and greeted his mother. Diedra hugged him and kept her arms around both his neck and Kelly's. "What do you kids say? Can you put me up for the night?"

Glenna couldn't take any more. As Chad stepped within reach, she grabbed him. "Beau, I'm not feeling well. A headache. I have a headache. Chad is going to take me home."

Chad gave her an astonished look, and she buried her fingers into his arm inside the letter jacket. He nodded. Diana frowned at him and swept her fall of golden hair away from her face.

Beau stared at Glenna. "What headache? You didn't have a headache a minute ago."

"That was then and this is now." She made her face smile at Diedra and said, "It was nice meeting you."

Beau called after her as she walked away with Chad and Diana, but she didn't look back. She already felt as if she was the plainest woman in the room and that she had made a fool of herself by falling in love with Beau. Everyone knew they had come together, and after the dance was over they would notice that he left with Diedra. She couldn't hang around for that.

Chad was fuming as they left the Community Hut. "Who was that woman, anyway? I never saw anything like that except on TV."

"Her name is Diedra Fletcher. She's Beau's ex-wife." The words drained all Glenna's energy.

"So what's he doing with her when he had a date with you?" Chad demanded.

Glenna rubbed her head where a real headache was starting. "I suppose she came to see Keith and Kelly."

"Is she staying at their house?" Diana asked as they reached the car. "Did you see that dress?"

Glenna was positive everyone in the room had seen it seconds after Diedra entered the room. "I assume she is staying there. I don't know."

"There's not a really nice motel in town," Diana assured Chad. "My parents say it's a shame that the nearest decent motel is miles from here."

"I have no idea what her plans are." Diana's wealth of information about the motels in the area piqued Glenna's curiosity about her, but she didn't want to delve into that now. She had all she could handle thinking about Diedra.

"It's those damned Fletchers," Chad fumed. "They're all into stirring up trouble. Didn't I tell you they were like that, Mom? Didn't I tell you?"

"Frequently. Don't say 'damn.'" Glenna only wished she could be magically transferred to her house and that her riotous thoughts would stop pounding through her head.

"She looks like a streetwalker," Chad said darkly. "I've never seen anyone wearing a dress like that."

Diana giggled. "It looked as if she jumped into it and nearly missed."

Chad laughed and winked at her. Glenna tried not to slide lower in the back seat. Somehow she had to retain her composure until she was safely at home.

At last they reached the house. It had never looked so secure to Glenna. Chad stopped in the drive. "We're going back to the dance," he said as his mother climbed out of the back seat via Diana's door.

"All right. Good night, Diana." She returned Diana's wave as she slammed the car door.

Chad's headlights pierced the darkness as he backed out and drove away. Glenna put her key in the lock and let herself in.

She had left a lamp burning as she always did when she would be out past dark. It made the room seem welcoming and safe. As if her feet were made of lead, Glenna trudged over to the stairs and slowly made her way up. The house was so empty. Safe, but empty. Halfway up, she sat on the steps, lowered her face into her hands and began to cry.

She loved Beau, and she was afraid she would lose him. Diedra did look like what Chad had termed a streetwalker, but it would have been a very expensive street. She hadn't appeared cheap, just far too sexy for a school dance. Men liked women who looked that way. Beau had been struck speechless. He had told her that Diedra had left him for another man. Maybe he was pleased that she had come back. That thought broke Glenna's heart.

Feeling very tired and alone, she stood and went to her room. As if she needed the extra pain, she went to her full-length mirror and stared at herself. The dress she wore was elegant, not flashy by any means. Her hair was cut in a simple style that required minimal care, and she never wore much makeup. Her childhood freckles had faded from her nose, but her skin would never have that deep cream color that seemed indigenous to brunettes like Diedra. She ran her hands over her breasts. They weren't small, but she lost out in that department, too.

Despondently, Glenna sat on the edge of her bed. Behind her the phone started ringing, but she ignored it. If it was a friend calling, he or she would leave a message on the answering machine. If it was Beau, she didn't want to talk. She knew after seeing Diedra that she had lost him, and she was in no hurry to have it confirmed.

As if in a daze, she undressed and pulled on a flannel nightgown that was more comfortable than flattering. She turned out the lights and lay down, but she couldn't sleep, not with the memory of the way Beau had stared at that red dress and the body in it. She couldn't sleep when her heart was breaking.

CHAPTER TEN

BEAU GLARED AT THE PHONE as if *it* were responsible for Glenna not answering his call. When her recorder clicked on he waited with growing impatience for her message to end, then said, "Me again. I know you must be home. Will you at least tell me why you won't speak to me?" He hung up with more force than was necessary.

He had hardly slept the night before. Diedra's unexpected appearance at the homecoming dance had been upsetting, especially to Keith, who had recognized his mother's dress for the seductive weapon it was. Beau had convinced Diedra that he would not leave the dance with her, allow her to stay overnight with him or resume anything resembling a friendship. Kelly had been furious with him and wasn't speaking to him this morning. Keith wasn't speaking to anyone at all.

Glenna had obviously left the dance because of Diedra's surprise appearance, but Beau couldn't understand *why*. Surely she couldn't think he would want to be with Diedra instead of her. He loved Glenna and had told her so. He ran his hand through his hair as he often did when he was upset and confused.

The doorbell commanded his attention. Glenna. Maybe she hadn't answered the phone this morning because she was on her way to his house.

Kelly beat him to the door and threw it open. Diedra, not Glenna, stood on the porch. Kelly beamed. "Come in, Mom. Dad, look. Mom's here."

Diedra glanced at her daughter, but her attention was on Beau. "I need to talk to you," she said.

Beau reluctantly motioned for her to come into the den. He watched as she appraised the room with apparent disdain, and he was reminded again of her expensive tastes. "Have a seat."

Diedra sat on the nearest chair and leaned forward so that her tight sweater outlined her breasts to their fullest advantage. "I miss you, Beau. I want us to try to work things out."

"See, Dad? I told you." Kelly was nearly jumping from foot to foot in her excitement.

Beau said quietly, "Your mother and I need to talk, honey. Why don't you go up to your room and give us a minute?"

Kelly frowned. "I want to stay here. I never get to see Mom anymore."

Diedra finally spoke to her daughter. "I won't leave without seeing you. Your Dad and I need to talk in order to work things out."

Kelly's face brightened, and she was all but skipping as she left the room.

"Why did you tell her that?" Beau asked. "You know we aren't going to work anything out. Our marriage was a mistake from the beginning, and we aren't going to work out anything."

Diedra pouted prettily in a way that reminded Beau too much of Kelly. "Don't say that. I drove all the way from Denton to see you."

"I thought you came to see the kids. Kelly certainly thinks so."

"Them, too. I made a mistake, Beau. I never should have left you. I didn't realize how wonderful you are. It really is a jungle out there."

"Then you should feel right at home. I gather Ted left you."

"I don't want to talk about him. I want to talk about us. You could at least have let me stay here last night. That motel is the pits."

"I didn't want to chance having you sleepwalk and end up in my bed by accident."

"No?" She smiled obliquely at him, flirting with her eyelashes.

"No." Beau stood. "You're wasting time you could be spending with Keith and Kelly. I'm not going to come back to you. As a matter of fact, I've found someone else. I intend to ask her to marry me."

"Not that redhead in the gray dress! Oh, Beau, not really. Why, she's not nearly as pretty as I am."

"She is to me. I'll go get Keith. Kelly's room is at the top of the stairs." He turned to go.

"I'm not giving up without a fight," Diedra said as she, too, got to her feet. "I want you back."

"No, you want a meal ticket. A man who will support you while you sleep your way through half of Denton and most of Dallas."

She smiled as if she was daring him. "Jealous?"

"No. Just smarter than I used to be. I'll get Keith."

"Don't bother. I can see there's no reason for me to waste my time here." Diedra flounced to the door and yanked it open. "Goodbye, Beau. But you'll be sorry you didn't choose me instead of that redhead."

"I doubt it. Goodbye, Diedra. Don't hurry back on my account."

She slammed out the door. Beau glanced up the stairs to see Kelly standing there, looking like a lost three-year-old. He had no idea how long she had been there or how much she might have overheard.

"Mom left?"

Beau sighed. Once again Diedra had left a mess for him to clean up, but apparently Kelly hadn't heard any of their conversation. "Yes, honey. I guess she forgot she was going to come up to talk to you."

"My Mom wouldn't forget me. You're just saying that to make her sound bad." Kelly glared at him accusingly. "You sent her away."

"No, I didn't. She left mad because I refused to come back to her."

"Well, why won't you? She's my mother, mine and Keith's. We love her."

Beau knew this was going to require delicate handling. Neither of the children knew exactly why Diedra had left. "I know you love her, and you should, but I don't. I haven't for a long time."

"You used to love her, but you ran her off."

"I didn't chase her away. She made the decision to leave, and I didn't know about it any earlier than you and Keith."

"I don't care. It's all your fault that I'm so unhappy and that I can't even see my own mother! She was trying to make up."

"Kelly, it's not that simple. We didn't just have an argument. We got a divorce."

"But don't you love her at all? You used to love her."

"Love isn't something static. You don't fall in love with someone without something changing. Sometimes it grows, but sometimes it dies."

"Sure! Like Mrs. King doesn't have anything to do with it!"

"Glenna had nothing to do with my refusal to go back to your mother." He regarded his daughter steadily and added, "But it's true that I love Glenna and that she loves me, too."

"Then why did she run off and leave you at the dance, huh?" Kelly kicked at the stair-rail spindle. Her voice sounded thick, as if she was trying not to cry. "Just tell me that."

Beau wished he knew the answer himself. "Adults sometimes make decisions that seem odd, I know, but—"

"Right!" Kelly wheeled and ran toward her room, finally breaking into sobs. "Like you sending Mom away so we can't talk to her!"

He started to follow her and comfort her, but he heard Keith come into the room.

"Mom was here?" Keith asked in confusion. "She already left? Without even seeing me?"

"Keith, I'm sure she wanted to see you. I guess she was in a hurry."

"Sure." He turned and walked quickly from the room.

Beau sat on the stairs, scowling at the front door. Diedra had struck again. As usual, she had left a pile of emotional debris in her wake. He slammed his fist against his leg and tried to tamp down the rage he almost invariably felt after even a brief conversation with his ex-wife. She kept the children in a state of emotional turmoil, and Beau was positive that she neither knew nor cared.

Decisively he stood and strode from the house. Keith was on the patio shooting baskets, but he paid no attention to his father as Beau hurried by. Keith didn't even turn when Beau started the car. Beau knew Keith was far more upset than he would admit. He wished his son were still small enough to take onto his lap and comfort. Beau tightened his grip on the steering wheel and backed the car out of the drive.

He drove straight to Glenna's house. Thankfully, Chad's car was not in the driveway. It wasn't that he wanted to avoid Chad, but he needed time to talk to Glenna alone. He parked and went to the door at the rear of the house where he thought she was most likely to be. Through the window he could see her moving around in the kitchen, so he knocked on the door.

At first he thought she wouldn't answer, but after a brief hesitation, she crossed the room and opened the door. "Yes?"

Beau frowned. "What do you mean, 'yes'? Why did you run away from me last night? And why haven't you answered your phone?"

She turned away, and he followed her into the house. "I shouldn't have done that, I guess. I just felt so... insecure. So dowdy."

"Dowdy? You? Don't tell me you were intimidated by Diedra! She doesn't mean anything to me."

"I saw her." Glenna stared at him as if she were trying to make him understand. "I can't compete with her."

"It's the other way around. Glenna, I love you. Did you think I told you that just for fun? Surely you give me more credit than that!"

"I love you, too. That's why I won't stand in your way if you want her." She paused. "Did she spend the night with you?"

"Of course not! Did you think she might?"

"I heard her ask, and she sounded pretty sure of herself."

"Of course, she did. Diedra can't conceive of any man not wanting her. I sent her away, and you'd have known that if you hadn't left so fast."

Glenna lowered her head. "I was afraid you were going to patch things up with her."

"I'm not that stupid. She had affairs almost from the first day of our marriage. Do you think I want to repeat that?" He paced to the sink and leaned against the counter. "I'm so confused lately. At one time I knew exactly where I was going and what I wanted to do. Now all I can think of is you."

Glenna lifted her head and watched him as he began pacing again.

"Last night I wanted to talk to you so much I could hardly stand it. I called, and when you didn't answer, all sorts of things ran through my head. You had left town. You were in an accident. You would never speak to me again. Glenna, don't ever do that to me again. I can stand anything except not being with you."

"I'm sorry," she said softly. "I never thought of it that way. I thought I was the only one hurting."

He caught her eye and said, "Marry me."

"What? We said we weren't going to rush into anything."

"I know we did. Marry me anyway."

Glenna pressed her fingers to her lips. "I never expected to look like this when you asked me. I was going to be wearing makeup and have my hair combed and be wearing something glamorous."

"You look beautiful. Will you marry me?"

"How can I answer that now? I love you to distraction. I want to say yes, but... But what about Chad and Keith and Kelly? How can we marry now with our children not even speaking civilly to each other, much less to us? You know they're already upset with us for dating. Can you imagine what our home life would be like?"

"I know what it's like now."

"The boys are almost grown. Maybe we should wait until they graduate."

"No good. The boys won't graduate for another year, and Kelly isn't even in high school yet. Then there's the possibility that all three will stay right here and attend college. We shouldn't have to wait another ten years to be together."

"No. I want to marry you, and I don't want to wait that long." She smiled at him and he stopped pacing. "I don't want to wait at all, but . . ."

What she was saying was beginning to sink in. "To tell you the truth, when I decided to ask you to marry me this morning, I wasn't thinking of our children at all. I was only thinking of myself and how much I love you and want to be with you always. I don't want to move you into a war zone. You're right about the kids. They won't take this well at all."

"That's putting it mildly."

Beau sat down and rested his forearm on the table. "What do you think we should do?"

"I think we should get our kids on friendlier terms with each other first. Then we can work on the rest."

"How do you propose to do that?"

Glenna sat opposite him. "I wish I knew. But whatever we do, I think we'd better go slowly. If we push them, we may make it even more difficult."

"I guess." He wasn't pleased with her answer, but he knew she was right. And it wasn't going to be easy. "Diedra came by for a final shot before leaving town. She managed to have Kelly in tears and Keith closed off in silence before she left."

"I'm sorry. Surely she didn't intend to have that effect on them."

"Diedra never thinks beyond herself. She came over to talk me into giving our marriage another try. I refused, naturally, so she gave me a few verbal punches and left. She didn't say goodbye to Kelly, and she never saw Keith at all."

"Oh, no!"

"Now Kelly thinks I forced Diedra to leave without telling her goodbye. Who knows what Keith is thinking. It may be days before he speaks. Even then, he probably won't tell me what made him mad or what hurt his feelings."

Glenna was outraged. "I can't imagine a mother treating her children that way."

"Diedra isn't a mother, she's the eighth plague of Egypt. Kelly can't see that, of course, and she has no idea about Diedra's excessive fondness for men. I think Keith at least suspects, and at his age it would be rather odd if he hadn't noticed his mother's inappropriate behavior around men, but he never mentions it. The divorce was hard on them both, especially since I didn't tell them the real reason. I couldn't. It would have hurt them even more to know that their mother had chosen to shack up with a man named Ted Plitt rather than to live with them."

"I'm sorry she hurt you, too," Glenna said gently. She reached out and covered his hand with her own.

Beau was silent for a while. He had never acknowledged his own hurt. "Yeah. For a while I thought I just wasn't good husband material. After all, if I couldn't keep Diedra at home nights, it must have been my fault."

She smiled. "Take it from me, it wasn't your fault that she ran around on you. You're better than great."

He grinned and looked at her. "You don't have any doubts about me, do you?"

"I don't have any doubts at all about us. You know, it's funny. I never expected to remarry or have a man in my life once Jordan was dead. He took on a bigger-than-life image for me—for all of Sweet Gum, actually.''

''I know. I hear about him at every turn. If you think Diedra is a hard act to follow, you should try measuring up to Mr. Perfect. Tell me the truth. Didn't he have any vices?''

Glenna smiled. ''Of course, he did. He could be stubborn to the point of being ridiculous. He was so terribly competitive that he always won at games, and that can be very demoralizing even if he did win fair and square. And he was much too lenient with Chad. The only discipline Chad ever got was from me.''

''Good cop, bad cop. That's not a good way to parent.''

''No, it isn't. Only recently I have come to realize that I was tired of always playing the heavy. Jordan had me convinced it was my responsibility, but at the same time, he made it clear that he thought Chad would grow up perfect whether I taught him how to behave or not. It's great for a person's self-esteem to be considered that perfect, but it's too much for a child to handle.''

''I never had that problem. Keith and Kelly were never perfect. They have both waded through mischief all their lives. They're good kids, but they have needed guidance. I think all kids do.''

''Exactly. But Jordan would never have agreed with that.''

''Neither would Diedra. She seemed to assume they wouldn't become real people until they were grown.''

''At least our philosophies of child raising match so far. Maybe there's hope for us yet.''

At that moment Chad came through the back door. When he saw Glenna and Beau holding hands, his face contorted with contempt. "What's he doing here?" he asked his mother.

"We're talking. I thought you were going over to the football field."

"I did. Mom, you won't guess what the coach is going to do! I saw Ditto Barnes at the field house, and he told me he overheard the coaches talking about putting Keith in as starting quarterback in the next game and moving me to halfback. That means I'll have to be catching Keith's passes—and I don't think he can throw the ball straight enough for me to get under it."

Beau said calmly, "Keith's got an excellent passing arm. He was quarterback in Denton."

Chad simply glared at him. To his mother he said, "When are we eating lunch?"

"You just had breakfast. We'll eat at noon as usual." She turned to Beau. "Will you stay and eat with us? I'll even put on makeup."

Beau grinned. "Why not? It'll give me a chance to get to know Chad better."

Chad gave him a level look. "Why would you care whether you get to know me or not?"

Glenna squeezed Beau's hand to signal to him that she preferred to answer. "Because he just asked me to marry him."

Chad's face contorted in an almost comical grimace. "He what! Mom, are you crazy? You told him off, didn't you?"

"No, I told him I thought it was a great idea." She cast a smile at Beau, but in her eyes he could see the strain she was feeling.

"You can't do that! What about Dad?"

"He's dead, Chad. I'm not. I don't want to spend the rest of my life alone. Would you?"

"I'd rather be alone than with a Fletcher," he retorted.

Glenna's face paled. "That's enough! Apologize to Beau and stop acting like a spoiled brat."

"You never called me a brat until he came along."

"No, but I often thought it. You're not a small boy any longer, and you can't continue acting as if you are." She refused to let Chad's glowering expression make her quail.

Chad turned to face Beau and met his eyes squarely. "Okay. I'm sorry. But I'm only saying it for Mom's sake." He turned and slammed out of the house.

"Only Chad could make an apology sound like an affront. I really am sorry, Beau."

"Don't be. You haven't been exposed to my kids much, yet." He considered that thoughtfully. "I love my kids and I love you. You love Chad and you love me. Somehow there has to be a way for all of us to love each other."

"I hope you're right. If you come up with a solution, I'll marry you in a minute."

"And if I don't?"

"I have confidence that you will."

Beau smiled at her as he stood and pulled her into his embrace. "You look prettier in that old robe than Diedra did in her shiny red dress."

Glenna laughed. "You must be in love."

As they kissed, Beau thought what an understatement that was. Love was too small a word for all he felt for Glenna. His only concern was what to do to get their kids on their side.

"WHY DO WE HAVE TO FEED her supper?" Kelly asked again.

"We don't. Glenna is perfectly capable of feeding herself. We're only going to serve it."

Kelly scowled at her father. "You know what I mean."

"Yes, I do, and I'm tired of repeating my answer." Beau inspected the table one last time. He wanted everything to be just right. "She should be here any minute. Is the spaghetti water boiling?"

"Yeah," Kelly said dismally.

He pulled Kelly to him and managed to hug her for a moment before she wriggled free. "Don't look so down in the mouth. The firing squad won't be here until after we've had dessert."

"That's not funny, Dad."

"I know, honey, but old folks like me will laugh at anything."

Kelly finally smiled.

"That's better. Go find Keith and tell him dinner will be ready ten minutes after Glenna arrives. He's probably out shooting baskets on the patio."

Kelly pretended to straighten the forks beside the plates so she could linger a while longer. "Dad, if I ask you a question, will you tell me the truth?"

"Of course." He stopped what he was doing and looked directly at his daughter.

"Are you having an affair with Mrs. King?"

Beau's mouth dropped open. "Why on earth would you ask a thing like that?"

"Because Cathy Compton says you are. She told me that she and her mother drove by Mrs. King's house one night and saw you two kissing on the porch."

"Kissing isn't the same as having an affair, honey. You can tell Cathy and her mother that for me."

"Then you're really not?"

Beau thought carefully. "Kelly, the word 'affair' has a rather sordid meaning. There's nothing sordid about the way I feel about Glenna."

"How do you feel about Mom?"

"I don't love her and she doesn't love me. You wouldn't want us to live in the same house and fight all the time, would you? Don't you remember what that was like?"

She nodded but wouldn't meet his eyes.

"I know you miss her." He pulled her to him and stroked her dark hair the same way he had when she was small. "You're growing up so fast. Sometimes I want to freeze-frame you and Keith and keep you here with me forever. But that wouldn't be good for any of us, would it?"

She shook her head.

"You have interests besides school and things here at the house, and I do, too. So does Keith. It's only natural. Glenna is also part of my world."

"I don't want her to be."

"Is it fair to ask me to stagnate when I wouldn't do the same to you?" he asked gently.

Looking uncomfortable, Kelly made one of her lightning-swift subject changes. "Conan asked me to go to the movies tomorrow afternoon. I told him I could. Can I?"

"That's fine." Beau stood up, relieved that the conversation had taken a definite turn.

"He kissed me."

"He what?" Beau was surprised to discover how much this revelation dismayed him.

"He kissed me. At the homecoming dance. We went outside after Mom left, and he kissed me."

"I see. I gather this was the first time this has happened?"

Kelly nodded. "I didn't like it very much. His mouth was all wet."

"I'm sure he'll learn how when he gets a little older." He hadn't expected to have to face this issue until Kelly was past the car-date stage.

"He says this means we're going steady now."

"Going steady?" Beau wondered if he should talk to Kelly about how far to allow a boy to go and why. Glenna was due to arrive at any moment, and he had a pot of boiling water on the stove. "This really isn't the best time for us to discuss this. Maybe tomorrow we could talk."

Kelly smiled and her face dimpled. "I don't need to have that talk, Dad. Mom and I discussed this stuff a long time ago."

"You did?" Somehow this didn't reassure him. "Just the same, maybe you and I should go over it again."

Kelly rolled her eyes as if she couldn't believe he was being so parental, then giggled when he poked her in the ribs. As Beau laughed with her, he hoped her good mood would continue long enough for Glenna to see how lovable Kelly could be. However, when the doorbell sounded, Kelly sobered.

"Go get Keith," Beau said over his shoulder as he went to answer the door.

Glenna met him with an uncertain smile. "Chad wouldn't come. I won't tell you his exact words."

"That's probably just as well. Kelly has gone out back to get Keith. Come on in." He made a sweeping gesture with his arm and said, "This is the living room. If you care to remember it, take a good look now, because we seldom use it. Come on back to the kitchen."

"I never use mine, either. I have a family room, so I'm considering turning the living room into a study. I have so many books, I'm running out of storage space." She leaned nearer and in a conspiratorial whisper asked, "How is it going with the kids?"

"So far, so good. Kelly was upset at first, but she seems to be mellowing. Keith is still as silent as he's been since his mother's visit."

They reached the kitchen just as Kelly and Keith came in from the patio. Both children stared at Glenna as if they hadn't expected to see her here. Finally each mumbled hello. Glenna responded, trying not to gush or to be too cool. She was afraid anything out of the ordinary on her part would be construed by them as negative.

"Go wash up," Beau said as he put the spaghetti into the boiling water.

When they were gone, Glenna said, "I feel as if I'm meeting your parents. What if they don't ever develop a liking for me?"

"It's okay. I just rent these kids. We'll trade them in for some others." He winked at her and grinned.

"If that were possible, Chad would be on a used-kid lot already. He really acted like a pill when he saw I was coming over here whether he came or not."

"It's good for him. Builds character. When I was growing up, that was what my dad said about anything unpleasant. I must have character coming out my ears."

"You *are* a character," she retorted. "Can I help?"

"You can warm the bread in the microwave and reassure me that you like garlic. I had already put it on before I thought to ask."

"Spaghetti wouldn't be right without it." Glenna went to the microwave, and after looking over the unfamiliar buttons for a moment, she punched in the proper sequence.

"The den is through there," Beau said, gesturing with his chin. "We practically live in that room."

"Ours is the same."

She turned to find Beau watching her with a questioning look on his face. "What?" she asked, her lips tilting up.

"I was just wondering whose house we would live in."

"Mine has three bedrooms."

"So does this one. Either way that would mean Chad and Keith would be sharing a room. Can you imagine that working out?"

"Heavens, no! I never thought about that." She was quiet as she mentally checked over her house plan. "Well, my house is larger, but I guess I should wait before I turn the living room into a study. It might have to serve as a bedroom."

"I like the idea of that. Us living together."

"So do I, but we have three hurdles to cross first."

He groaned. "Three teenage hurdles. I remember. By the way, Keith collects coins, and he just found a silver Kennedy half-dollar."

"I'll remember to ask him about it. What about Kelly?"

"She's into clothes and hair and all that."

"I remember the clothes. I hope I learned something from that." Glenna heard the children approaching and squared her shoulders. "I'm going to give this my all."

"YOU DID YOUR BEST," Beau consoled Glenna over the phone.

Glenna slid her head lower on her pillow and drew up her knees under the bed covers. "I never seem to say anything right around Kelly."

"How were you to know her mother gave her that sequined sweatshirt for her birthday? I never liked that style much, either."

"But did I have to say so right out loud? She's going to hate me forever."

"Keith took it all in stride. After you left me he even said you weren't too bad."

"Great." She gazed dismally at the ceiling. "Actually, I enjoyed talking to Keith. I didn't expect him to know so much about the space program."

"He wants to work for NASA someday. He's considering going into engineering."

"That's great. Chad hasn't thought that far ahead yet. He just wants a football scholarship and Diana."

"He has time to decide. I didn't know what I wanted to be when I was that age, either."

"You don't think Chad is just awful, do you? I wouldn't blame you if you did, the way he acts every time you're around."

"No, I don't think he's awful. I think he's trying to protect what he sees as his way of life. I can't blame him for that. I wish he weren't so hard on you, but he'll outgrow that."

"I hope you're right. I miss the old Chad. He was such a sweet child."

"He's growing up," Beau reminded her. "If he didn't act somewhat rebellious, it would be too hard to let him go."

"You're right. I used to wonder how I could bear for him to be grown and gone."

"We have each other. Together we can fight dragons."

"I hope you're right. Teenagers are the closest thing to dragons that I've ever seen."

Beau laughed. "Good night, Glenna. I love you."

She smiled and twisted the cord around her finger. "I love you, too."

CHAPTER ELEVEN

GLENNA SLIPPED HER HAND into Beau's and matched her steps to his. The night was cool, but Indian summer was delaying winter for a while longer. "I love this time of year," she said dreamily. "All the trees are such pretty colors. We've had just enough cold weather to make them turn."

"This part of Texas is beautiful, there's no doubt about it," Beau agreed. "I've always liked it. That's why I went to work at the University of North Texas. It may be even prettier here."

"I've lived here all my life," Glenna said. "I don't regret it for a moment."

"If you had moved away, I might never have met you." He smiled at her in the darkness.

She returned his smile. "That would have been a shame. Lucky for me I stayed in a small town where it's easy to get to know newcomers."

"I appreciate your consideration toward a complete stranger. Now if only our children would fall into line."

Glenna sobered. "It's not happening, is it? What are we going to do?"

"I wish I knew. To hear them talk, you'd think I'm dating Lizzie Borden."

"And you're Jack the Ripper at my house." They walked in silence for a minute, the silvery moonlight illuminating their way. "At least we have interests in common. I'm glad you went with me to the Parents Anonymous meeting tonight. Are you really interested in becoming a group leader?"

"I want to help eliminate child abuse, and from all you've told me about this organization, and from what I've seen tonight, I don't know of a better way. I never thought child abuse was so widespread that even a sleepy little town like Sweet Gum would have such problems."

"It's a problem everywhere. That's why I got involved."

"How are you holding up as volunteer coordinator?"

"Okay, I guess. This was only my second weekly meeting, and I'm still learning how to do the job. If I had had more time to think about doing this, I might have been better prepared. Of course, Sally had no idea her husband would be transferred with so little warning. There was no time to find someone with experience to take his position as coordinator. The president of the PA board says he's trying to locate one, but the truth is, I like the job. Jordan's mother is appalled that I gave up all her clubs for involvement in an organization of my own choosing, but that's the way it is. If the board wants me to stay on, I may be willing." She glanced at Beau. "What do you think?"

"I think you're doing a great job. If you like what you're doing, stick with it." He looped his arm around her shoulder as they turned the corner toward her house.

"You don't mind?"

"Why would I mind? It's certainly worthwhile. I'll do all I can to help you."

She sighed with contentment. "That's one reason I love you. No matter what I want to do, you back me up. I never feel like I'm merely an adjunct to you."

"No one should ever be made to feel that way. Look at all the talents and creativity you have that were stifled because you couldn't work outside the house."

Her brow knitted thoughtfully. "I was never exactly told I couldn't work. It was more or less assumed that I wouldn't. If I had, though, I'm sure I would have been expected to get a job with well-defined hours. I would have had trouble justifying a job involving travel, as this one does occasionally. By the way, will you be able to go to Austin next weekend for that seminar on working with troubled teens?"

"Yes, my schedule is clear then." He grinned. "Maybe we can use what we learn to handle our own teenagers."

"We could use some help."

When they reached Glenna's house, instead of going inside, they walked around to the summerhouse at the far end of the flower garden. Hand in hand, they climbed the shallow steps and stepped into the shadows. The open walls afforded a view of the surrounding lawn and gardens, which were flanked by a tall privacy fence.

"I never knew anyone who had a summerhouse," Beau said as he sat on the wicker love seat and drew Glenna down beside him.

"This is my haven. My escape place," she explained as she snuggled against his warm side. "Jordan built it when Chad was a toddler. It gave me a place to hide out for a minute or two and still be within earshot of the swing and slide. I think escape places are essential to motherhood."

"To fatherhood, too. I had more of a hand in raising my children than most fathers. Even before my divorce, I was the principal parent." He glanced at her and kissed the top of her head. "I wish there were some way for us to get married right away."

"I know. I think about it constantly. At times I think I'm crazy not to rush to the altar at breakneck speed. But then I worry that problems with our kids might make our everyday lives a nightmare."

"I know. That concerns me, too. And I've also been worried about how, even in an ideal situation, marriage changes things between a man and woman. Neither is the same after having lived together for a while. What if I'm not able to make this one work, either? Maybe I really do have failings as a husband."

"When I'm having my doubts, I never even consider that possibility. Just because your first marriage didn't work, it doesn't mean no marriage will. It takes two people to make it a success."

"So I hear."

"My worry is only about the children."

"That's worry enough."

"Maybe we should just get married and let the chips fall where they may."

He tilted her head up so he could see her face. In the darkness he couldn't see her eyes well enough to tell if she was serious. "Do you mean it?"

She nodded. "I love you, Beau. Whenever I'm near you, I feel all soft and warm and secure, and when we're apart, I feel as if there's a piece of me missing. I spend my days looking forward to seeing you again and wondering what you are doing or thinking."

"You've just described my daily schedule exactly. My friend Joe says I've become impossible to talk with on any subject that doesn't involve you or marriage. He's even beating me at tennis these days."

"I wish my friend Margo were that supportive. I can't figure out what's wrong with her. She insists I would be making a mistake to remarry."

"I've never met her. How does she know I'm not right for you?"

"She doesn't. That's just it. She acts as if I'm running around on Jordan every time I tell her I've seen you."

"That's another problem. Will anyone in this town accept me as your husband? I'm bound to have trouble competing with his memory."

"I know. Everyone seems to think our romance is their business. People I barely know have been stopping me on the street to tell me how much they admired Jordan."

"Surely it won't continue forever." He couldn't make his voice sound convincing.

"I'm not so sure. I wonder if this has been going on all the time and I never noticed it, or if the entire town is conspiring to make me remain Jordan's bereaved widow forever."

Beau shook his head. "I have to admit, I've never seen anything like it."

"What about you? Are you jealous of Jordan?"

Beau thought for a moment. He knew his answer must be honest. "At times it bothers me. At others it doesn't. He's gone and won't be back, but I know you loved him. Sometimes I wonder which of us you'd choose if he showed up now on your doorstep, all hale and hearty."

"I've asked myself that, too." Glenna's voice was strained. "At first I was upset because I wasn't sure who I would pick. Lately, however, I've made myself face facts. Jordan was as close to perfect as Sweet Gum will ever produce, but that isn't necessarily enough to guarantee a lasting marriage. I wonder now if I wouldn't eventually have wanted more for myself than to walk in Jordan's shadow. I had to admit that he would have had trouble accepting anything else." She reached up and caressed Beau's face. "With you I can be myself, and you love me for it. I don't have to pretend to like football or even to understand it."

"Football knowledge or even interest in sports isn't important to me in a wife," he agreed with a smile.

"In all the time we were married, Jordan never once noticed that I don't know one end of the field from the other. You saw through me in minutes. Jordan would never have wanted to give his time to help with abused children, but you volunteered as soon as you knew there was a need. Jordan would have sent a check to support their work, but he wouldn't have given up his evenings." She paused. "I'm pretty sure he wouldn't have let me go, either."

"Marriage shouldn't be for only one person. It has to be a partnership. Fifty-fifty."

"That's why I know I would choose you," she said softly.

Beau suddenly realized how much he had worried about having to share Glenna's love with the ghost of Jordan King, and he was almost afraid to believe his anxiety had been needless. "You really would? You know you could lie to me about this to make me feel good, and I would never know the difference."

"I would choose you. I wouldn't have agreed to marry you if I hadn't known I would choose you over him. It wouldn't have been fair to you. I might have started comparing the two of you, and that would have been the beginning of the end for us."

"You mean you don't compare us?"

She smiled. "Not anymore. You're not perfect, and that's what I like about you."

"So what do you think? Should we go ahead and tell everyone we're going to get married? Are you ready to brave our kids and the entire town?"

Glenna drew in a deep breath. "I think so. I mean, yes. I'm ready. Are you?"

He nodded. "I love you, Glenna. I know it's going to be hard at times, but together we can face anything and walk away the winners."

Glenna snuggled into his arms and laid her head on his chest. "You're not like anyone I ever have known before. I remember the first time I heard you read poetry. It was Elizabeth Barrett Browning, and I found myself holding my breath because it was so beautiful. I had never heard anyone read the way you do. Someday, will you read poetry to me again?'' She smiled at him. ''Even if I did drop your class?''

''I'll do even better than that.'' He gazed into her eyes and quoted,

> '''Let me not to the marriage of true minds
> Admit impediments. Love is not love
> Which alters when it alteration finds,
> Or bends with the remover to remove.'''

Beau bent and kissed her lightly, and his breath was warm on her cheek.

> '''O, no! It is an ever-fixèd mark,
> That looks on tempests and is never shaken;
> It is the star to every wand'ring bark,
> Whose worth's unknown, although his height be taken.'''

He smiled and caressed the smooth curve of her cheek. His deep voice moved her almost to tears.

> '''Love's not Time's fool, though rosy lips and cheeks
> Within his bending sickle's compass come;
> Love alters not with his brief hours and weeks,
> But bears it out even to the edge of doom.'''

He bent to kiss her again, and Glenna swayed toward him as if he were a lodestone to her soul. He continued in a soft but compelling voice.

"'If this be error and upon me proved,
I never writ, nor no man ever loved.'"

"That's beautiful," she whispered. "I've read Shakespeare's sonnets, but I never heard the words until now. It's as if you created them just for me."

"If I were a poet, I'd write stanzas to immortalize our love. A century from now other lovers would read my words and marvel that any man ever loved so much."

"I love you, Beau. My words sound so simple, but they're the best I know."

"Sometimes the simplest words mean the most," he replied, his eyes caressing her face. "Especially if you look at me like that when you say them. I love you as I never dreamed it would be possible for me to love. You're an integral part of my life, and I would change nothing about you. If I were to describe the perfect woman for me, it would be you."

"I feel the same way. I love you exactly as you are. Sometimes I wonder how, in all the world, we managed to be at the right place at the right time for us to meet. What if I had never decided to take a class at the college or if you had gone to teach at another university? Would we ever have found each other? Something within me tells me that somehow you were born to love me, and that I was born to love you, but it's like a miracle that we've found each other."

"A miracle? I think we would have found each other even if we had had to travel to the ends of the earth."

Glenna smiled. "I think you're right."

SHE KNEW she should tell Chad when they were alone. His reaction was predictable. Although she wanted to share her joy with someone, she wanted to be sure of telling someone who would be supportive of her. It didn't take her long to realize that no one she knew could be counted on for that support. Margo, maybe, but only if Margo would be willing to forgo her own opinion in favor of Glenna's joy. It would be a chance, but Glenna had to tell someone.

"I know it's late. I didn't wake you, did I?"

"No, no. We were watching TV. Is something wrong?"

"No, everything is wonderful. Beau walked me home tonight after the Parents Anonymous meeting. We went out to the summerhouse and talked. Margo, we're going to be married."

There was a long silence. "Hello? Margo? Are you still there?"

"I'm here."

Glenna heard Margo put her hand over the phone and say something to her husband. The words were lost, but Glenna could hear the tone of her voice. She tightened her grip on the phone. "I had hoped you'd be happy for me."

"Glenna, you're making a big mistake. You barely know this man. You've known him what, two months?"

"About that, yes." She waited for Margo to continue.

"You shouldn't rush into anything like marriage. You'll be setting yourself up for a divorce. Texas is a community-property state. If you don't have a prenuptial agreement to protect you, a sharp divorce attorney could get him half of all you own. And I seriously doubt he would be willing to sign such an agreement."

Glenna could hear Bob in the background asking his wife questions, but Margo was ignoring him. "Prenuptial? That's nonsense. Beau doesn't want half of all I own. He wants me. We're in love, Margo. It doesn't always take years for love to develop. Sometimes a couple can be lucky and know it right from the start."

"You're making a serious mistake," Margo repeated.

Glenna took a steadying breath. "I had hoped you would be more supportive. I really need a friend right now. Aren't you happy for me at all?"

For a moment Margo was silent, and Glenna hoped she was changing her mind.

"As your friend, Glenna, all I can do is offer you advice. Take a vacation and try to get this in perspective. I mean, how can you consider taking up with this man when you were married to *Jordan?* What does Chad have to say about this?"

"I haven't told him yet."

"There! You see? If you thought he would be all for this, you would have told him before you breathed a word to anyone else."

"Margo, I love Beau. I want to marry him."

"I think you're just lonely."

Glenna felt like crying. "Have you ever been lonely? I don't mean just for the day or when Bob has been out of town for a week. I mean the kind of lonely that could last the rest of your life. Chad is almost grown, and he'll soon begin a life of his own that will have little to do with me. And that's as it should be. But I want a life, too. Do you know how much comfort you can get from curling up to only a memory at night?"

"You see? Have an affair if you must. Better yet, buy a puppy or a kitten. Don't marry a stranger just because he asks you to."

Glenna felt herself pulling away from the friendship. "I'm not. I told you I love Beau. I told him tonight that I want to marry him."

There was another long silence, and Glenna knew Margo was biting back her words rather than escalating the disagreement. "I guess I shouldn't have called. We've been friends for so long, I just assumed that you would see how much this means to me and stand by me. I see I was wrong."

"I want you to be happy. It's just that I know you're wrong in thinking that this person will make you happy."

"No. No one can make me happy. I have to do that for myself. And when I'm with Beau I'm happy. Happier than I've ever been. I guess I should say goodbye, Margo."

The silence stretched out between them. Finally Margo said, "Goodbye, Glenna."

Glenna hung up, but her hand remained on the phone for several seconds. More than a conversation had ended. So had her friendship with Margo—a friendship that had endured for so long she could hardly recall a time when it hadn't been there. The loss made her sad, but she knew Margo was wrong and that if the friendship had been all she had assumed it to be, it would have weathered her marriage to Beau.

Glenna lay back in her bed. Tomorrow she would tell Chad.

ARLENE AND GEORGE KING had invited Glenna and Chad over for dinner. As always, Glenna felt nervous with all the snowy linens and silver candlesticks and china. Even after all these years, she felt out of place here. Chad seemed completely unperturbed. He was never so much his father's son as he was at his grandparents' table.

"More peas, Glenna?" George asked.

"No, thank you." She could barely taste the food at all, and she wasn't sure she could finish what she had in front of her. At home she wouldn't have given a second thought to leaving a little food uneaten, but here she always felt compelled to clean her plate. Mealtime with the Kings had always been uncomfortable for her, though she had never said a word about it to anyone. She was curious how Chad, who was equally at home in the casual style Glenna favored, could be so comfortable amid the Kings' elegance and pomposity. Jordan had had that same knack. For the first time she wondered if it was a lack of sensibility rather than a cultivated taste.

"Marie Murdock called today," Mrs. King said, her voice perfectly modulated to carry her words to the people seated at the table but not to the maid in the kitchen. "She said she saw you the other day, Chad."

He grinned and helped himself to another roll. "I see her all the time."

Glenna nodded. "Chad is over at Diana's house more than he's at home lately. I hope he's not wearing out his welcome."

"No grandson of mine could possibly be unwelcome at the Murdocks'," Arlene assured her proudly. She gave Chad one of her closed-lip smiles.

"He's been coming in at all hours, too. I'm surprised the Murdocks let Diana stay out so late. Even on a school night he may not be home until eleven or later."

"He's a boy," George announced from the end of the table. "Let him do as he pleases. Right, Chad?" He winked at his grandson. "He'll be a husband soon enough. Let him sow a few oats while he can."

"I would just as soon he didn't sow them at midnight on a school night," Glenna said firmly. "His grades have dropped."

Mrs. King leaned toward Chad. "You didn't make the honor roll this term?"

"I made one lousy B." Chad frowned at his mother as if he blamed her. "If I had been able to study later with Diana, I would have made an A as usual."

"Right," Glenna said with a tinge of sarcasm. "I figured you were studying over there."

"If he says he was studying, he was studying," his grandmother stated. "I believe Chad just as I believed his father. Neither would ever lie to me."

Glenna shot her mother-in-law a doubtful glance, but the woman was patting Chad's hand and didn't see it.

"All the same, he needs to be home earlier."

"Why?" Chad asked daringly. "You aren't home much yourself these days."

Glenna was so amazed he would speak to her this way in front of his grandparents that her mouth dropped open.

Mr. King good-naturedly poked at Chad. "Go easy, boy. It's best to humor the ladies."

Glenna frowned at him. "I don't need to be humored, Mr. King." Had Jordan only been humoring her all those years when she had thought they had so much closeness?

Mr. King winked at Chad, who winked back. Glenna lowered her eyes to her plate, hoping she wouldn't let slip what she was thinking.

Mrs. King's features remained placid, but her eyes became calculating. "That does bring up something I've been meaning to ask you about, Glenna."

"What's that?"

"I know there's probably no truth to it, but there's a rumor around town concerning you."

"Oh?" Glenna said as she laid her fork down carefully. She was positive the rumor had to do with Beau, and she certainly didn't want to discuss him over the Kings' dinner table, but her mother-in-law left her no choice. "What rumor?"

"Excuse me," Chad said as he shoved his chair back. "No dessert for me. I'm in training. I'll be watching TV."

Glenna watched him go, with Mr. King right behind him. Dread swept over her. Was the rumor so lurid that her father-in-law didn't want to be in the room while it was being discussed? Arlene and George had as close to a virginal marriage as Glenna had ever seen. She tried not to appear nervous.

Mrs. King folded her napkin and set it beside her plate. "If you're finished eating, we could go into the den. It's so much cozier there, and we can talk undisturbed."

The fine hairs on the back of Glenna's neck began to prickle. She felt as if she were being summoned to the principal's office. Her mother-in-law never closeted herself in the den with someone unless the subject was a serious one. She considered trying to avoid the discussion but rejected the notion, because doing so likely would build needless suspicion in Mrs. King's mind. Dutifully she followed her mother-in-law to the den.

The Kings' den was as dissimilar from her own as it could be. Whereas Glenna's was meant for daily use and was decorated for comfort, the Kings' was as formal as their dining and living rooms. The walls were block-paneled oak. The furniture was leather and the rug Oriental. The lamps had dark green shades, and there was a fire in the fireplace even though the night wasn't cold. Glenna sat in a chair opposite Mrs. King.

The imperious woman leaned forward, her forearm resting on her crossed knee. For a moment,

Glenna was absurdly reminded of a scene from a movie in which Andy Hardy and the judge were having a father-to-son talk. But then the gravity of the subject at hand brought her back. What were people saying about her and Beau? They had been as careful as possible in Sweet Gum. The only time she had made love with him had been that golden weekend in Dallas. Had word of what happened there somehow leaked out in town?

"Marie is concerned," Mrs. King began. "And I must say, I agree with her that you shouldn't go through with it."

The marriage plans? "I had intended to tell you about it in a day or two." Abruptly Glenna stopped as it dawned on her that Marie Murdock shouldn't know anything about the marriage plans. Margo was the only one she had told, and as far as she knew, Margo and Marie weren't friends. "How did Marie know?"

"It was that article in the paper." Mrs. King disdainfully shook her head and leaned back in her chair. "I've never been so upset."

"What article?" Glenna was confused. How and why would the paper run an article about her engagement to Beau?

"The one in Sunday's paper. The picture takes up a third of the page and there you are right in the middle of it." She reached beside her chair, picked up a copy of the paper and handed it to Glenna. On the page was a picture of Glenna accepting a donation check on behalf of Parents Anonymous given by one of the local social clubs.

Glenna was both relieved and bewildered. "So? The donation was from one of the clubs you belong to. Do you feel Parents Anonymous is not a worthy cause? I'm confused."

"Of course, it's worthy. It's that you are involved in it."

"I told you I was working with them."

"On the board, yes, but not like this." Mrs. King's face registered as much contempt as she ever allowed herself. "Your picture is right there in the paper."

Glenna shook her head. "I'm afraid you've lost me. You're upset because I'm a volunteer coordinator for Parents Anonymous? That's what is bothering you?"

"Of course. You should have heard Marie. I was terribly embarrassed. She wanted to know how long you had been an abusive parent."

Glenna blinked and leaned forward. "Pardon?"

"That's exactly what she said."

"But that doesn't make any sense. I'm not an abusive parent. You know that."

"I told her you aren't, but there's your picture in the paper."

Glenna made a valiant effort to control her temper. "I work at PA, just as a lot of other people do who have had no reason to need their counseling services."

Mrs. King looked relieved. "I told Marie as much, but you know how she is. She was considering telling Diana she would have to break up with Chad."

"I wish she would. That girl is as wild as they come. Chad is no more studying at her house until midnight than I am!"

"Let's not change the subject. I believe it would be for the best if you resigned from the Parents Anonymous board."

"I'll do no such thing! Do you have any idea how hard it is to get volunteers for anything, let alone volunteers to work with families in crisis? They need me."

"Think of Chad. If Marie made this mistake, others must have, too. Quit for his sake."

"No way."

"For Jordan's, then. We'll send a donation and you can bow out gracefully."

Glenna knew the proposed donation would be a large one, but she shook her head. "As much as they need the money, they need me more. I'm the coordinator for all the group's activities, and the paperwork goes through me. My predecessor left without giving any warning. I won't do the same. I enjoy what I'm doing, and for once I feel as if I'm important in my own right."

"You should have heard Marie's voice. I was so mortified. You could tell she believed every word she was saying."

Glenna's temper finally overtook her reasoning. "I can tell you something that will likely upset you even more. I had intended to talk to you about this at a more propitious time, but maybe you should know now. Someone has asked me to marry him."

Shock registered in her mother-in-law's face, despite her obvious effort to maintain her reserve. "No! Who is it?"

"I doubt you know him. Beau Fletcher is his name. He's a professor of English literature at the college."

"A teacher? You've been dating a teacher? I never suspected such a thing." She paused. "Wait a minute. Does he have a son named Keith? A young ruffian."

"His son is named Keith, but if he's a ruffian, so is Chad. He also has a daughter named Kelly."

"I hope you told him no and set him straight about taking such liberties with you!"

"As a matter of fact, I agreed to marry him. Chad doesn't know yet, but I'm going to tell him on the way home."

"No! Glenna, you can't do this!"

"Yes, I can. I can't live all my life for other people. There are still things I want to do and see. I want to be with Beau. I've fallen in love with him." Glenna rose and closed the distance between them and put her hand over Mrs. King's. "I know this has been upsetting to you, and for that I'm sorry, but there was no simpler way to say it."

"You're going to remarry?" The woman still looked stunned. "But what about Chad? What will this do to him?"

"Frankly I dread telling him, but it has to be done. He won't be happy about it."

"I should think he wouldn't. What about us? Don't you owe any of us some loyalty?"

Feeling deeply regretful, Glenna straightened and said, "No, Mrs. King, I don't," then turned and walked away. At the door, she paused. "I'm sorry I've upset you. I really am."

Mrs. King glared at her for several seconds, then turned her head away in a typical gesture of eloquent dismissal. Glenna went out and quietly closed the door.

Chad was ready to leave. Visits with his grandparents were frequent, and he was usually ready to go as soon as she was. Glenna waited until the car was moving before she said, "I have something to tell you."

"Grandmother must really have lit into you," he observed. "What was all that about?"

"It was nothing. She said Marie Murdock called to ask if I'm an abusive parent."

"What?" Chad's face lit up with amusement. "She said that?"

"Yes. Can you believe it? She saw my picture in the paper with PA and thought I was involved in it because I abuse you."

"So that's why she asked me the other day if I was getting enough to eat at home. I wondered."

"She did what!" As Glenna jerked her head around to look at Chad for some sign that he was joking, she swerved and almost drove off the road into someone's yard.

"I think it's funny." He chuckled. "Abusive. You."

Glenna smiled in spite of herself. "I'm glad to see you don't think I am. Lately, with all our disagreements, I wasn't sure you were still in my camp."

"Sure I am. You just come on too strong sometimes." Chad leaned his tanned arm on the armrest and slumped into the sunlight. "For a mother, you're not bad." He grinned and winked at her.

Glenna was delighted that she and Chad were having a normal conversation for the first time in months, and although she hated to spoil his good mood, she had to tell him about her pending marriage before he heard it from someone else. "Chad, I have something to tell you that I just told Mrs. King. I want you to hear it from me and not her."

"You look serious. What's going on?"

"Beau asked me to marry him and I said yes."

"What!" Chad's good humor was instantly gone. "You did what?"

"We haven't set a date. I told you I was considering it. Remember?"

"Sure, but I didn't believe you'd actually do it." He glared straight ahead. "I'm not going to be in the same family as Keith. No way. I'd go live with Grandmother and Grandfather first."

Glenna held her breath. Chad would be seventeen soon, and at that age he could move away from home and she couldn't stop him. After a while she said, "I hope you love me enough not to do that."

"You wouldn't try to stop me?" he demanded.

"I think you know as well as I do that I can't stop you if you're determined to go. I'm hoping you'll decide not to leave me."

Chad frowned and picked at the chrome strip beneath the window. "You'll have Beau and his bratty kids. What'll you want with me?"

She smiled. "You're *my* bratty kid. We're a team."

She quickly glanced at him and caught the glimmer of a faint smile, but he gave her no reassurance.

CHAPTER TWELVE

BEAU SMILED AT HIS children. He still thought of them that way even though Keith was as tall as Beau and Kelly looked more like a young woman than a child. "You're growing up too fast," he mused aloud.

"Is that what you wanted to tell us?" Kelly asked. "My favorite show is coming on."

"No, there is something else. As you know, I've been seeing Glenna King." He paced the width of the den as he rubbed his hand over his hair. This wasn't proving to be as easy as he had hoped. "I guess I ought to come right out with it. Glenna and I have fallen in love. I've asked her to marry me."

The resulting explosion was all he had expected. When he finally was able to get a word in edgewise, he said, "I know this is coming as a surprise to you, but it's all happened rather fast."

"You barely know her," Keith argued. "You don't even know her middle name!"

Beau became thoughtful. "You're right. That has never come up in conversation. I'll ask and let you know what it is."

"I don't care what it is! That's not the point."

"I know, son. I wanted to tell you two as soon as I started falling in love with her, but you weren't receptive to hearing it."

"What about Mom?" Kelly demanded.

"Your mother and I have been divorced for more than a year. This shouldn't affect her one way or another."

"But you can't ever get married to her again if you're married to someone else!"

"Kelly, I never intended to remarry her. We got a divorce because we were no longer in love or able to live together without fighting. I'm sure you must remember how it was the last year or two. I gave it my best shot, but the marriage couldn't work."

"How do you know this one will?" Keith asked.

Beau shook his head. "There are never any guarantees. I knew your mother a long time before we married. We simply weren't compatible. I think I have a better idea now of the type of person I can live with."

"You would have a fit if I said I was going to marry a girl I had only known for a couple of months," Keith pointed out sullenly.

"Yes, I would. You're only sixteen. But I'm thirty-eight, and I have had more years of experience at living. I'm not going to tell you I'm positive that Glenna and I will always be happy. I doubt any couple is happy all the time. We'll have arguments, and there'll be times when we all will need our space, but that's all a part of marriage."

"I don't know why you even bothered telling us," Kelly said, sulking. "It doesn't matter to you what we think."

Beau went to her. "Yes, it matters a great deal. But I can't let you and Keith decide how I will live my life. Some things are beyond your realm of knowledge."

"There you go, using big words again. You just do that so Keith and I won't know what you're talking about." She kicked the back of her foot against the couch. "I don't want Mrs. King here."

"I think you had better start calling her Glenna. We discussed it, and that seems to be the best. She won't be Mrs. King much longer."

"I hate her name and I hate her. I won't call her anything, because I won't ever speak to her!"

"That's something else I wanted to talk to you about. Once we're married, I don't want you two making her life miserable." To Keith he said, "I know you and Chad have trouble getting along, but I'm hoping you can put your differences aside."

Keith pulled back. "We have to live with Chad King?"

"Of course. Where else would he live but with us?"

"I'm not sharing a room with him. No way."

Beau nodded. "We assumed you would feel that way. This house would be too small for two more people."

"You want us to move, too?" Kelly stared at him.

"We'll move in with Glenna. We plan to turn the living room into a bedroom for Keith." He smiled at Keith. "I thought you would like that. It'll be bigger than your room here, and it's near the phone."

Keith looked at the floor without answering.

"I don't want to move to her house." Kelly crossed her arms over her chest and pouted as if she were still a child. "I want to go live with Mom."

"We've been all through that," Beau said patiently.

"You're just being mean to me! That's all you ever do anymore!"

Beau sighed. "Kelly, don't do this. I'm not being mean to anyone. I was afraid you'd react like this, but I had to tell you. We haven't set a date yet, but it will be in the near future. I want you to get all this anger out before you see Glenna again. I mean what I say about you not making this any harder than it has to be."

Kelly leapt to her feet. "I am too going to make it hard. I'm going to chase her away if she comes here! We don't want her." She looked at her brother for support but he offered none. In frustration she shouted, "If you marry her, you'll be sorry!"

Beau watched her run from the room and heard her clatter up the stairs. "I knew she would take it hard. How are you doing with it?"

"I'm not real happy, but I've been expecting this." Keith glanced in the direction of his sister's room. "Kelly is really mad."

"I know." Beau sat on the couch where she had been. "I'm worried about Kelly. Her grades are continuing to drop. She's never happy anymore. Does she confide in you?"

"Me? No. What problems could she have? She doesn't even date. Not really."

"I've been thinking that it would be good for her to get some counseling. There's a man here in town who is said to be good." He rubbed his eyes and sighed. He hated to think that Kelly might need professional help.

"You mean a shrink?"

"He's a psychotherapist. Maybe he can help Kelly with her problems. She won't talk to me, either."

"I doubt she'll talk to some stranger if she won't talk to you."

"I have to try something." He smiled at his son. "Thanks for taking this so well."

Keith shrugged. "I know you'll never go back to Mom. I'm glad of it. I never told you, but I saw and heard things that you don't know about. I know why you and Mom really got a divorce."

"I had hoped you didn't."

"I never told Kelly. She's just a kid. It would have hurt her too bad."

"What do you really think about me marrying Glenna?"

Keith thought for a minute. "I don't like Chad, and I probably never will. I don't have anything against her, though. She's pretty and she makes you laugh. Will Chad change his name to Fletcher?"

"No, he'll stay Chad King."

Keith nodded. "I guess if he can adjust, I can, too."

"Thanks, son." Beau watched Keith get up and leave the room, and to his relief his son went toward the den instead of the basketball net on the patio.

A few minutes later, Beau went upstairs and knocked on Kelly's door. After the second knock she said, "Go away. I want to be alone." Her voice was muffled and strained as if she was crying.

Beau's hand dropped to his side. He had known Kelly would take it hard. He wished he could somehow take away her pain, but, of course, he couldn't.

He went to his room and dialed Glenna's number. "I told them."

"What did they say?"

"Kelly reacted worse than I expected, Keith better. I can understand algebraic equations, and I can decipher Latin, but the workings of a teenage mind is beyond me."

"Tell me about it. I told Chad on the way home from the Kings' tonight."

"How did he take it?"

"Exactly as I expected. I told him while the car was rolling so he would have to stay put and listen. He wants to live with his grandparents."

Beau tried to quell the spark of hope that unwillingly sprang to his mind. "Oh?"

"Naturally I told him we don't want him to be away from us. At his age, however, we really have very little say in it. He will be seventeen in a couple of months. He said he would think about it. Beau, what will I do if he decides to leave home?"

Instantly Beau regretted his moment of selfishness for thinking that it might be easier on the rest of them if Chad *did* go to live with his grandparents. How could all this distort his thinking to such a degree? "You mustn't worry about that. Together we'll talk him out of it. You know how stubborn I can be."

"So is Chad. I'm so confused. I want to marry you, but frankly I'm afraid. Chad may move out, and your kids hate me. Maybe we've made a bad decision."

"No, we haven't. Chad is probably all bluff. Teenage boys are good at it. My kids don't hate you. I told you Keith took it better than I expected."

"Oh?" Her voice became hopeful. "What did he say?"

"He said he wants me to be happy. He knew more about his mother's activities than I realized. He was hurt by the divorce, but for different reasons than I assumed. I told them that we would be moving into your house, and he took that well, too."

"What about Kelly?"

Beau wished she hadn't asked. "She didn't do well with it at all. She wants to go live with her mother."

"She shouldn't do that. If Diedra is half as promiscuous as you've said, she'll be a bad influence on Kelly."

"I know. I refuse to let her even consider it. Fortunately I know Diedra won't encourage her to move back in with her. Diedra loves her freedom too much. Besides, Kelly is nowhere near seventeen yet. I still have control there. If Diedra changes her mind and tries to get custody, I'll have her declared an unfit mother and have her visitation rights terminated."

"I hope it never comes to that."

"Me, too. But I'll do whatever I have to do to protect Kelly from harm. Right now she's just upset."

"Do you think she'll ever accept me?"

"I don't know. I'm going to call Bill Prescott and see if I can get her in for therapy. She has problems that are too big for her to handle alone, and she won't let me help."

"He's good. I saw him after Jordan died. He has a way with young people, I've heard. You might mention my name when you call."

"The old King passport?"

"No, I went to high school with him."

"In that case, I'll use your name. You know, there are other things about Kelly that bother me. Her grades are dropping steadily and I have reason to wonder whether she's skipping school."

"Oh? Why is that?"

"I find food missing from the kitchen. At first I assumed that I had simply forgotten how much pie had been eaten or whether any sandwich meat was left after I made lunches that morning, but now I'm beginning to wonder. The school is only a block from here. It would be easy for her to show up for roll call and walk home."

"Would she do that?"

"I don't know. She's normally a bright girl. It would explain her grades being so low. It wouldn't be hard for her to write notes excusing her absences and signing my name. I doubt the school has the time to verify signatures."

"You're right. Since you're gone all day, there would be no one home to notice if she's there or not. Maybe I should start driving over during the day to check."

"No, you'd better not. I don't want Kelly to think you're my policeman. She's having enough trouble accepting you as it is. Do you think I could get the school to call me if she turns up absent for any of her classes?"

"Maybe. Would you like me to call? I know the woman who works in the office."

"No, I'll do it. I don't want to start off by having you do the unpleasant errands for me."

When she spoke again he could hear the smile in her voice. "I wish we were already married. I would much rather talk to you face-to-face than over the telephone."

"So would I. Are you in your bedroom?"

"Yes."

He grinned. "What are you wearing?"

"It's a silver-blue gown, all slinky and silky. I wish you were here."

"I wish I were, too. Is Chad at home?"

"Yes, for a change. His timing is impeccable."

"Maybe you could open a window and I could climb the trellis."

"I don't have a trellis. Besides, you'd probably fall and break your neck."

"I'm in my room, too. It sure is lonesome without you tonight."

"I've never been in your room. How could you miss me there?"

"It's easy. I miss you everywhere."

"This all seems like a miracle. Three months ago I didn't even know your name."

"By the way, what's your middle name?"

"Kathleen. Glenna Kathleen O'Murphy. My father was Irish. Could you guess?"

"You're full of surprises. I should have guessed by the red hair."

"It's not really red. I'm almost blond."

"You're perfect."

"What's your middle name, while we're on the subject?"

"You'll laugh."

"No, I won't."

"It's Emory."

Glenna laughed. "Sorry. Your parents named you Beau Emory?"

"Worse than that. It's Beauregard Emory. I told you that you'd laugh. That's why my son is Keith Edward—a nice common name. Actually I'm named after both my grandfathers. Both are family names from way back."

"I see."

"You're smiling. I can hear it," he accused.

"I'm trying not to," she said with a laugh.

"I ought to come over there and see for myself."

"I wish you could."

"Yeah," he said with a smile. "I wish I could, too."

"I think we ought to set the date. Our kids will be more likely to believe us then."

"All right. How about next Tuesday?"

"Be serious. How about Christmas?"

"I don't know. Would you feel as if you never got an anniversary gift, just Christmas presents?"

"I think I can manage it if you can. It would make it easier for you to remember the date."

"I'm good at dates. How about this—we'll marry on Christmas Eve but we'll celebrate our anniversary on the date we met."

"You remember that?"

"Of course. It was the first day of school."

"Okay."

Beau paused. "I hate to ask this, but Christmas Eve wasn't your other anniversary, was it?"

"No. It was June. How about you?"

"July. Okay, Christmas Eve will be the day. I can't wait to open my gifts this year."

Glenna laughed. "Should I tie a tag around my neck that says 'Do not open until Christmas'?"

"You'd better not. I'm not sure I can wait that long."

"Good. I wish Chad had a date tonight. He's been gone every night for two weeks, but tonight he decides to stay home."

"It won't be long. Do you want to keep the wedding small?"

"Goodness, yes! I doubt my mother and stepfather will come. He has health problems, and she never travels without him."

"My parents will be there. You'll like them."

"Do they know about me?"

"Not yet. I'll call them after I hang up." Beau knew his mother would like Glenna. He also knew they would accuse him of rushing into marriage. "I'd like Joe and Sue Ann Tarrant to come, too. Joe and I have become good friends."

"I don't know them. Margo and Bill Clark won't come. Margo and I had words earlier today. She can't handle the idea of me remarrying."

"Looks as if it might not be any of her business."

"We've been friends for so long. I know she meant well. At least I'm trying to tell myself that."

"I want you to meet Joe and Sue Ann. You'll like them."

"It's usually the kiss of death to say that."

"I'll call them and see if we can all get together this weekend. I think you'd enjoy being with them."

"Okay. I want to meet your friends and family."

Beau smiled. "It's late, and I ought to let you go, but I hate to hang up. There always seems to be so much to be said. I could spend the rest of my life talking to you."

"And you will. We won't be apart much longer. Christmas will be here before you know it."

"I don't suppose you'd consider a Halloween wedding instead?"

"Good night, Beau."

"Good night, Glenna. I love you."

"I'M NERVOUS." Glenna brushed at her skirt and smoothed her hair for the tenth time.

"Don't be. Joe and Sue Ann are easy to get along with."

"What if they don't like me?"

"Then I won't marry you," he teased. "Lighten up."

"That's easy for you to say." She stood close to him as he opened the gate that led into the Tarrants' backyard. She could already smell barbecue cooking.

Joe was bending over a smoking barbecue grill, and Sue Ann was putting a salad on the table. They smiled when they saw Glenna and Beau. "Come on in," Sue Ann said. "I thought I heard your car door shut."

Beau introduced everyone and added, "It smells great."

"It should. Joe's been at it for hours. I hope you like brisket."

"We do."

Glenna felt warm all the way through when Beau linked her likes and dislikes with his. Their love was still so new she was sometimes surprised when he knew her opinion on things. "I've never been able to cook it," she added. "Maybe you could give me your recipe?"

"Better yet," Beau said, "just invite us over to eat it often."

"I'm surprised you put up with him," Joe said, waving his cooking fork at Beau.

"He pays me," she said seriously.

Joe grinned. "I like this one."

Glenna wondered if that meant she wasn't the first woman Beau had brought to the Tarrants' backyard.

Sue Ann swatted at her husband's arm. "You sound as if he has paraded a stream of women through here." To Glenna she said, "Just ignore him. I do."

Joe pretended to be wounded. "And after me slaving over this hot grill for you all afternoon. I get no respect."

"Have you seen Keith or Kelly? I thought they would have already been over here," Beau said as he helped himself to a potato chip.

"Kelly came by and said she's eating at Cathy Compton's house. They rented a movie she wants to watch. Keith said to shout over the fence when it's ready."

"My kids make themselves at home," Beau said as he shook his head. "You'll probably be glad to see us go."

"Not really," Joe told him. "We've gotten used to you."

Glenna found she was already liking the Tarrants. There was none of the awkwardness that usually accompanied meeting new people. She felt as accepted as Beau was.

"Will you help me with the iced tea?" Sue Ann asked Glenna. "I guess it's really too cool for it, but we drink it year round."

"I do, too." Glenna followed Sue Ann into the house.

The kitchen was smaller than her own, but it was evidently the hub of the house. Two girls of about the same age were playing a video game on the small TV in the corner. Sue Ann introduced them as Jody and Kay Lynn. Glenna smiled and the girls smiled back, then went on with their game.

"I don't know how parents survived without TV," Sue Ann said as she took glasses from the cabinet. "Our girls live in front of it."

"So does my son. It's a mixed blessing."

"I understand. Girls, the food is almost done."

"Can we eat in here?" Jody asked. "We want to watch a show that comes on in ten minutes."

"Okay," Sue Ann said. "Will you put ice in the glasses while I dilute the tea? I made it strong so I would be sure to have enough. I think it could almost walk to the table on its own."

Glenna put cubes of ice into the glasses. "Do you know Beau's children very well?"

"Keith and Kelly? Sure. They're over here half the time."

"What are they like?" Glenna glanced at the two girls, but they seemed to be interested only in the game. "I'm so nervous around them that I can barely talk. I want them to like me, but I don't think they do."

Sue Ann nodded. "I understand. My sister married a man with a family, and she had problems with the kids, too. Seems to go with the territory. But Keith and Kelly aren't hard to get to know. Keith is a bit shy, so he's often quieter than Kelly. He's a thinker, not a talker."

"He is?" It had never occurred to Glenna that Keith might be shy or that he was quiet because it was his way and not because he didn't want to be around her. "What about Kelly?"

Sue Ann frowned. "I wonder about Kelly sometimes. She seems to be so full of anger. Maybe the divorce hit her harder than it did Keith. That's what Beau thinks. I don't understand Kelly, to be perfectly honest. She's not a bad kid, but she has her own way of thinking about things. You know what I mean?"

"I think so. My son is like that, in a way. He's not too pleased at having a stepbrother and stepsister."

"Adjustments are hard on teenagers."

"They aren't a picnic for adults, either." Glenna thought of Margo and the friendship that seemed to be over.

"Beau says Christmas Eve is the big day."

"That's right. Will you and Joe be able to come?"

"Wild horses couldn't keep us away." Sue Ann put all but two glasses on the tray. "Girls, your tea is here on the counter. Don't spill it on the carpet."

"Okay," Kay Lynn said without turning her head.

By the time they went outside, Keith had arrived. Glenna smiled at him and he ducked his head, but this time she saw it as a gesture of shyness, not rejection. "Are you hungry?" she asked him. "It smells so good."

Keith risked a smile. "Sure does. Kelly says to tell you hello. She went to her friend's house."

Glenna nodded. "Tell her I said hi and that I missed her." She tried to act as normally as she would have if her heart hadn't been in her throat. She was so afraid Beau's children would never accept her.

Glenna sat by Beau, and he pressed his thigh close to hers under the table. As the plates of barbecue and potato salad were passed around, Glenna saw Keith studying her covertly. She pretended not to notice and laughed and talked as usual. Once she saw him smile at the banter between Beau and herself and she was heartened. She vowed silently to somehow win him over. Then there would be only Kelly to worry about. She pressed her leg against Beau and smiled at him.

CHAPTER THIRTEEN

CHAD SHOVED HIS BOOKS into his locker and kicked the door shut with a clang. Diana jumped at the noise. "What's with you?" she complained. "You look as grouchy as my father."

"I've got every reason to be. Do you know what my Mom laid on me last night?"

"What?"

"She and Mr. Fletcher are getting married. On *Christmas Eve,* no less. Merry Christmas."

"That's rotten. Is he just awful?"

"Probably. I barely even know the guy. If he's anything like Keith, he's the pits."

"I saw him once at a ball game. He's really good-looking."

"Not to me, he isn't." Chad leaned against the lockers and shoved his hands into the pockets of the letter jacket he had earned the year before. Diana was wearing his current one, and despite his glum mood, he couldn't help but notice how cute it was that the jacket reached almost to her knees.

"I can't even imagine you and Keith Fletcher as brothers." Diana pulled a packet of gum from her pocket and offered a stick to Chad.

He pushed the gum away. "He won't be my brother. Just my stepbrother."

"Still," Diana mused, "it's weird. He has a sister, too, doesn't he? You'll be like the Brady Bunch."

"In your dreams. His sister is named Kelly or Jelly or something like that." Chad pretended indifference, but he was intensely curious about the people with whom he would soon be sharing his house. Diana giggled. "And get this! Kelly gets the extra bedroom and Keith gets the living room. The living room!"

"So?"

"It's only about two times the size of my room, that's all. He'll be two feet from the front door and only six feet from the telephone. Every time you call, you'll probably have to talk to him first. That's if his dorky sister isn't on it nonstop."

Diana's blue eyes widened and she shook her golden mane. "That's awful! Won't your mom put in an extra line? My parents did. They said that's the only way they can ever get any calls. Like they get calls! My phone rings three times more than theirs does."

"My mom won't do that. I've already asked her and she said no."

"That's mean. When I'm a mother I'm going to let all my children have private lines. I think it's only right."

"Yeah. There's the first bell. I'll walk you to class."

"I can go alone."

Chad gave her an appraising look. "Since when?"

"I don't know. I just think we spend too much time together." She fingered a loose corner on her folder.

"We're going steady. We're supposed to be together all the time."

"I know that. I just want to go to class by myself today."

"Wait a minute. Doesn't Keith have a class next to yours this period?"

"Maybe. So what?" Her voice was too casual.

"So maybe you're going to meet him and don't want me around."

"You don't own me, Chad King." Diana tossed her shining hair and glared at him.

"Now look here, Diana. Do we mean something to each other or not? I was under the impression that you're my girl."

"Maybe I am and maybe I'm not."

Chad felt anger pounding in his temples. "Why did you pick a time like this to start a fight? Don't I have enough troubles without you doing this?"

"Don't you blame me for your trouble. Blame your mother."

"Leave my mother out of this."

"Well, you're the one who brought her up. It's her fault that you're so upset."

"I'm warning you, leave Mom out of this!"

"I'm really scared now," she jeered. "See me shake? I'm trembling all over."

"Give me back my jacket."

"What!"

"You heard me. If you don't care any more for me than this, we're breaking up."

"I don't believe you. Breaking up?"

"That or you say you're sorry for what you said about my mother."

Diana stared at him as if she couldn't believe her ears. "You talk about her like that all the time."

"That's different. I can do it, but you can't."

"Well, that's just great, Chad. Just great!" She shucked the oversize jacket from her shoulders and thrust it at him. "Here! Take the sorry old thing. I'll find a better one." She flounced away.

"Good! You do that! See if I care," he shouted after her. He wadded the jacket, shoved it into his locker and slammed the door again. He and Diana had been arguing a lot lately, but he had never thought it would lead to them breaking up. He had expected Diana to apologize the way she usually did and to soothe his ruffled feelings. He glared after her, but she was already lost in the crowd.

Diana lost no time. She had planned to break up with Chad and be at Keith's first class long before now. She threaded through the crowd and arrived at the door in time to lean against it mournfully before Keith arrived.

"What's the matter?" he asked when he saw her downcast face.

"Oh, hi, Keith. I didn't know you were in class this period. It's nothing, really."

"Hey, are you crying?" He bent closer to see her eyes beneath the fall of her hair.

Diana had not been able to summon tears, so she turned away. "It doesn't matter."

"Did you and Chad have a fight?"

She gave a mournful little laugh. "I guess you could say that. We broke up."

"You did? You broke up?"

She nodded. "I'll probably never have a date again. Every boy in school is scared of him and they won't date me."

"I'm not afraid of him." He didn't pause to think. "Will you go out with me Friday?"

Diana looked up with hope shining in her eyes. "Me? You want to go out with me?"

"Sure. Why not?"

"I'd love to, Keith." She smiled and the dimple played in her cheek. Then she sighed. "Chad took back his coat, and I don't have a coat to wear home. I've heard it's going to turn cold this afternoon. I'll probably freeze on the way. I walk, you know."

"Here." Keith shrugged out of the jacket he wore. It had the colors from his old high school and patches sewn down the sleeve to show what sports he had lettered in there. "I'll drive you home."

"Oh, Keith, I couldn't." She touched the jacket as if it were precious. "I couldn't take your jacket."

"I'm wearing a heavy sweater and you're not. I don't want you to get cold."

She smiled at him in a way that could melt less susceptible hearts than his. "Thank you, Keith. Should I meet you in the lot after school?" She knew full well where he always parked.

"Sure. I drive a red Mustang."

"Great. I'll meet you there." She hurried away so everyone would see she was wearing Keith's distinctive jacket and tell Chad. She loved the feeling of having two of the cutest boys in school fighting over her.

"ALL RIGHT, what's going on?" Coach Jack Hevener glared from Chad to Keith. "You two played as if you were from rival teams today. What's going on?"

"Nothing." Keith frowned at the chalk-smudged blackboard to keep from looking at the coach or Chad.

"Nothing," Chad echoed. He looked at the row of empty showers.

"Don't give me that." Hevener frowned at the boys. "I hear you broke up with Diana Murdock," he said to Chad. To Keith he added, "And that she's wearing a letter jacket now with Denton high school's colors."

Chad and Keith exchanged glowering looks.

"That's what I thought. Now I don't give a rip who's dating whom or why. All I'm interested in is having a football team that works together. Keith, you were deliberately overthrowing the ball to Chad, and Chad, even when you were in reach of the ball you fumbled it as if it was a bad pass. I'm not as dumb as you boys seem to think."

"It's not my fault he can't throw," Chad burst out.

"No one at my other school ever complained," Keith shouted.

"Okay. That does it. Hit the track. You're both going to run laps until you can make peace."

"But, Coach!"

"Not a word, King. To the track." He glared at the boys as they began dragging themselves to their feet, then shouted, "Move it! Now!" In a flash, they were out the door that led to the field.

Hevener went to the stands. He hadn't wanted to spend an extra hour or so at school, but he supposed it beat raking the leaves or doing the other chores his wife considered to be his due. He studied the two boys as they circled the track. Anger was apparent in their movements. King was a good athlete, and Fletcher was proving to be one, too. Fletcher was able to keep abreast with King even though the other boy was trying to leave him behind. Hevener pulled a piece of hard candy from his pocket and unwrapped it. Putting the paper in his pocket, he sucked on the candy to calm his stomach. Years of being a coach had taken their toll.

After two hard laps the coach called them over. "Ready to be friends?"

Chad was out of breath, but he glared at Keith and wheezed, "Not on your life." Keith said nothing, but from his defensive posture, the coach was sure of his answer, as well.

"Okay, keep running." Hevener sat down and leaned his elbows on his knees. The boys were stubborn. He had to give them that. Both of them had heart.

After a couple more laps, he called them back. "How about it, boys?"

"Okay." Chad glared at Keith.

"No way," Keith said. "He just wants to stop running."

"Aren't you about worn out?" Hevener asked. They had just finished football practice, and he knew the boys were tired.

"Not me," Keith said. "How about you, Chad?"

"I can run you into the ground and not work up a sweat."

Hevener didn't point out that both boys were already sweating profusely. "Okay. It's up to you. Take off again."

He was curious to see how long it would take for the boys to run off their animosity. He had never known any to last that long, but he had no intention of letting them off until he was convinced that they had given up the feud. He knew Diana Murdock and could spot her type a block away. She wasn't worth ruining a team over.

The next time he called them over, the boys' attitudes had changed. Neither took a jab at the other. He knew they were finally willing to listen to what he had to say. "Let's walk. I don't want your muscles to cool too quickly."

Companionably, Hevener strolled between the boys around the tarmac track. "You two boys are the best athletes I've had the privilege of coaching in years. And I'd say you're the most evenly matched. If you could get to be friends, you'd make an unbeatable pair." He waited for either to deny the possibility, but when they didn't speak, he continued. "What was the problem between you two? Was it Diana Murdock?"

Chad spoke up. "We broke up before school this morning, and even before first period started, she was wearing *his* jacket."

"We aren't going steady. She said she was cold, so I loaned it to her," Keith answered. "I tried to tell you that, but you wouldn't listen."

"Chad," Hevener said as they passed the goalposts, "the thing to remember is that you two broke up. When you aren't going together, she's fair game for anyone else."

"I'm telling you, we aren't going steady," Keith repeated. "I asked her out for Friday after she said you broke up, but she encouraged me. And was pretty quick to say yes."

Chad frowned but this time not at Keith.

Hevener nodded as if this issue was resolved. "What else?"

"My father and his mother are getting married," Keith mumbled.

"What? What's that?" Hevener thought he must have misunderstood.

"That's right," Chad confirmed. "On Christmas Eve, of all times."

"So." Hevener couldn't think of another response. He had figured Glenna King would never remarry. "I gather you two are making it as hard as possible on your parents?"

Neither boy answered.

"That's what I thought. Now look. It's going to come about and there's nothing you can do to stop it. When people get it in their heads to marry, nobody can talk 'em out of it. Right? Have you had any luck?"

Both boys shook their heads.

"Okay then. The only thing to do is to give in gracefully. I'm not saying you two should act like you're best friends, but give your folks some space. Making everybody miserable won't solve anything." He glanced from one to the other. "Well? Am I right?"

"I guess," Keith admitted grudgingly. He added, "I don't have anything against Mrs. King—Glenna—I just don't want my dad getting married again."

"How about you, Chad?"

"I don't even know Beau Fletcher. Not really. I've just seen him a time or two at the house. I don't think it's right for Mom to marry. I mean, how could she have loved Dad and want to marry somebody else?"

Hevener nodded. He had seen exhaustion on the track bring out confessions before. "Think about it, Chad. You and Diana Murdock broke up. Do you ever plan to date anyone else?"

"Well, sure."

"It's the same with parents. It's natural for men and women to want to be together, or for most it is. Nearly everyone remarries after a divorce or a death. You can't expect them to devote the rest of their lives to just being parents to you. Why, you boys will be out of school next year, and on your own."

"Not me," Chad disagreed. "I may go to college here."

"So will I," Keith said. "I won't leave Dad for at least five years. And then there's Kelly for him to raise."

"Now think about what you're saying," Hevener said in a reasonable tone. "How would you feel in their shoes?"

Chad finally grinned. "I'd feel like a cross-dresser in Mom's."

Keith laughed in spite of himself.

"See? I knew you could laugh together. Like I said, lighten up on your parents. A family can be a lot like a football team. Everyone has a different assignment, and if he does it well, and works well with everyone else on the team, the family can have a winning season, and some even a championship season. If you two don't learn to cooperate with each other, everyone else on this football team of ours will suffer. It's not so different with a family. A winning season makes everyone happy. Your folks and the rest of your family deserve to be happy. Give them a chance. They aren't going to stop loving you just because they have someone else in their lives. It doesn't work that way. The members of our football team change every year, but when we all pull together, we can still have a winning season."

"How do you know it works the same way with families?" Chad asked. "Maybe that's different."

"I know because I got a divorce, and later I married a woman with a little girl. I kept on loving my kids, and now I love my stepdaughter as well."

Both boys seemed to be giving some serious thought to what they had heard, and as they were nearing the field house Hevener said, "You boys bury the hatchet. Life's too short to spend so much of it being mad." He clapped them each on the shoulder. "I'll see you at practice tomorrow, and this time I want to see team spirit.''

Chad nodded, and so did Keith. As he showered, Chad reflected that whether Keith was telling the truth or not about why Diana was wearing his letter jacket, he at least seemed sincere about their parents' marriage. And some of what Coach Hevener said had made sense, even though Chad couldn't agree with it all. He and Diana had broken up, and that meant she was free to date anyone she pleased. With a little time to think about it, and with the first pangs of disappointment now passed, Chad realized he had little real regret. It had always made him mad when Diana flirted with other boys, even though she claimed she was only talking to them, and now he wouldn't have to worry about that anymore. This time the thought that Diana might be going steady with Keith brought a smile to Chad's face. Doubtless she would lead him for a spin, flirting with every boy in sight, and he would have to deal with it. Maybe Keith and Diana deserved each other. One day, Chad was certain, Diana would leave Keith for someone else the way she had left him, and Chad's pride would be salved. He was whistling as he went to his car.

"ARE YOU SURE Chad is at football practice?" Beau asked as he sat on the couch next to Glenna and pulled her closer to him. "I don't want him to come in and find us necking."

"I'm positive." She snuggled up to his side and curled her legs onto the cushions. "I've noticed a change in him lately. He almost seems to be accepting the idea of us getting married.''

''So is Keith. What do you suppose is going on? Keith was late getting home from practice a few days ago, and when he came in he actually asked me if he could come over and see you sometime.''

''It's a miracle. But let's not examine it too closely.'' Glenna tilted her head and kissed the curve of his jaw. ''Are we really going to be necking on the couch?''

Beau cradled her face in the palm of his hand. ''Only because I think it would be pushing our luck to go upstairs.''

She nodded. ''When I get you alone upstairs I don't want it to be rushed. I plan to take your clothes off slowly and kiss you from head to foot. Then I plan to really turn you on.'' She grinned at him.

''You just did. And what am I supposed to be doing while you amuse yourself with my body?''

''Anything you want.''

''You'd better change the subject or we're going up to your bedroom whether Chad might catch us there or not.''

''I think you and I should get some sort of medal for restraint. After Dallas you're hard to resist.''

Beau smiled. ''I always hoped I'd fall in love with a bawdy wench. I got my wish.''

''I was never bawdy until you came along. I used to be logical and levelheaded and perfectly normal.''

''I question that.''

''It's true.'' She ran the tip of her tongue down the pulse beneath his jaw. ''You taste so good. You're Beau-flavored.''

Beau turned her in his arms so that she lay cradled across his lap. He gazed into her silver eyes. "You're like an addictive substance. I can't get you out of my system."

"Good." She put her arms around his neck and drew him nearer. She stopped with her lips a breath away from his. "I don't ever want you to feel any other way." She kissed him lightly. "Last night I dreamed you were there beside me. I woke up aching for your touch and you weren't there. Do you really think it's necessary for us to be so upright from now until Christmas?"

"No, I don't. I just haven't figured out a way to circumvent two houses with children in them. Sweet Gum is too small for us to chance going to a motel. Do you have any ideas?"

"I know where the teenagers go to park," she teased. "Does your car have a roomy back seat?"

"Maybe we could find a reason to leave town for the weekend."

"As closely as our kids are watching us? They would nail us in a minute." She laughed. "Here we are, two adults, and we can't think of a safe place to ravish each other's bodies. Can you believe this?"

"I know! Kelly is spending the night with Cathy Compton this Saturday. Keith has a date with a girl named Janie Rogers."

"I thought he was dating Diana."

"No, I'm glad to say he saw through her tactics pretty fast. He's taking Janie to a dance, and he won't be home until late. We can go to my place."

"That sounds safe. I can't believe we have to sneak around like this. How do other single parents manage?"

"Got me. I'll come get you at seven. We can grill steaks and spend the evening doing lascivious things to each other."

"Sounds great." She rubbed her nose against his. "You smell good and you taste good. You *are* good."

"Glenna," he whispered. "How did I ever find you? When I think of all the places I considered moving to, I feel a shiver. I might never have found you."

"Yes, you would have. You told me you would have searched to the ends of the earth. We were meant to be together."

"Yes. It's as if you're a part of me." He drew her closer and kissed her.

Glenna's blood warmed as his mouth moved over hers. She had never known anyone could kiss as sensuously as Beau. Her lips opened to him, and his tongue coaxed hers as he probed her mouth. His hand covered her breast, and she trembled with desire as her nipple beaded tighter. She wanted him so much she could hardly control herself.

Beau's fingers grew bolder and he unbuttoned her blouse. He ran his fingers over the lace of her bra. The heat from his fingers seemed to sear her, and a breathy sound of surrender escaped her lips. Her mind tried to focus on how long Chad was likely to be at football practice. "Maybe we have time to go upstairs," she whispered.

"We'd have to hurry. I don't ever want to have to rush when I'm making love with you." He lowered his head and leaned her against his legs and ran his tongue over the lace of her bra, coaxing the scarcely concealed nipple back to throbbing firmness.

"The way I feel, we would *have* to hurry." All her thoughts and emotions were jumbling together. She was aware only of his touch and what it was doing to her. "I couldn't bear to wait to have you."

"I have a lot to teach you." He kissed her again as his hand slipped into the cup of her bra and toyed with her breast. "I'm going to show you how to be satisfied over and over."

"You made a good start on it in Dallas," she murmured. "That's never happened to me before."

He smiled. "That was only the beginning."

Glenna's entire body seemed to be on fire. "We have time. Surely Chad won't come straight home. He never does."

"I guess I could hurry, but just this once." He grinned at her. "I want you as much as you want me."

Hand in hand, they ran upstairs, racing each other to Glenna's bedroom. Beau kicked the door shut and watched her undress as he pulled his clothes off and tossed them to the floor. Having him in the room that was her private domain excited Glenna beyond all bounds. He seemed to so fill the room, there was no space left for loneliness.

He finished undressing first and jerked the bed covers back with one sweep of his arm. "I had a feeling you would have pink sheets." He looped his arm around her and pulled her to the bed.

Glenna felt the leashed control that held his strength in check, and her excitement grew. The idea that they were taking a chance by being in her bedroom made her pulse race. She ran her hands over his lean body and gloried in his firm muscles and warm skin. "You feel so good!"

He kissed her and rolled them over so that she lay on top of him. Glenna trembled from wanting him, and she rocked her hips seductively as she threw her leg over his hips. Beau groaned and his kisses became demanding and hot.

She positioned herself and slid him into her body. Becoming part of him made her catch her breath and roll her head back to savor all the sensations. Beau cupped her breasts in his hands and played his thumbs and fingers over the sensitive buds. Almost at once Glenna felt her body rushing to fulfillment and she quickened her movements. Soon waves of hot release pounded through her and she braced her hands on his chest.

As the waves subsided, she opened her eyes and gazed at him. He was watching her with enjoyment. Their eyes locked, he rolled over so that she was half beside him, half under him. Once more he began to summon her responses with the urging of his own. Glenna opened her mouth to tell him she had already reached her peak, but he silenced her with a searing kiss. He ran his hand over her ribs and along the swell of her hips. By shifting his position slightly, he managed to fill her even more deeply.

His hand moved between them in tantalizing, circular strokes across her belly until he reached the source of her ecstasy. When his finger touched her intimately, Glenna felt as if she would explode with desire. She whispered his name as her need increased with each movement of his hips and stroke of his finger. Then he took her to one glorious pinnacle after another, giving her more pleasure than she had known was possible. Finally he joined her and they spent their love together.

When his breathing had subsided to the point where he could speak, Beau said in a whisper, "See? I told you once is not enough."

Glenna felt as if she might cry from sheer happiness and satisfaction. Never had she felt so complete as she did at that moment. "I love you," she murmured. "I love you so much."

Regretfully Beau rolled from her. "I want to stay here and make love to you until morning comes around. Do we really have to wait until Christmas to get married?"

"Unless you want to be the one to explain to the children that we are too hot for each other to wait that long."

"Okay. We'll wait. But we're spending our honeymoon far away from anyone we are kin to by birth."

"We get a honeymoon?" She hadn't thought of that.

"You bet we do. I don't have to be back to class until the second week in January. Pick a place you've already seen or have no interest in seeing, because we may have time for nothing but each other."

"That sounds perfect to me. It should be someplace close so we don't lose a lot of time in travel."

"My thoughts exactly."

"How does Dallas sound?"

"You took the words right out of my mouth. We can tell the kids we went to Colorado or someplace more traditional."

"I'll forget to pack my camera. That way we don't have to produce snapshots."

"I love you, Glenna." He leaned over her and kissed her slowly and lingeringly.

"I love you, too, but we had better get dressed. I have a feeling we've been up here longer than we think."

They dressed and were sitting on the couch drinking coffee by the time Chad came home.

"Hi," he said awkwardly, as if he was trying to be polite but wasn't sure what to say to them. "What's going on?"

Glenna smiled. "Not a thing. Anything new going on at school?"

Beau only smiled.

CHAPTER FOURTEEN

GLENNA WAS RELUCTANT to call Margo, but their long years of friendship made the call necessary. She dialed the familiar number and waited for Margo to answer. "Margo? This is Glenna."

Margo paused. "Hello, Glenna."

Glenna felt strange having such a cool conversation with her longtime friend. "Look, Margo, I don't like the way things are going between us. I wish we could be friends like before."

"I have no idea what you're talking about. Of course, we're still friends." Margo's voice held a sharp edge that belied her words.

Glenna sighed. "How have you been?"

"Fine, thank you. And you?"

"I'm fine. How're Bob and the boys?"

"Fine."

Margo's coolness left Glenna strangely bereft. "Beau and I have set a date. We're going to be married on Christmas Eve."

An almost palpable silence stretched between them.

"Margo? Are you still there?"

"Yes. Christmas Eve, you say?"

Glenna wished she hadn't called. She had suspected from the last time she and Margo talked that their friendship was over, but for all the years they had been closer than sisters, she wanted to try to patch things up. "That's right. We'll be married in the chapel rather than the sanctuary, since it's to be a small wedding. Will you come?"

"I'm so sorry, but I have other plans."

Glenna wished the words didn't hurt so much. "I know Christmas Eve is difficult with children and all, but I meant for you and Bob to bring the boys. It's not as if they're still interested in Santa Claus."

"Of course not. No, we have other plans. On Christmas Eve I think it's best for families to be at home together."

"I agree." Glenna's voice became as coolly impersonal as Margo's. "Even though we've often gone to each other's houses on Christmas Eve to assemble bikes and swing sets, I think it's time for us to be with our own individual families. Beau and I will miss you."

"Thank you for asking me." Margo sounded as detached as if Glenna were a stranger.

"Goodbye, Margo," Glenna said, then hung up. For a long while she sat there and stared at the phone. So many of the people she had thought would be forever in her world had dropped away. The Kings weren't speaking to her, either, and her mother had told her she was making a mistake and that she wouldn't fly across three states to see her do it.

Glenna lifted her chin. She loved Beau and she knew it was no mistake. Nothing else had ever felt so right. Not even her marriage with Jordan. But she hadn't thought she and Beau would be so... alone. Unexpectedly she was reminded of something she had read in high school by Thoreau about being a majority of one. She wished she had understood it so thoroughly then—she would have made a better grade in that class.

"KELLY?" BEAU CALLED as he went through the house. "Are you here?"

Keith looked up from the book he was reading. "I haven't seen her."

"What do you mean you haven't seen her? Hasn't she come in from school?"

"Nope. I've been here the whole time and I haven't seen her at all." Keith went back to his reading.

Beau frowned. "I told her to come straight home today." He had had an uneasy feeling all day but he had tried to ignore it, thinking it stemmed from the fact that he and Kelly had argued before school. She had again said he would be sorry for deciding to marry Glenna. Then she had become uncharacteristically quiet. He had hoped that meant she was beginning to accept his decision.

Not wanting to alarm Keith, Beau went to his bedroom to call Kelly's friend Cathy Compton. "Hi, Cathy. Is Kelly over there?"

"No, I haven't seen her all day." Cathy sounded as concerned as Beau. "I thought maybe she was sick or something. Isn't she at home?"

"No. If you see her, or if she calls you, will you tell her to call me right away?"

"Sure thing, Mr. Fletcher."

Beau hung up and looked up Conan Hudson's number. If Kelly had skipped school to be with Conan, he was going to ground her for the rest of her life. "Conan? This is Kelly Fletcher's father. Could I speak to her?"

"She's not here, Mr. Fletcher. Maybe she's over at Cathy's house."

"I just called there. Do you have any idea where else I might try? Does she have a new friend?"

"No, sir. Just me and Cathy, mainly. Maybe she's out riding her bike."

"Maybe so. By the way, did you see her at school today?"

"No, I thought she was staying at home today."

"Why would you think that?"

"Well, because she called me before school and said that she was."

"I see. Did you go to school today?"

"Yes, sir."

Beau couldn't tell if the boy was telling him the truth or not, but his worry doubled. What if something had happened to Kelly? He read in the paper about kidnappings and young girls being attacked all the time. "Did she say why she was skipping school?"

Conan said reluctantly, "She acted like she was upset or something."

"Did she say why?"

For a long moment Conan didn't speak. Finally he said, "She mentioned something about you getting married to Mrs. King. That's all I know about it."

"Thanks, Conan. If she calls you, tell her I'm looking for her."

Beau hung up and went to Kelly's room. As usual his daughter's room was in a jumble from the night before. She had tossed the bedspread over the rumpled covers and pillows, and the red sweater she had worn the day before was on the floor, halfway under the bed. Her collection of stuffed rabbits was in one corner beneath a poster of a rock group. Another rock group in lurid makeup hung over her desk. Beau wasn't interested in the clutter. He went to Kelly's closet and opened the door.

A search revealed that her canvas flight bag was gone. Beau's stomach turned over. Was it possible that Kelly had run away from home? As fast as the thought surfaced, he shoved it away. Runaways came from other families.

He went downstairs and out to the garage. Kelly's bike was gone. Dread seized him. He had always believed runaways were kids who had it so bad at home that they left for their own survival. That it didn't happen in homes like his. True, Kelly was opposed to his intention to marry Glenna, but she knew he and Keith loved her, and Glenna had never done anything to turn the girl against her. No, surely she hadn't run away because of the announcement of their marriage plans. But in the dark recesses of his mind, he knew it was true.

"Keith, has Kelly mentioned any new friends to you? Someone she might have gone to see?"

Keith put down the book. "No, as far as I know she just runs with Cathy Compton and Conan Hudson. Is she in trouble?"

"It seems she skipped school today."

Keith's eyes widened. "No kidding? Kelly skipped school?"

Beau rubbed his eyes as he tried to think. "Who is her homeroom teacher? Mrs. Nesbitt, that's it." He went to the kitchen and looked up the Nesbitts' number in the phone book. A short conversation revealed that Kelly had indeed been absent.

"Maybe she's with Conan," Keith said.

"I've already called him as well as Cathy. Neither of them has seen her."

"Maybe they're lying."

Beau looked at his son and hope sprang anew. He hadn't thought of that. "Maybe so."

"I could go over there and see."

"I'd appreciate it. If she isn't there, will you drive around? You might see her on the street."

"Sure, Dad." Keith put a marker in the book he was reading and set it aside.

Beau went to the kitchen and wrote Kelly a note telling her to stay home in case she returned before they did.

Keith drove away in the direction of the Hudsons' house; Beau went to Glenna's.

"What do you mean she's missing?" Glenna said as he came in. "How can she be missing?"

"Her overnight bag is gone, and so is her bike. I couldn't tell if any clothes were missing or not."

"But why would she—" Glenna's words stuck in her throat. She knew why Kelly might have run away, and she was flooded with feelings of guilt. "What I meant was, where could she have gone?"

"Keith is driving around looking for her." He went to the couch and slumped down, staring at the opposite wall, lost in thought.

Glenna turned off the TV and sat beside him. "She must be here somewhere. She couldn't go far on a bicycle."

"She was pretty upset when I left for class. She said I'd be sorry." Beau's concern was becoming edged with panic. "Do you think there's a chance someone might have . . . you know, kidnapped her?"

"No. No, of course not," Glenna said quickly. "Not in Sweet Gum. We have never had a kidnapping here. She must be trying to worry you, that's all."

"Punish me is what you meant. And she's doing a damned good job of it."

Beau was obviously quite distraught and blaming himself for Kelly's actions. Glenna, too, felt guilty and wanted to say something to make all this easier on Beau, but she didn't know what would help. She only prayed that Beau didn't blame her for the decision they had made to announce their wedding plans now rather than later.

Chad apparently heard their voices and came to the doorway. "What's going on?"

Glenna put her hand over Beau's and turned to her son. "Kelly is missing. Have you seen her?"

"No." He came into the room and looked at the adults. "Maybe she's at a friend's house," he said, trying to sound hopeful.

"I've called the two people she runs with and they haven't seen her. She skipped school," Beau added.

He hated the way the words sounded. The words were too frightening to be linked to his precious daughter.

"I doubt she's been kidnapped," Glenna repeated. "It's more likely she's hiding somewhere."

"I hope you're right."

"Have you tried her mom?" Chad asked.

Beau glanced at him. "She couldn't ride a bicycle all the way to Denton. It's a long drive by car."

"Her mom might know where she is, though. Kelly might have talked to her."

Beau nodded slowly. Chad was being more helpful than he would ever have expected, and his suggestion was a good one. "You're right," he said. "Maybe I ought to call Diedra."

Glenna handed him the phone, and he dialed Diedra's number. After what seemed to be a long time, he heard a recording informing him that the number he had dialed was no longer in service. He hung up and called information. Diedra's new number rang, but the phone went unanswered.

"She changed her number?" Glenna asked as they waited to see if Diedra would pick up the receiver. "Has she moved?"

"I have no idea. It's still a Denton exchange. She changes her number from time to time to prevent her ex-boyfriends from finding her. Or maybe she just does it to irritate me when the kids can't find her. Probably both." He hung up and frowned at the phone.

"Kelly must be here in town," Glenna said reasonably. "She'll get hungry by suppertime and come on home."

"I can't wait around that long to find out if she's okay." Beau stood and paced to the window. "What if something has happened to her?"

"If it had, the police would have contacted you."

"Maybe Diedra came after her."

Glenna went to him. "Surely she wouldn't do that without telling you."

"Sure, she would. Diedra's still angry at me because of my rejection of her at the homecoming dance."

"No mother would put her child in the middle that way, surely."

"The term doesn't apply to women like Diedra. Giving birth doesn't automatically make you the sort of mother Norman Rockwell painted."

Glenna put her hand on his arm and Beau pulled her close. He needed to feel her strength and support.

Chad watched his mother and Beau, and saw the worry and concern on their faces. Rather than becoming instantly resentful of their togetherness, Chad discovered he was seeing them in a new light. Before, he had always been so immersed in his own problems and preferences that he had not seen them as people. The man was genuinely worried about his daughter, and Chad's mother was being compassionately supportive. He still didn't want Glenna to marry Beau, but this new way of seeing them had given him food for thought.

"I guess I could go look for her," he said casually, expecting Beau to turn down his offer.

Instead Beau turned to him hopefully. "You'd do that?"

"Sure. I don't want some kid getting hurt. I know all the places kids go around here."

"That would be great, Chad," Glenna said. "Call if you hear or see anything."

"Okay." To cover the fact that he was upset over the idea of someone running away, he sauntered from the room. He had never known anyone to actually run away from home. Sure, he and his friends talked about it when they were mad at their parents, but it was tacitly understood that none of them would ever really do it.

He got in his car and revved the engine for a moment so he could hear its comforting roar. He rested his arm on the back of the seat and backed out of the driveway. For a while he drove up and down the streets between his house and the Fletchers', though he doubted Kelly would have had any interest in coming in that direction.

One by one he visited the hideouts that were favorites of the younger teenagers in Sweet Gum. When Kelly wasn't to be found, he began wondering if she had run away for real. He had seen enough movies to know that kids tried things like that. In the movies the runaway boys usually had terrific adventures and became heroes to their peers, but the runaway girls were usually found dead. The thought wasn't comforting.

As he neared the football stadium, he slowed. This wasn't a hangout favored by his crowd, but some of the others came here, usually to neck behind the field house or to share pot in the shadows below the stands.

He parked beside the gate and walked into the stadium. In case he should run into anyone he knew, he kept his stride measured and purposeful so he could pretend he was only doing this for his mother's sake.

The field house was locked, as he knew it would be, and no one was behind it. He circled under the stands and walked in the stripes of sunlight that angled through the bleacher seats to the bare dirt below. The ground was littered with cigarette butts and other trash, but he saw no one at all. At the far end he went up the steps and started down the broad walkway between the seats and the fence that protected the fans from injury or participation during a game.

Halfway down, Chad saw another boy come up the far steps. He slowed. He wasn't in the mood for trouble. Not with his mother already upset over Kelly. He watched his rival for any signs of animosity.

Keith stopped when he saw Chad, but he didn't leave. Instead he waited for Chad to come within talking distance. "Have you seen my sister?"

"No, I told Mom I'd help look for her."

Keith stared at him as if he couldn't believe his ears. "You're looking for Kelly?"

"Yeah, what about it?" Chad didn't want to fight, but he wasn't going to let Keith know that.

"I'm just surprised, that's all."

"What did you think I'd do? It'll be getting dark soon, and she doesn't have any business being out after sundown."

Keith grinned. "That sounds like a line from a vampire movie."

Chad carefully returned the grin. He still wasn't sure what Keith would do.

Keith looked across the field toward the seats used by Sweet Gum's opponents. "I've looked everywhere I can think of. I even went back by the house to see if she had come in after we left."

"She wasn't there?"

Keith gave him an exasperated look. "If she had been, would I still be hunting for her?"

Chad shrugged. "Have you been to the Dairy Dip?"

"Not yet."

"Let's go. We can use my car. No point in both of us wasting gas if we're going to the same place."

Keith hesitated but then nodded. "Okay."

Chad felt ill at ease as they walked to the car. He had never thought he would be offering Keith Fletcher a ride anywhere at all. "Pull up on the door handle when you shut it. It's contrary."

As Chad started the car, Keith said, "Good sound. Is this the original engine?"

"No way. I replaced it with a Cobra. Listen." He revved it until the car vibrated.

Keith was appreciative. "My car needs a tune-up. Dad was going to help me, but he's been too busy lately."

Chad grimaced. "My mom has been the same kind of busy."

Keith looked out the side window. "What do you think about them getting married?"

"I think it's the pits."

"So do I. He says they're going through with it, though. I guess I'll have to make the best of it. That's probably why Kelly took off."

"Yeah. You think she really ran away?"

"Hell, I don't know. Who knows what a girl thinks? She's dumb enough to try it."

Chad drove in silence for a while. "I hear Diana has a date with Mike Clark this weekend."

"Yep."

"I thought you two were going steady."

Keith shook his head. "Not me, man. I saw how she did you. I want a girl I can trust out of my sight."

Chad made no comment. He was surprised to find Keith wasn't a nerd or afraid to talk about Diana with him. His estimation of the other boy began to rise.

"IT'S GETTING DARK," Beau commented. "Maybe I ought to call the police."

"That might be a good idea." Glenna went to the phone and dialed. When the switchboard answered, she handed the phone to Beau. As he told the woman what had happened, Glenna looked out the kitchen window.

She was more worried than she was letting Beau see. Although Sweet Gum had a relatively low crime rate, it wasn't impossible that something could have happened to Kelly. When Beau was off the phone, she turned expectantly.

"They haven't had a report of any accidents, and no one has reported seeing a girl of her description. Until she has been gone forty-eight hours they can't consider her to be officially missing." He ran his fingers through his hair. "Forty-eight hours! I can't wait that long to search for her.

"Try calling Diedra again."

Beau dialed the number they had been calling in-
termittently for more than two hours. As before, there
was no answer. "I'll bet Diedra has come to get Kelly.
Why else would she be gone so long?"

"It's possible that she's just gone out. I'm often out
at this time of day, you know." Glenna went to him
and put her arms around him. "Kelly will be fine.
We'll find her any minute now. Try your house again."

She watched him dial and wait for Kelly to answer.
When he shook his head and hung up, she took the
phone and called the Hudsons' number. Instead of
speaking to Conan, she asked for his mother. "Bar-
bara? This is Glenna King. Fine, thanks. Beau
Fletcher is here and we're trying to locate his daughter. Is she over there?" Glenna shook her head at Beau
rather than keeping him in suspense. "Do you have
any idea where she might be? Yes, we are getting worried. Okay. Will you call if you hear from her? Fine.
Thank you. 'Bye."

"No luck?"

Glenna shook her head. "I was hoping we might
learn something by talking to the parents. What's the
Comptons' number? Maybe Cathy's mother will know
something."

The call proved to be no more fruitful than the last.
Glenna reluctantly hung up the phone. "Are you sure
she never mentioned where she might go if she ran
away?"

"All she ever says is that she wants to go back to
Denton."

"I'll call the state Department of Public Safety. Maybe she doesn't realize she can't get to Denton by bicycle."

After she made the call, Beau put his arms around her and buried his face in her hair. "I want to hug her and to ground her and never let her out of my sight again, not to mention wring her neck."

"I know. We'll find her. She can't stay hidden forever." Glenna hoped she sounded more positive than she felt. The TV was full of reports of missing children who were never found. She held Beau tightly. His misery was as real to her as if it were her own. "I'll make us some dinner."

"I can't eat."

"Some coffee then. Chad will be home soon, and he may have heard something."

"Wouldn't he have called if he had?"

"You're right. He would."

"If Diedra is behind this . . ."

"Now, Beau, you have no valid reason to believe she is. Has she ever threatened to take either of the children?"

Beau shook his head. "No. She has refused to see them at all most of the time. They cramp her social life."

"Then she probably hasn't changed her mind now."

Beau looked at her. "Then where is Kelly?" When Glenna had no answer, he said, "See? It's better for me to assume she is with Diedra."

"I guess you're right." She went to get the can of coffee from the pantry. "I'll bet Kelly is at some new friend's house and that she'll show up at her usual curfew."

"I hope so."

Glenna measured coffee into the pot. "Beau, do you think we should go ahead with our marriage plans since Kelly obviously feels so strongly about us?"

"I'm not giving you up. Kelly is a child. She can't be the one to make a decision like that for us. No child has that amount of maturity. Besides, it's not just you. She's been depressed since the day Diedra left."

"It does seem to have hit her exceptionally hard."

"Diedra told Kelly she would take her with her if she left. Instead, she was gone when Kelly and Keith came home from school. She didn't even leave them a note. In her note to me she said she had decided to leave that way because it was easier on her. Kelly insisted that I show her the note, and she tried to convince herself that Diedra had left her one, too, but that it had been lost. She went through a lot of denial.

"That's one reason I moved to Sweet Gum. I thought it would be best for Kelly to get away from the memories. She couldn't ride down a street without saying Diedra shopped there or had an account in some store she saw. Obviously the move didn't help."

"It's not your fault." Glenna went to him and sat in his lap as she waited for the coffee to perk. "You're a good father, Beau. The best I've ever seen. Diedra was emotionally abusive to the children. Kelly is caught up in the abused-child cycle. She thinks she has to be validated by her mother before she has real worth, and, of course, that validation will likely never come. We see it in Parents Anonymous all the time."

"I know. I just don't know how to deal with it."

Glenna put her forehead against his. "Have you given any more thought to getting Kelly into counseling?"

"I called the man you suggested, but she refused to go. When I get her back, I'm going to insist."

"I think that's a good idea."

She heard the sound of two cars driving up, and she stood and went to the door. When she saw Chad and Keith arriving together, her mouth dropped open. Beau looked equally amazed when the boys came inside.

"I ran into Keith and we've been looking for her together," Chad said offhandedly, as if there were nothing unusual about them being together. "Any word here?"

Glenna shook her head.

Chad glanced at Keith and said, "I'll show you the living room. If you're going to live in it, you might as well see what it looks like."

"Okay." Keith nodded to Glenna as he followed Chad through the door.

"Did you see what I saw?" Glenna whispered to Beau. "Can you believe it?"

Beau looked as dumbfounded as she felt. "If I could figure out teenagers, I could make a million dollars overnight."

She peeped through the crack between the door and the frame. Chad was showing Keith his and his father's sports trophies in the glass case in the corner of the dining room. Keith was asking questions about the events as if he and Chad were friends.

"Maybe there's hope for us yet," Beau said from behind her.

She turned to find he had come to the door and was peering through the crack above her head. "Maybe I ought to make sandwiches. The boys must be hungry."

Beau nodded. "I never knew Keith when he wasn't." He drew in a deep breath. "What if Kelly doesn't have any supper? What if she stays out all night?"

"Kelly is a sensible girl. She must have had a plan of some sort. She's probably at a new friend's house right now. After we eat, let's go to your house in case she tries to call and won't leave a message on your recorder."

"That's as good a plan as any."

Glenna looped her arm around him. "I'll stay with you until we find her. We're in this together."

He kissed the top of her head. "I love you. I don't know how I would manage this without you."

Glenna hoped he was serious about sending Kelly to a therapist when she was found. She thought the girl might have problems that were more serious than they had suspected.

CHAPTER FIFTEEN

NIGHT HAD FALLEN before the phone rang. Keith beat Beau to the phone by only a step. By the expression on Keith's face, Beau knew it wasn't Kelly. Keith handed his father the phone.

"Hello?"

"Mr. Fletcher? This is Cathy."

"Have you heard from Kelly?" The words rushed from his mouth despite his attempt to control his anxiety.

"No, at least not really."

The girl sounded frightened and reluctant to talk. Beau took a deep breath to calm himself. "What do you mean?"

"My mom said I should call you. She's real mad at me for not telling you sooner."

"Telling me what?" He was finding it difficult not to roar at the girl.

"Kelly *did* call me this morning before I went to school. She made me promise and swear not to tell you. If she hadn't, I would have told you right off."

"What did she say to you?"

"She said she was going to run away. I didn't think she really meant it. Then when she wasn't at school, I figured she was skipping school just to worry everybody. But when you called the second time, I went to Mom and told her and she said I should call and let you know where Kelly went."

"Where? Where did she go?"

"She went to her mother. That's what she said, anyway. She said she had saved some money for a rock concert, but that you said she couldn't go, so she was going to use that for a bus ticket to Denton."

Beau covered the receiver with his palm. "Keith, go see if Kelly's money jar is empty." Keith hurried from the room. "I appreciate this, Cathy."

"I hope you aren't mad at me for not telling you sooner. Mom said you have every right to be."

"I just want to get Kelly home safely." He told her goodbye and hung up.

Keith came back with an empty juice jar shaped like a cat. "She took all her money."

Beau went to the door. "Let's go. She took a bus to Denton."

Glenna and Keith followed close on Beau's heels.

THE RIDE TO DENTON seemed to take forever despite the fact that Beau was paying little regard to the speed limit. Glenna occasionally glanced at the boys sitting in the back seat. They were unusually quiet, but each seemed to be accepting the other's presence. Dusk was gathering by the time they arrived. Glenna was sure the question of whether Kelly had arrived safely was uppermost in all their minds, though no one dared put it into words. Glenna's next most frequent thought was what would happen to her relationship with Beau if, God forbid, something terrible had happened to

Kelly. Did Beau really feel that Glenna was responsible for Kelly's disappearance? She didn't know—and she wasn't so sure she would blame him if he did.

As Beau turned into the residential neighborhood where Diedra was living, Keith leaned forward expectantly. "Look, Dad! On the lawn," he said.

They all saw it. The For Sale sign was trimmed with tape that glowed in the car's headlights.

"Mom has moved?" Keith sounded stunned. "She never told us she was moving."

Beau pulled into the drive. "Maybe she hasn't yet." But as his headlights played on the house, they saw that the windows were vacant and the house was dark.

Keith hit the back of the seat with his fist so hard Glenna jumped. "Why did she move and not tell us? Why would she do something like that?"

"I don't know, son." Beau frowned at the vacant house. "Let's go to the bus station and see if anyone there remembers Kelly arriving. She obviously isn't here."

The bus station was quiet at that time of night. Glenna looked around but didn't see Kelly. Beau went to the row of phones on the wall and dialed Diedra's new number. As Glenna came to his side, she noticed the muscles in his jaw were clenched, and she put her hand on his shoulder to show her support.

"Hello? Diedra? Is Kelly there?"

Glenna prayed the answer would be yes.

"What do you mean by that?" he said, then covered the mouthpiece of the phone and explained to Glenna that Diedra had heard from her.

As he listened in silence, Glenna saw his building anger reflected on his face. "You did what?" There was another silence. "Keith wants to know why you moved and didn't tell him." His entire body became rigid as he listened to her reply. "I'm not going to tell him that," he said in a voice too low for Keith to overhear. "I'll see if she bought a ticket. 'Bye." He hung up and glared at the phone.

"What did she say?" Glenna asked.

"Kelly was here earlier today. Diedra said Kelly called her and asked her to come and get her. Diedra met her here at the bus station, but told her she had moved and couldn't take her home with her. Although Diedra didn't tell Kelly the reason, it seems Diedra has a new boyfriend and they are leaving in the morning for Cancun. Because the man thinks Diedra is younger than she is, Diedra was afraid for him to know she had a teenage daughter."

"That's terrible!"

"Diedra gave Kelly money for a return ticket and left her here. She said that she thought if Kelly could figure out how to get here from Sweet Gum, the return trip couldn't be any more difficult."

"Her mother didn't even see that she got on the bus safely?" Glenna was outraged.

"She said she had to get back to her boyfriend."

Keith and Chad came to them. Keith said, "Was that Mom? What did she say?"

"Yes, it was. She talked to Kelly here for a few minutes, then gave her money for a return ticket and told her to go back home."

"Did you ask her why she moved?" Keith sounded hurt and angry.

"I did, and she said it was none of my business. I assume she was going to write you and Kelly to give you her new address."

Glenna knew he assumed nothing of the kind but was trying to make it easier on Keith.

"Let's see what bus she took," Beau said as he clapped his son on the back. "She may already be home."

They went to the ticket counter, and Beau asked the man if a girl had bought a ticket to Sweet Gum. "She's about five feet two and has dark hair and brown eyes. Her name is Kelly Fletcher."

"We don't ask names, just sell tickets. Nope, I haven't seen any girl like that leave on a bus. The only bus that goes through Sweet Gum from here left out at two o'clock. I was on duty then, and I'd have remembered if anybody got a ticket for Sweet Gum, you know?"

Glenna put her hand on Beau's arm and felt the tension in his muscles. "You're sure?" she asked.

"Yes, ma'am. I ain't sold a ticket for Sweet Gum this whole week. A lot of people pass through there, but they don't want to get off and stay." He grinned as if he had made a joke.

Beau turned and stalked back to the phones. After he dialed, he glared at the wall until Diedra answered. "She never got on the bus."

"Well, that's not my fault," Diedra snapped. She lowered her voice. "I wish you'd quit calling me. Charley is getting suspicious."

"I don't give a damn if Charley is swallowing his socks! Kelly is missing."

"There's no need to be so melodramatic. She's probably just doing it to worry you."

"Can't you understand? Kelly is gone and I can't find her. Don't you even care?"

"Of course, I care. She's my daughter, isn't she? I'm just not going to get hysterical over it. It's not as if she's in a strange town. She knows people here from school. She's probably at one of their houses and will be home tomorrow."

"What if she isn't? Did she mention anyone in particular to you?"

"No. I'd call Becky Smithson and Mary Jean Peters if I were you."

"Meaning you aren't going to try to locate her yourself?" Beau's voice was barely controlled.

"Look, I'm trying to pack for Cancun. Our plane leaves early tomorrow morning, and I have a lot of things to do. You have custody of the kids—you do it." She slammed down the receiver.

Beau jiggled the disconnect button in vain. He slammed down the receiver and turned to see Keith standing behind him. By the look on Keith's face, it was plain that he had heard enough of the conversation to know what his mother had said.

"She really doesn't care about us at all," he said. He turned away, but not before Glenna noticed the dampness in his eyes. "She doesn't even care about Kelly."

Beau tried to make his son feel better. "She was busy. It's not that she doesn't care."

Keith shrugged. "I know better than that. I don't care how busy she is, she could come help us find Kelly. What could she be doing that would be more important than finding her daughter?"

Beau shook his head and didn't answer.

Glenna touched Keith's arm, wishing she could salve his pain. "Maybe we should call the police."

Beau made the call while she and the boys stared into the darkness. Beau soon joined them. "They say it's too soon for her to be listed as missing and they can't do anything to help. I gave them her description anyway. Maybe someone will spot her."

Glenna had no idea what she could do to help him. "Could she have passed us on the road? Maybe she's home by now."

"The last bus for Sweet Gum left here at two. If the ticket agent was wrong and she was on it, she would have been back in town before we left. Now that it's dark, she might have gone home if she was already in Sweet Gum." Beau sighed and went to the phone again to call his house.

"No answer," he reported when he returned.

"Let's go back to the house where Mom used to live," Keith suggested. "Kelly's best friends lived just down the street. Maybe she went there. We'll at least be doing something."

Beau nodded. "We can't just wait to see if she'll show up here."

In the old neighborhood, as Keith and Beau checked with the families of Kelly's two friends, Glenna and Chad waited in the car. "They sure are worried," Chad observed.

"Wouldn't you be?" Glenna felt almost as frantic as Beau.

"I just can't understand her mother acting the way she is. You wouldn't ever do me like that."

"You're right. I guess you don't have it as bad as you sometimes think. But you acted as if I had treated you terribly when I told you Beau and I were getting married."

"I don't really think that. I mean, I'm not thrilled with having Keith as a stepbrother, but I guess it's your life. I just said all that stuff to keep you on your toes." He poked her arm and grinned, trying to tease her out of her depression. "Hey, you aren't crying, are you?"

Glenna wiped her cheek. She hadn't realized she was. "No," she lied.

Chad shifted in the back seat. "I guess I was wrong about Keith and Beau. They aren't jerks after all."

Glenna smiled. "No, they aren't jerks." She looked across the lawn at Beau, who was standing beneath the neighbor's porch light. His shoulders were slumped as if he was tired, and she could tell by the way the woman at the door was moving her head that she hadn't seen Kelly. Keith stood with his hands jammed into his pockets. She had never before thought of him as a son. Next month she would become his stepmother—unless the problems with the children kept that from happening. The mere thought that things might not work out was devastating. Keith and Kelly obviously needed a mother to love them, and Glenna needed Beau. Glenna had to force the unpleasant possibility from her mind.

With a dejected look on his face, Beau came back to the car. "No luck. I gave Becky's mother my address and phone number just in case. Mary Jean's father said Diedra moved weeks ago and that they haven't heard from Kelly since the divorce."

"Can we go to our old house again?" Keith asked. "I just need to look at it."

Beau turned around in the driveway and returned to the dark house near the other end of the short street.

"It looks different, doesn't it? I remember it being bigger." Keith opened his door and said to Chad, "Come on. I'll show you where my room was."

Glenna started to stop them, but Beau said, "Let him look. He won't see it again." He rubbed his eyes as if he was exhausted. "Where in the hell can Kelly be?"

"I don't know." She gazed at the house where Beau had lived with Diedra and their children.

"I was never happy here," he said as if he were following her thoughts. "Diedra picked this house because it was the largest one the realtor showed us. It's the largest one in the neighborhood, for that matter. I tried to tell her it would be hard to resell the largest or the smallest house on a street, but she wouldn't listen."

"Did you live here long?"

"About seven years. It seemed like forever. Kelly was in the first grade and Keith was in the third." He smiled at the memories of his children. "I built them a playhouse in the backyard. I wonder if it's still there."

Glenna pointed. "See that window? It's broken."

Beau followed her gaze. He leaned forward. "Someone could put their hand through and open the door from there." He looked at Glenna. "You don't suppose..."

They got out of the car and hurried to the front door. It was locked, but Beau reached through the broken window beside it and opened it. The boys heard him and came to see what was going on.

Glenna eased into the darkness, squinting to make out what she could of the interior, which was illuminated only by the dim glow from the streetlights outside. The house already was beginning to take on the mustiness common to vacant houses, but by far the strongest odor was that of stale cigarettes, doubtless left behind by Diedra or one of her boyfriends. Glenna felt as if they were intruding on Diedra, and moved closer to Beau.

Moments later, Keith returned with the flashlight Beau had sent him to get from the car, and together they moved toward the back of the house. Glenna felt terribly uneasy being there and wouldn't have been surprised to see a police car arrive at any moment.

At the end of a short hall, Keith shined the flashlight into the room that had been Kelly's. All the furniture was gone, of course, but Glenna could see the brighter patch of carpet where the bed had been. The room was small and had only one window. The walls were scratched from the jostle of furniture and pricked with small holes where posters and other memorabilia that kids collect had been attached. It looked unwelcoming.

"It sure looks different," Keith said again. "My room was down here." He led the way down the hall.

Glenna followed them a few steps, but stopped short. Across from Keith's doorway was the bedroom evidently used by Beau and Diedra. Suddenly she didn't feel up to viewing any more of the house. Surely if Kelly was here, she already would have come to them.

Through the darkness, Glenna made her way toward the front door, but took a wrong turn and wound up in the den at the rear of the house.

Through the wide patio doors on the opposite wall, Glenna could see into the backyard. Curiously, she crossed to the doors for a better look. Toward the back of the lot was a child's playhouse, faintly lit from the streetlights out front. She smiled at the evidence of Beau's parental love.

As she narrowed her eyes and peered at it more closely, she thought she saw something move past the small window in the front of the playhouse. Without a second thought, she unlocked the door, removed the piece of broomstick from the track at the bottom and slid it open. The noise of the door's rollers grinding on the track reverberated loudly in the emptiness of the house, momentarily startling Glenna.

"Glenna?" Beau called out. "We'd better go. She's not here."

"I'll be there in a minute, okay?" Glenna stepped onto the concrete patio and, after a moment, made her way to the playhouse. She tried the door, but it seemed to be locked. "Kelly?" she called out. "Are you in there?"

To her surprise, the door opened and Kelly stepped out.

For a minute they stared at each other. Then Glenna said, "We've looked everywhere for you."

Kelly folded her arms across her chest and frowned at the sky, then at the ground. "I don't know why. Nobody loves me."

The childish sentiment touched Glenna. "Then why did we drive all the way from Sweet Gum to find you?"

Kelly had no answer. "Where's Dad?"

"Inside. They thought you might be in your old room."

"I was for a while, but I got scared. The house is weird without furniture in it."

Glenna started to call out to Beau, but she paused. This might be the only chance she would have to talk to Kelly alone. "Why did you run away?"

"Because everybody hates me." Kelly sulked and kicked her toe at the ground. "Dad is going to marry you, but I thought Mom would want me."

"I know. Your dad talked to her. It must have hurt you for her not to take you in."

"She would have if she hadn't had other plans." Kelly's eyes darted to Glenna's, daring the older woman to dispute her statement.

"I'm sure you're right," Glenna said. "Your dad has been worried sick over where you had gone. Do you dislike me that much? So much you would run away rather than live with me?"

Kelly sighed and kicked the ground again. "I don't know. Why are adults always asking questions like that? I don't know how I feel. You aren't my favorite person in the world. You have to know that much.''

"I figured that out.'' Glenna hoped she wasn't making a big mistake in telling Kelly, but she said, "When I was a little girl, my parents were divorced and my mother married a man I couldn't stand.''

Kelly finally looked at her but didn't speak.

"He was always on my case about one thing or another. It was all I could do to be civil to him.''

"And now you love him like a father, right?'' Sarcasm dripped from Kelly's voice. "Give me a break.''

"No, actually I dislike him more than when I was a child. The man is a bore and has a lazy streak a mile wide.''

Kelly was clearly confused. "So what's the point?''

"Only that I understand why you don't want me to marry your father. Stepmothers have had a bad name from Snow White onward. But most of us don't warrant it. Give me a chance, Kelly. That's all I ask. Then if you want to hate me, it's up to you.''

"You hate me for running away.''

"No, I don't. I think you were wrong to do it, and I'm upset that your father has been so worried, but I don't hate you.''

Kelly uncrossed her arms and shoved her hands into the back pockets of her jeans. "Keith won't ever agree to live in the same house with Chad and you. He hates Chad.''

"I think all that has changed. They're inside looking at Keith's old room now.''

"Chad is here?'' Kelly sounded genuinely surprised. "He came to look for me, too?''

"We all did." Glenna drew a deep breath and took a chance. "That's what families do."

A noise behind Glenna gave her a start. It was Beau hurrying toward them with both boys close behind. "Kelly!" Beau pulled his daughter into his arms and hugged her until she wriggled free.

"I can't breathe with you squashing me," she said, but her mouth tilted in a smile.

"You nerd," her brother said. "Are you crazy? We've been worried half to death over you. What a jerk!"

Kelly smiled at him. Keith gave in and smiled back.

"Are you okay, honey?" Beau asked. "How did you get here from the bus station?"

"Mom gave me money for a ticket to Sweet Gum, so I spent some of it on a cab."

"Why didn't you come home? What did you want to come here for?"

Kelly said reluctantly, "I thought Mom still lived here. I thought if I showed up on her doorstep, she would have to let me in." She looked at the dark house. "I guess she moved."

Glenna wanted to put her arms around the girl, but knew Kelly would push her away.

"I was scared to come home," Kelly added. "After me running away I figured you wouldn't want me around. Especially since you know I can't stand *her.*" Kelly jerked her chin toward Glenna.

Beau started to reprimand his daughter, but Glenna put her hand on his arm.

Kelly spoke again. "I never expected her and Chad to come with you to look for me. I never even thought *you* would come." She glanced at Glenna. "Maybe I was wrong."

Glenna said gently, "I want you to come back to Sweet Gum. I know we have a lot to work out, but I think we can."

Kelly frowned at her. "Nobody knows how I feel. All of you seem to think I can just move in and everything will be all right and we can be the Brady Bunch or something. I don't want a stepmother or a stepbrother, and I sure don't want these two."

Beau put his arm around her. "I know you're upset, and I know this is a bigger problem than can be solved tonight. I've talked to a counselor, and he's agreed to let you come and talk out your problems with him."

"I won't talk to some strange dweeb who'll go straight to you and tell you everything I said."

"He won't tell me anything unless you give him permission. Whatever you talk about with him will be kept confidential."

"All my friends will think I'm nuts."

"Unless you tell them, they won't know. They won't find out from me. Besides, many people go to a counselor at one time or another, and no one thinks anything about it."

"Besides, we all know you're nuts already," her brother added.

Kelly made a face at him.

"I'm just glad to find you're safe and sound," Beau said. "Come here." He hugged her as if he hadn't seen her in weeks.

Glenna hesitated, then joined the hug. Beau laughed and pulled Keith in as well. Chad looked as if he expected the others to push him away, but he sidled up close enough for Glenna to drag him in with the others.

From the middle of the hug Kelly said, "What a bunch of dweebs. I'm glad nobody can see us."

As they walked to the car, Beau and Glenna lagged behind.

"What did you two talk about before we found you?" he asked.

"I told her I have a stepfather that I don't like and that it's up to her whether she learns to like me or not."

"You didn't say her dislike would keep us from marrying, did you?"

"No, because it won't, although it might be a good idea to postpone it until spring. I just wanted her to know she has the option of disliking me." She looked at the shadowy figures of their children rounding the corner of the house. "Do you think she will?"

"If she really disliked you, she wouldn't have let you hug her. I think there's hope. You aren't the problem, it goes a lot deeper than that. I have a feeling once she gets into therapy, she'll feel different about many things."

"I hope you're right. I always wanted a daughter." Glenna put her arm around Beau's waist. "I think Chad will shape up, too."

"I'd bet on it. I'm not telling you it will always go smoothly and that we'll never have rough times, but I think in time we can become a family."

"I need to convince Kelly that I'm not trying to take her mother's place."

"It's a place that would be easy to fill. You've seen how nonmaternal Diedra is."

"You know what I mean."

"Yes, I know, and I love you for it. Some women would have tossed in the towel before they ever got started. You've never seen Kelly at her best."

"Just as you've never seen Chad at his, but you're willing to try."

"I'm willing to do more that that. You and I are a team. The kids will all be grown and gone someday, and we'll be left together."

"Let's hope by then we've become a real family."

"I'm counting on it."

Arm in arm they went around the house to where the children were arguing over who had to sit in the middle. Beau and Glenna exchanged a glance and laughed.

EPILOGUE

GLENNA DRESSED for her wedding, listening to the faint murmuring of family and guests below. Sue Ann and Beau's mother were down there helping to straighten out last-minute details, and Glenna's mother had gone to help them. Glenna was glad for the few minutes alone. She buttoned her ivory silk blouse and tucked the shirttail into the waistband of her pale yellow linen skirt, then slipped on the matching jacket.

From the window overlooking the backyard she could see the white trellis, lavishly draped with greenery, that had been erected at the fence as a backdrop for the ceremony. Her garden flanked the trellis on either side, and all the spring flowers were blooming in brilliant profusion. The preacher was already there, talking with Joe Tarrant, Beau's father and Keith. As she watched, Chad joined them, and when her son playfully punched his soon-to-be stepbrother in the arm, she smiled. Keith responded with a similar gesture. They would be all right.

By leaning forward and peering to the right, Glenna could see Kelly. She and Conan were sitting in the garden swing, self-consciously exchanging smiles.

Kelly had come a long way since she had started going to counseling. Glenna knew they weren't out of the woods with her yet, but the improvement in Kelly's attitude was remarkable. Glenna wondered if she would ever be as close to Kelly as she now was to Keith. It was odd, she thought. Because she had always wanted a daughter, she would have assumed that her relationship with a stepdaughter would have been closer than that with a stepson. But maybe, she thought, she felt closer to Keith because he reminded her so much of Beau.

As if Beau had heard her thoughts, he stepped away from the gathering crowd and looked at her window. Glenna unconsciously started to move back so he couldn't see her, but then she stopped. As much as they had been through, she didn't believe it would bring bad luck for him to see her before the ceremony. She and Beau were making their own luck these days.

The Kings wouldn't be there. She hadn't expected them to be. That morning, Arlene had confirmed, with a coolly polite phone call, that she and Mr. King were otherwise engaged. Secretly, Glenna was glad. They were a part of her other life, not the one she shared with Beau.

The one regret she did have was that Margo and her husband, Bob, weren't there. Glenna remembered how she and Margo had once pledged they would be at each other's weddings. She had attended Margo's wedding, and Margo had made it to her first one. She supposed that would have to be enough. Glenna missed Margo more than she had told Beau. He would have felt badly about being the cause of their friendship ending.

The door opened behind her and Glenna turned to see her mother and Sue Ann come in.

"Come away from that window," Betsy said, as if her daughter were still a child. "Beau will see you, and you need all the luck you can get these days."

"Is everyone here?" Glenna asked.

"I think so. The ceremony is to start in ten minutes. Max is fit to be tied. He knows you don't allow anyone to smoke in the house, and he says he's allergic to the flowers outside."

Glenna made no comment.

Sue Ann took the white Bible from the dresser and handed it and the simple bouquet to Glenna. "You look beautiful. That suit is perfect."

"Thank you. Is my hair okay?" Now that the moment was upon her, Glenna was getting nervous.

"You look fine," Betsy said as she bent to examine her own reflection in the mirror. "Let's go down."

Glenna drew in a deep breath. She could hear Joe trying to get the crowd in order in the backyard. Was Beau as nervous as she was? He must be, though he wouldn't admit it. She had teased him about that at the rehearsal last night, and he had been firm in his denial of any last-minute jitters. She could always see through him, though, and she knew he was eager for the ceremony to be over. So was she.

"We should have arranged for music," Betsy grumbled as she brushed an imaginary thread from Glenna's shoulder.

"Music outside reminds me of a circus," Glenna said as she had every time her mother had brought the subject up. Her eyes met Sue Ann's, and they exchanged smiles.

"A circus, indeed! And it ought to be in a church, not the backyard as if it were some picnic."

"Beau and I were both married in a church the first time, and we want this wedding to be different," Glenna explained one more time. "Reverend Pickworth likes the idea."

"I never cared for that man," Betsy muttered under her breath.

Glenna leaned forward and kissed her mother on the cheek. "Cheer up. You're gaining a son. And two grandchildren."

Betsy sighed but she smiled. "Are you ready?"

Glenna nodded. First Betsy, then Sue Ann, preceded her from the bedroom and down the upstairs hall. Memories followed Glenna all the way.

Most of Beau's belongings had been moved into the house during the past few days. Kelly and Keith would stay here with Chad and his grandmother until their parents returned from their honeymoon. The arrival of their belongings had removed the last of Jordan's imprint from the house. Glenna felt one last farewell rise in her throat as she passed the room where Jordan had kept his desk and file cabinets. This was now Kelly's bedroom. Putting the past behind her forever, she went downstairs.

As she crossed the manicured lawn and walked toward Beau, a movement caught her eye. Four latecomers were shutting the gate. Glenna's glance met Margo's and she smiled. Tears of happiness welled in her eyes, and she swallowed to keep from crying. Margo had come after all. Their friendship might never be the same as it once had been, but maybe they could build a new one. She waited until Margo, Bob and their two sons found seats, then started down the grassy aisle.

Beau was waiting for her. The closer she went to him, the lighter she felt, as if she were leaving behind the burden of her old life and stepping forth into the new one. Despite her mother's insistence, she had refused to let Max give her away. Glenna was bringing herself to Beau, and she liked the idea of being her own woman—as independent as he was himself.

When she reached Beau's side, she put her hand confidently into his and gazed into his eyes. On the right side of the altar, Keith and Chad stood behind Beau. Kelly and Sue Ann were on Glenna's left. Up until the last minute she hadn't been sure Kelly would stand as her witness. But Kelly was there, and she was even smiling.

Glenna gave Beau's hand a squeeze, and as he returned the gesture, she could feel her soul touch his. With their hands joined, they turned to the preacher, who began to impart the familiar words of the wedding service.

Harlequin Superromance ®

Come to where the West is still wild in a summer trilogy by Margot Dalton

Sunflower (#502—June 1992)
Robin Baldwin becomes the half owner of a prize
rodeo horse. But to take possession, she has to travel
the rodeo circuit with cowboy Matt Adams, living
with him in *very* close quarters!

Tumbleweed (#508—July 1992)
Until she met Scott Freeman, Lyle Callander was about
as likely to settle in one spot as tumbleweed in a
windstorm. But who *is* Scott? He's more than the
simple photographer he claims to be . . . much more.

Juniper (#511—August 1992)
Devil-may-care Buck Buchanan can ride a bucking
bronco or a Brahma bull. But can he win Claire
Tremaine, a woman who sets his heart on fire but
keeps her own as cold as ice?

**"I just finished reading *Under Prairie Skies* by
Margo Dalton and had to hide my tears from my
children. I loved it!"** —A reader

Harlequin Superromance®

Coming in July from
Harlequin Superromance
A new novel from the author of
RAISING THE STAKES

THE WOMAN DOWNSTAIRS
By Judith Arnold

Ex-cop Alec Fontana came to Albright College to
investigate a charge of sexual harassment on campus.
But all he could think about was his mysterious
neighbor, and the hauntingly beautiful music
she played....

Pianist Lauren Wyler resented the eavesdropper
upstairs terribly—until they met, and discovered they
shared much more than an address....

THE WOMAN DOWNSTAIRS
A story of love and passion
Superromance #509

WD92

Take 4 bestselling love stories FREE

Plus get a FREE surprise gift!

OVER THE YEARS, TELEVISION HAS BROUGHT
THE LIVES AND LOVES OF MANY CHARACTERS INTO
YOUR HOMES. NOW HARLEQUIN INTRODUCES YOU
TO THE TOWN AND PEOPLE OF

One small town—twelve terrific love stories.

GREAT READING... GREAT SAVINGS...
AND A FABULOUS FREE GIFT!

Each book set in Tyler is a self-contained love story; together, the
twelve novels stitch the fabric of the community.

By collecting proofs-of-purchase found in each Tyler book, you can
receive a fabulous gift, ABSOLUTELY FREE! And use our special
Tyler coupons to save on your next TYLER book purchase.

Join us for the fifth TYLER book,
BLAZING STAR by Suzanne Ellison, available in July.

Is there really a murder cover-up?
Will Brick and Karen overcome differences and find true love?

Harlequin Superromance®

COMING NEXT MONTH

#506   OF DOLLS AND ANGELS • Virginia Nielsen
When William Tyson walked into her life,
Sara Eaton's heart flipped and visions of wedding bells
danced through her head. But at the same time, she
wanted to crawl into a hole and hide. Because suddenly
she was stuttering again . . . as badly as she had as a
teenager.

#507   GULF BREEZES • Anne Logan
The beautiful yacht had been anchored just beyond the
beach in the Gulf of Mexico for several days with no
sign of anyone aboard. Samantha Bradford sailed out
to investigate and found herself trapped on board with
the handsome but injured captain. Marc Dureaux's life
was in danger and now, it seemed, so was her own.

#508   TUMBLEWEED • Margot Dalton
Until she met Scott Freeman, Lyle Callander was about
as likely to settle in one spot as tumbleweed in a
windstorm. Now Lyle's heart was lost. But who was
Scott Freeman? He was more than the simple
photographer he claimed to be . . . much more.

#509   THE WOMAN DOWNSTAIRS • Judith Arnold
Ex-cop Alec Fontana came to Albright College to
investigate a charge of sexual harassment on campus,
but he couldn't keep his mind off his mysterious
downstairs neighbor and the hauntingly beautiful
music she played. Pianist Lauren Wyler resented the
eavesdropper terribly . . . until mutual concern for a
young student's welfare brought them together.

FREE GIFT OFFER

To receive your free gift, send us the specified number of proofs-of-purchase from any specially marked Free Gift Offer Harlequin or Silhouette book with the Free Gift Certificate properly completed, plus a check or money order (do not send cash) to cover postage and handling payable to Harlequin/Silhouette Free Gift Promotion Offer. We will send you the specified gift.

FREE GIFT CERTIFICATE

ITEM	A. GOLD TONE EARRINGS	B. GOLD TONE BRACELET	C. GOLD TONE NECKLACE
# of proofs-of-purchase required	3	6	9
Postage and Handling	$1.75	$2.25	$2.75
Check one	☐	☐	☐

Name: _____

Address: _____

City: _____ State: _____ Zip Code: _____

Mail this certificate, specified number of proofs-of-purchase and a check or money order for postage and handling to: HARLEQUIN/SILHOUETTE FREE GIFT OFFER 1992, P.O. Box 9057, Buffalo, NY 14269-9057. Requests must be received by July 31, 1992.

PLUS—Every time you submit a completed certificate with the correct number of proofs-of-purchase, you are automatically entered in our MILLION DOLLAR SWEEPSTAKES! No purchase or obligation necessary to enter. See below for alternate means of entry and how to obtain complete sweepstakes rules.

MILLION DOLLAR SWEEPSTAKES
NO PURCHASE OR OBLIGATION NECESSARY TO ENTER

To enter, hand-print (mechanical reproductions are not acceptable) your name and address on a 3″ × 5″ card and mail to Million Dollar Sweepstakes 6097, c/o either P.O. Box 9056, Buffalo, NY 14269-9056 or P.O. Box 621, Fort Erie, Ontario L2A 5X3. Limit: one entry per envelope. Entries must be sent via 1st-class mail. For eligibility, entries must be received no later than March 31, 1994. No liability is assumed for printing errors, lost, late or misdirected entries.

Sweepstakes is open to persons 18 years of age or older. All applicable laws and regulations apply. Sweepstakes offer void wherever prohibited by law. Prizewinners will be determined no later than May 1994. Chances of winning are determined by the number of entries distributed and received. For a copy of the Official Rules governing this sweepstakes offer, send a self-addressed, stamped envelope (WA residents need not affix return postage) to: Million Dollar Sweepstakes Rules, P.O. Box 4733, Blair, NE 68009.

HS3U

ONE PROOF-OF-PURCHASE
To collect your fabulous FREE GIFT you must include the necessary FREE GIFT proofs-of-purchase with a properly completed offer certificate.

(See inside back cover for offer details)